...OF A MYSTERY

"Like its predecessors, *Dead Heat* is worth reading. It has a civilized aura (Spraggue is, after all, a Brahmin) combined with tough police routine. Characterizations are well worked out, and when evil gets its comeuppance, the reader may start cheering."

The Washington Post

"Even more entertaining than...*Bitter Finish*...A complex murder plot, a startling final revelation... and fast-moving, lightly humorous entertainment throughout, featuring an uncommonly well-developed assortment of minor characters."

The Kirkus Reviews

"You'll learn interesting things about an actor's use of phonetics and phonetic symbols, in a book that moves swiftly and with a degree of toughness as it strips away layers of official corruption."

Houston Post

"*Dead Heat* is Linda Barnes' third Michael Spraggue novel....it makes you want to seek out the previous two....she writes about Boston and its environs with the verve of the delighted, appreciative outsider."

The Detroit News

Also by Linda Barnes
Published by Fawcett Books:

BITTER FINISH

BLOOD WILL HAVE BLOOD

CITIES OF THE DEAD

A TROUBLE OF FOOLS

DEAD HEAT

Linda Barnes

FAWCETT CREST • NEW YORK

A Fawcett Crest Book
Published by Ballantine Books
Copyright © 1984 by Linda Appelblatt Barnes

Library of Congress Catalog Card Number: 83-13800

ISBN 0-449-20689-0

This edition published by arrangement with St. Martin's
Press, Inc.

Manufactured in the United States of America

First Ballantine Books Edition: November 1985
Fourth Printing: May 1989

To my parents, Hilda and Irv Appelblatt

My thanks to Steve Appelblatt, Richard Barnes, James Morrow, and the staff of the Bill Rodgers Running Center for information and criticism generously given.

ONE

With sweaty fingers, Spraggue yanked a crumpled scrap of paper from the pocket of his running shorts. He didn't have to read it; he knew it. Awkward block printing on dime-store stationery. Today's date, in numerals and slashes, in the upper right-hand corner. CHESTNUT HILL RESERVOIR. Beneath it, RUN FOR YOUR LIFE. Beneath that, 3 P.M. And at the bottom, the scrawled signature that took most of the sting out of the threat, A FRIEND INDEED.

Frowning, he shoved the note back in his pocket, glanced around hoping to get a glimpse of the author.

The scene would have been picture postcard stuff if not for all the ragtag runners. The reservoir's shape could have been fashioned by nature rather than bulldozer. Furled along an irregular rocky coast, the water seemed suspect—too perfect a blue, barely rippled by the mid-April breeze. If you ignored busy Beacon Street slicing through the middle, the grounds resembled those of an English country estate, with the tiny, boxlike gatehouses and support structures along the shore serving as outbuildings to the two ornate Chestnut Hill Pumping Stations.

Afternoon sunshine glinted off the surface of the pond and forced the runners to squint. Those who had come equipped with sun visors smugly pulled them down. Spraggue, lacking visor or sunglasses, momentarily shut his eyes, sun-struck, and stubbed his toe on a lurking rock. One more discomfort hardly seemed to matter.

Today's most aggravating scenario, he thought, plodding determinedly onward, would encompass aching muscles—worse—a torn Achilles tendon, the direct result of pretending a thirty-five-year-old body could still move like an eighteen-year-old one. Blistered feet. One car towed from its dubious mooring in a zone prominently marked by No Parking signs—worse—held captive by the dread yellow Denver Boot, bane of Boston drivers. He tried to recall whether he had the requisite five unpaid parking tickets stuffed in the dash compartment. And to top it all off, the anonymous letter writer wouldn't show.

The trail narrowed and changed from shin-splintering cement to a foot-mangling mixture of gravel and turf. A murderous incline made the fronts of his thighs shriek in protest, the backs of his thighs cringe in anticipation of the eventual decline.

The path swarmed with runners, atoning for training time lost to the freak April blizzard, chests emblazoned with the logos of sportswear manufacturers or the locales of popular road races: New York; Denver; Charleston; Falmouth; Eugene, Oregon. Fukuoka, Japan was represented by a slight, exuberant Oriental in spotless white running shorts. Through sun-dazzled eyes, the runners—despite their mismatched apparel and dirty sneakers—looked uniformly young, incredibly thin, disgustingly fit. Feeling like some creaky relic, Spraggue increased his pace. He'd have asked the attractive, bronzed woman running alongside him when they'd started letting babies run the Boston Marathon, if he'd thought he could summon sufficient breath to string together the ten or so necessary words. He knew that if he tried, he'd gasp like a salmon jerked out of a stream. He dug his balled fist into his right side, searching for the source of a gnawing ache.

Could the bronzed woman have composed the curious note, delivered it to Aunt Mary, the only person always able to contact him? Was that why she paced herself so steadily beside him? Even as he had the thought, she gulped in a deep breath, and sprinted ahead.

On the whole, he hoped his mysterious correspondent was a woman, a fascinating dark-eyed woman, with sculptured cheekbones and a ready, aching smile.

Didn't any of these runners perspire?

Hath not old custom made this life more sweet
Than that of painted pomp? Are not these woods
More free from peril than the envious court?

To keep his mind off a right baby toe that felt like a swelling balloon, off the letter writer's three o'clock deadline, he recited bits of *As You Like It* under his breath. Not his own lines, but those of the banished Duke Senior, words appropriate to the rustic surroundings. And he scrutinized the faces of approaching runners, chiding himself for paying greater attention to the females. It wasn't that he believed the anonymous note to be a feminine invention, he admitted. It was pure loneliness, pure longing.

He considered the possible benefits of consoling himself with one of his female colleagues at the Harvard Rep. The exquisite, if predatory lady who played Celia to his Oliver, perhaps. Was there any hope for an honest relationship with a woman with whom he feigned falling in love four times a week in Act Four, scene three?

The ache in his side took a fierce bite out of his appendix and his calf muscles picked the same moment to shift from minor grievance to screaming alarm.

"Spraggue! Over here!"

The rumbling voice was unmistakable. He turned his head and saw Pete Collatos, dark hair plastered in ringlets

3

against his skull, sprinting toward him. A terry-cloth band, circling his broad forehead, failed to keep the sweat from pouring down his swarthy face. Spraggue's mouth split in a rueful grin. So much for the mystery woman. He tried to breathe normally. His lungs burned.

Collatos' running companion, a strikingly familiar-looking man wearing last year's '81 Boston Marathon T-shirt, approached from the right and halted, jogging in place, breathing as softly and regularly as if he'd been relaxing in a lounge chair by the side of a crystal pool instead of racing hell for leather around the Chestnut Hill Reservoir.

Collatos wiped his hand off on his shorts before offering it for a handshake. "I thought you were one of those lousy, good for nothing, half-hour-in-the-morning-if-it-doesn't-rain runners. You gonna do the marathon this year?"

"No way." Spraggue searched for a sign that he'd met up with his anonymous correspondent, decided not to mention the reason for his unusual afternoon run. Not yet. "How's Boston's finest?"

"Hang on to your hat; I'm not a cop anymore," Collatos said. "Got laid off. Goddamn Proposition 2½." The ex-cop smacked himself on the forehead with the flat of his palm, a gesture Spraggue remembered from countless nights in a sweltering telephone booth of an office at police headquarters, and turned to the man jogging impatiently at his side. "Excuse me. Sorry, Brian. Meet one of the snakes I had to deal with when I was a humble civil servant. Michael Spraggue—Senator Brian Donagher."

That accounted for the overwhelming sense of familiarity. Spraggue mentally kicked himself for not tagging a name to the man earlier. But this Donagher looked much older than the brash upstart who'd run for U.S. Senate six years ago on a platform as liberal as that of any sixties Democrat and confounded all the pollsters by winning. He'd aged more than the time should have allowed. His hair

4

looked darker than it did on television, on his ubiquitous campaign posters. His blue eyes, twinkling out of a nest of fine lines that belied his youthful physique, seemed just as frank, his face as gaunt.

The senator displayed a flash of even white teeth as he extended his hand, crinkling up his face even more. "If you're the Michael Spraggue who spells his last name with two g's, I've met your aunt at a few fund raisers lately."

"Pleased to meet you," Spraggue said, returning the man's smile. "Get anything out of her?" He wished someone would suggest going out for a drink.

"A few tips on playing the stock market."

"You running the marathon?"

Donagher's face seamed into another smile. "You bet. God, I've missed running the damn thing. Last year, when I was sitting on my butt on that reviewing stand at the Prudential Center, I vowed that I'd run it this year, if I had to get the Senate to pass a special bill letting me out for training time."

"Planning to come in second again?"

"Give me a break. It's been five years since I made the top ten. Warming a chair in Washington isn't the best preparation for Heartbreak Hill. Look, why don't I keep on moving while you guys chat about old times? I've got a few more miles to rack up and I don't want my leg muscles stiffening."

"You sure it's okay?" Collatos spoke in an undertone, full of concern.

"No problem," Donagher reassured him, using the same hushed tone. "This isn't exactly midnight in a dark alley. I'll pick you up next circuit. Nice meeting you, Spraggue."

"Stay away from the press," Collatos hollered after him, grinning.

As soon as Donagher was out of sight, Spraggue collapsed onto a large flat rock by the side of the trail and rubbed his legs. "You're looking good," he said after a two-minute pause. He wasn't going to be the one to mention the note.

Collatos laughed. "It's that goddamned diet. Preparation for the marathon. Man, the day after the race, I'm gonna down three six-packs and stuff five large Regina's pizzas with sausage, onion, and anchovies down my throat."

"Remind me to avoid you on April twentieth. Are you carbohydrate loading?"

"Nah, it's some fancy diet some doctor concocted for Donagher. I run with him; I follow his diet."

And why are you, a former detective, running with the junior senator from Massachusetts? Spraggue wanted to ask.

"Sorry you got canned," he said instead. Was Collatos responsible for that note? He'd been so sure when he'd first seen him; it was the kind of gag Collatos would pull. . . .

"Hey, forget it." Collatos' irrepressible smile made Spraggue's legs throb painfully. "Oh, I was depressed at first. All that training down the tubes. Family tradition shot to hell. It's hard to kiss off the dream of twenty-five years and a good pension. But, hell, I wasn't in love with the department."

"Your ears still perk up when you hear a siren," Spraggue said.

"Can't help it." Collatos listened for a moment. "That's a fire engine, not a cop car."

"Sure it's not an ambulance?"

The ex-cop closed his eyes in concentration, frowned, shook his head emphatically.

"Too bad," Spraggue said, massaging his taut calf muscles. "I could use one."

"You gotta stay in shape," Collatos scolded. "Build up the miles gradually. Anyway, after I got laid off, not even a week after I'm out in the cold, I've got a new gig all sewn up."

"Doing what?"

"I'm telling you." Spraggue remembered how hard it was to push Collatos forward in a straight line. He leaned back on his hands and carefully flexed his ankles.

"I never even had a chance to reflect on my future," Collatos said. "My sister had a whole list of professions for me to try out; she even wanted me to go back to school. I was planning to take a two-week vacation, blow my severance pay in the sunshine, then maybe go into private practice, pirate a case or two from the cops. But the guys in the department, man, they really take care of you. Senator Donagher calls up, looking for a bodyguard. He's a runner; the guys know I run. Perfect match, they figure. The brass gives me top grades and here I am, training for the marathon while I earn more bucks than the dear old taxpayers ever shelled out."

"What's Donagher need a bodyguard for?"

"He started getting death threats in the mail. Makes him nervous."

"Doesn't seem nervous."

"I thought, maybe, besides just protecting him, I'd do a little snooping, find out who's sending the notes."

"To a politician? Where are you going to start? The voting register? Probably some crank sending bouquets to both sides."

"Nope. I checked. Bartolo's people say he's not getting that kind of hate mail."

"Either they're waiting for the campaign to heat up or there's no accounting for taste."

"You said it. I mean, why hate Donagher and not Bartolo? Donagher's an all right guy. For a pol, he's a prince. I told him he ought to hire you, Spraggue."

Spraggue's smile was grim, a straight line between two parentheses. "So that's what this little charade is all about," he said.

"I knew that note would get you," Pete said. "You're a sucker for that kind of stuff."

"Hold it right there. You're not a cop anymore; I'm not a private investigator anymore."

"You're shittin' me."

"Nope."

"You sure it's not just that your politics and Donagher's politics don't mix and match? I mean, he is one of the original soak-the-rich boys."

"It's nothing political," Spraggue said. "I voted for the guy. The old families in Massachusetts expect to get soaked. We just hate to flush our money down the nuclear warheads toilet. If Donagher had more power, I'd feel a hell of a lot better about my tax bill."

"Jeez." Collatos yanked off his sweatband, twisted it in his hands, and watched the drops of water seep into the ground. "Spraggue quits the snoop business. Nothing stays the same. You working? Or you just clipping coupons?"

"I went back to acting. I'm almost making a living at it."

"No shit. You on TV?"

"I specialize in plays that close on opening night and movies that never get released. Right now I'm with the Harvard Repertory Theater."

"And here I've been thinking I could hook up with you on this Donagher business. We worked together okay on that stolen car beef."

Spraggue remembered the reckless enthusiasm that had characterized that long ago investigation and felt sorry for whoever had sent Donagher the anonymous notes. Their writer would be hounded by Collatos for the rest of his life.

"Why not work on one more case?" Collatos said. "Keep your hand in?"

"My P.I. license is expired."

"Good," Collatos said. "That's probably the only thing that keeps Menlo from confiscating it."

"Menlo! They haven't fired that cretin yet?"

"You kidding? He was my boss on the arson liaison detail. When the rest of us got laid off, he got promoted!"

"God help the Boston Police!" Spraggue muttered under his breath.

Collatos twisted a grass stem between his thumb and index finger, kept his eyes glued on it while he said in a disappointed tone, "So that acting stuff keeps you busy?"

"Up to my ears."

Instead of responding, Pete stared abruptly up at the path. Spraggue followed the ex-cop's eyes and found himself confronting the woman of his fantasy, dark-eyed and exotic, moving at a languid pace around the pond. He jumped up as quickly as his stiffening legs would allow.

"You know her?" Collatos asked eagerly.

"Nope. But I'm planning to. Think it'll be too obvious if I collapse at her feet?"

Collatos grinned. "You're not up to your ears, you're over your head."

A shot cracked through the trees. Spraggue named it even before he stopped hoping it might be some backfiring truck. A sharp series of repeats, punctuated by screams, followed hard on the first explosion.

Spraggue found he could still run.

His eyes met Collatos' dark eyes for an instant and then both men took off, tracing the path Donagher had taken, the gravelly, narrow, uphill trail. Spraggue's toes bit into the turf and he leaned slightly forward at the waist to counter the incline. He saw a flash of metal in Collatos' hand, wondered where the ex-cop had managed to conceal a gun in his running clothes.

They topped the hill. "Brian!" Collatos hollered, and Spraggue wondered, too, where he got the breath for the full-throated bellow. The ex-cop stared wildly around and plunged full speed down the slope.

The Beacon Street traffic noises faded into insignificance in the background. The pain came back to Spraggue's side; he ignored it. They passed the life-course exercise stations scattered along the side of the trail without stopping to perform any prescribed number of sit-ups or push-ups. The path changed from gravel to cement, broadened, leveled out. Spraggue's breath rasped his throat, and he ran slightly bent now, not because of hilly terrain, but in an attempt to ease the stitch in his side. A burst of noise erupted just over the next rise. Someone shouted, "Stay down!"

"Brian!" Collatos hollered again. This time his voice shook and died.

"Pete!"

Collatos' relief was so great Spraggue could see the spasm pass through his whole body. He sagged momentarily, straightened, sped up, and Spraggue fell in behind him on the narrowing path.

"Don't come any closer!" The voice was Donagher's. Collatos ducked behind an overhanging boulder. Spraggue dodged after him, staring at the scene spread out in front of them. Donagher had taken shelter from the sudden barrage of fire by vaulting the fence that surrounded the reservoir and flattening himself behind one of the elms. Every other runner in the vicinity seemed to have followed suit. Faces peered out from behind bushes. The potential targets stayed low, some prone, the more daring on their knees. Those not staring at Spraggue and Collatos kept their eyes fixed across Lake Street on the old Boston College graveyard.

Donagher picked that moment to leap to his feet. "Behind the column," he yelled. "On the hill in the graveyard!"

Donagher pointed as he shouted and Collatos sprinted forward, crossing the road with a total disregard for traffic, climbing a formidable fence into the graveyard, and charging up the hill toward the tallest monument, gun drawn. In seconds, he was out of sight.

Spraggue considered pursuit, but his legs wouldn't deliver.

The runners ventured out slowly, forming a gawking ring around Donagher, whispering his identity, examining scratches and bruises. One elderly man had twisted an ankle clambering over the fence. He knelt, cursed, and rubbed his leg. Several witnesses, not sure what to do, giggled awkwardly.

"What happened?" Spraggue cut across the murmur of the crowd with the question.

"I'm not sure," Donagher said hurriedly. "Reflex action, I guess. A noise. I saw something moving in the graveyard—"

"Everyone hid, so I did, too," piped up a woman in an orange tank top. "Maybe it was just a car backfiring."

"No way!" This from a burly bare-chested man with an abundance of curly dark hair. "Shots. Rifle shots. I heard enough of 'em in 'Nam to last a lifetime. Man, I thought I was hallucinating, having a nightmare or something."

"Shouldn't somebody call the police?"

"Is everyone okay? Did anybody get hit?"

"That man running away, his face was all mashed-in looking, not like a normal face."

The last offering, rising over the hubbub of the suddenly talkative crowd, came from a blond teenager Spraggue recognized as one of the young females who'd passed him earlier in the day.

Stocking mask, Spraggue thought.

Donagher's pleasant baritone took charge. Spraggue didn't hear all the words because he was peering off for a returning Pete Collatos. But Donagher's tone smoothed and apologized. Spraggue caught a sentence here and there, something about "avoiding panic" and "unfortunate publicity" and "a black eye for a gracious city right before one of her most prestigious events."

Good luck, Spraggue thought. Try to keep these twenty people from spilling their guts to all their friends and relations. Just try. Wait until the newsmongers get ahold of it. Shots fired at senator from Boston College graveyard. He wondered how lurid the headlines in the *Herald* would be. GHOST SNIPES SENATOR in three-inch-high black boldface.

Collatos, still running, hove back into view.

He halted near Spraggue, panting like an overweight dog, and tried to speak.

"A car . . ." He got that much out, doubled over at the waist, bent his knees, and huddled into a ball.

Spraggue knelt beside him. "You all right?"

"Out . . . of breath . . ."

"You call the cops?"

Collatos nodded. So much for Donagher's eloquent plea to keep the incident under wraps.

Spraggue waited until Collatos had drawn a couple of shuddery breaths. "What kind of car?" he asked.

"On Comm Ave . . . dark . . . gunned the motor just as I got there."

"You see the guy get in it?"

Collatos shrugged.

"License plate?"

"Covered . . . with mud."

"Make?"

"Olds . . . maybe Buick . . . late model . . ." Collatos smeared the back of his hand across his forehead and drops of sweat spattered the ground. He grabbed Spraggue's shoulder and hauled himself up to a standing position. He tottered, caught himself, walked the ten paces over to where Donagher stood, and placed a tentative hand on the senator's arm.

"Sorry . . ." he said, still fighting for breath. "Sorry. Stupid to leave you . . ."

"Forget it," Donagher said, but his voice was hard and tight.

A siren closed in, different in tone and pitch from the one Collatos had identified earlier as a fire engine. A few stragglers in the crowd ran off, not eager to get involved. Most pressed in closer.

A patrol car, its blue lights spinning and flashing, shrieked around the corner and blocked the road. Two uniformed men jumped out.

TWO

He tore off his beard with the quick deft yank that experience dictated as the least excruciating way to perform a painful task. Then he cold-creamed and tissued the paint off his face, removing the heavy makeup that disguised one of Duke Senior's courtiers from the man the audience had earlier encountered as the wicked brother, Oliver. Spraggue glanced at the table in front of him to ensure that all was laid out in preparation for his five-minute transformation back to Oliver; fake mustache, dark red lining pencils, brown shadow, white liner, two fine-tipped camel's-hair brushes, medium powder, one grease stick in standard tan. He wouldn't have time to blend a particular shade for Oliver.

He smoothed on a light layer of grease and rubbed it in with face-washing motions, then selected the sharpest of his lining pencils by testing each of their points against his thumb. He raised both eyebrows to wrinkle his forehead and automatically traced the most prominent of the resulting lines with red pencil, highlighting each furrow with white. Pretty soon he could forget about the wrinkling ceremony, he thought. The lines were getting damn easy to spot without it.

Just as he'd established a ritual for the makeup table and an order, from hairline to chin, in which to line his face, so there was a structure to his mental preparation for each role. Now was the allotted time to slip back into the character of the evil elder brother: to replay Oliver's grim encounter with Duke Frederick at the new court; to reconstruct Oliver's plans to do away with his brother, Orlando; to relive Oliver's long journey to the Forest of Arden, culminating in his miraculous, plot-saving conversion to sudden goodness. Instead, Spraggue pondered the shooting at the reservoir.

The cops now had the names of some twenty runners who'd witnessed the brouhaha, complete with addresses, phone numbers, and a few addled, unmatching descriptions of the supposed perpetrator. The young woman who had brought up the stocking-mask possibility seemed the most reliable of a bad lot. The old man with the twisted ankle had offered twenty-two different conspiracy theories, the mildest being a plot by the sponsors of the New York Marathon to scuttle the Boston race. He also thought the sniping might be a diabolically clever ploy by the mob to get the cops out of the way while crooks reprised the Brink's heist.

Spraggue thumbed brown shadow across his eyelids. What bothered him was the reporters. Channel 4's news team had been on the scene like flies on honey even before the cops had finished flashing their badges. Asked better questions, too. Could they have been tipped off slightly in advance? Was the whole episode some cockeyed publicity stunt? Donagher was up for reelection in November and many were the pundits who claimed his return to marathon running was a cheap way of garnering momentum for his campaign start-up. Instead of shelling out hard won campaign contributions for newspaper ads, would some flunky in Donagher's organization point proudly to tomorrow's front page coverage in the *Globe* and the *Herald* and chalk up the cash savings for his committee? Spraggue decided that he'd investigate that angle long before he checked out any anonymous crank letters. He wondered what Pete Collatos would do. *If* Collatos kept his job. Spraggue hoped his friend hadn't gotten fired for his dereliction of duty.

Deftly, he hollowed out the area under his right cheekbone with dark shadow, edged it with white.

Any flunky responsible for the prank would have wept at Donagher's low-key reaction. The candidate had resisted every attempt by the cops to single him out as the target. A "random sniping incident" at the reservoir, that's what Donagher had called it. When pressed for motive, he'd discoursed on random violence in today's society. Hadn't mentioned any threatening letters. Out of twenty-five observers of Donagher's chat with the cops, Spraggue supposed the senator hadn't won more than twenty-five votes. Getting shot at all across the city seemed an uncertain way to win an election.

He peered up at the ceiling, cheated down into the mirror to line under his eyes. His Oliver makeup was a straight job in contrast to the character makeup he did for the rustic lord. No fancy tricks on this one, no putty noses or bushy eyebrows. Spraggue just reinforced the features he already had, evening out the faint asymmetricality that made his mobile face perfect for double casting.

Right now, Spraggue thought, he could play any age, from twenty to death, but his days as youthful Romeo were fast drawing to a close. On the street, his face never drew a second look. Makeup made a difference. The *Globe*'s reviewer had called his Oliver a *handsome rogue*, two words no one would have used to describe Spraggue. *Normal* was a more oft used term. Average, except for those amber cat's eyes.

Hurriedly buttoning up his deep red tunic, Spraggue reread the note he'd found tacked to his dressing-room door. "Michael," it said, "must see you. Finances. Real estate. Tonight. No excuses." The assistant stage manager had written down his aunt's peremptory message in appropriate red. He doubted his aunt had been quite so succinct; Mary had a reputation for volubility.

Tonight . . . Whether or not he made the appointment would depend on the mood of one Kathleen Farrell, the actress who played his beloved Celia. An after-theater snack might be in order: He'd missed dinner due to the cops' insistence on his testimony at the sniping scene, and his stomach rumbled like distant cannonfire. He'd almost been tempted by the gruesome fare the props crew dispensed for the Act Two rustic banquet scene. And after dinner . . . well, Aunt Mary might have to wait a bit. Maybe she'd have to forge his signature on whatever moneymaking scheme she was presently contemplating.

He shook himself from his reverie and addressed his reflection in the full-length mirror on the back of the door.

Good morrow, fair ones: Pray you, if you know,
Where in the purlieus of this forest stands
A sheep-cote, fenced about with olive trees?

He spoke those words in Act Four, scene three, every night *As You Like It* played, which was by no means a simple matter of every Tuesday through Sunday night with Wednesday and Sunday matinees. The Harvard Rep was just what its title proclaimed, a repertory company complete with its own bizarre calendar. This season they were running a three-show schedule: a Shakespeare, a Brecht, and an opera, the latter a new departure for the theater. Spraggue was cast in two out of the three, having neither the voice nor the inclination for opera. This week was more hectic than most: three *Caucasian Chalk Circle*s and four *As You Like It*s. The opera ran only once. At first, Spraggue had checked the schedule constantly to find out whom he was to play that night; now he took things a day at a time without much anxiety.

The Act Four speech he'd just recited was the opening of his big scene with Celia, a scene played not by the text, but according to Rosalind's later verdict that the two had "no sooner met, but they looked; no sooner looked but they loved." Each night Spraggue picked a different point in the scene to fall madly in love with Celia. He wondered how much of an effect that had on his feelings for Kathleen Farrell. Imitation spawning the real thing; art provoking life rather than imitating it. Hard to tell.

Kathleen, a blue-eyed siren with honey-colored hair, was breathtaking in the scene that night. Her voice was tuned to the back of the auditorium, but Spraggue couldn't rid himself of the notion that her eyes and thoughts were just for him.

He married her in the last scene. Was her curtain-call kiss warmer, longer than usual?

He recalled the first time he'd been shot at, years before, when he'd been a practicing private detective. He remembered thinking: If life is so capricious, if you can be wiped off the face of the earth by a stray bullet fired at a stranger by a stranger, enjoy each day, each moment. Confronting death made him think of pleasure, and pleasure made him think of sex. He wondered how Senator Donagher would pass the night.

Kathleen entered his dressing room still in her Celia garb, although her face had been scrubbed clean and her wig discarded. She carried her street clothes over her arm. Kathleen changed clothes wherever she happened to be—a habit that alternately delighted and irritated him—as long as her bra and panties stayed on. If those articles were to be removed, she retreated demurely to her dressing room like some innocent ingenue. Now she left the door open and began unhooking her bodice. Spraggue hoped the entire cast would not filter in to see which style of underwear she had selected for the evening.

"Hungry?" he asked, wondering if he were the first or the final male in the cast to try this less than novel approach. His was certainly not the only dressing room Kathleen had graced with her postperformance strip shows.

"Starving."

"The Harvest is still open. Or," he said, carefully not staring at any of the portions of Farrell's anatomy that were well worth staring at, "I could fix you some dinner at my place."

She glanced at him speculatively and said, "That would be nice" in a way that let him know all possible ramifications of his invitation had been taken into consideration.

"Fine" was all he said.

"Stage door in five minutes then." She vanished, leaving him to think delightful thoughts.

They were abruptly canceled. The hulking figure of Captain Hank Menlo of the Boston Police filled the doorway, blocking the light.

THREE

By the time he stalked out of Menlo's stuffy hole of an office at one thirty in the morning, Spraggue's earlier romantic mood was shot—nothing but a distant memory, as far away as Kathleen Farrell. He glared at the other occupant of the rumbling elevator all the way down to the lobby, causing the rookie cop to blush and pat his holster for reassurance. Ignoring the sergeant manning the check-out desk, Spraggue hurried down the stone steps of police headquarters, crossed a deserted Berkeley Street, and found, as he'd hoped, a lone taxi waiting in front of the Greyhound terminal.

"Harvard Square," he snapped as he opened the door.

"In a hurry?" The cabbie sounded hopeful: a bad sign. The cab had an accordion-pleated right front fender.

"No," Spraggue said sharply. A race down Storrow Drive hanging on to a filthy armrest in a taxi whose interior smelled like someone had recently bled to death in it didn't sound like any remedy for a foul mood.

The cabdriver shrugged and slammed his foot down on the accelerator like a flamenco dancer warming up for the finale. Spraggue clutched the armrest, wondered what the aging juvenile delinquent would have pulled had he been unwise enough to urge haste.

After the cabbie shot the red light at Beacon Street and surged onto Storrow Drive from a tricky left-lane merge without benefit of side or rearview mirror, Spraggue settled back and closed his eyes.

"Goddam Menlo," he muttered under his breath. He replayed the scene in his dressing room and got angry all over again.

"Imagine those two rookies just taking your name and address and letting you walk," Menlo had said while Spraggue had inwardly cursed the assistant stage manager responsible for keeping invaders away from the stage door. Menlo had folded his wallet and shoved it back into the pocket of his disreputable khaki pants; he must have used his badge to bully the woman into submission. Some admission ticket, that badge.

Spraggue could hear Kathleen, in her nearby dressing room, humming a tune from the show, a piping rustic melody. He resolved not to irritate Menlo in any way, not to give him the slightest excuse to ruin such a promising evening. He fastened a polite smile on his face; the evening's performance wasn't over yet.

"Long time, et cetera," he said mildly. "I convinced them I wasn't likely to skip town. And even if I did, they've got plenty of other witnesses, people who saw a lot more than I did."

"If they'd known who they were dealing with—"

"I'm not exactly on the F.B.I.'s most wanted list, Captain." God, it hurt to call Menlo "Captain." How the asshole had ever managed lieutenant was a puzzle.

"What the hell were you doing at the reservoir?"

"Ready, Michael?" Kathleen had chosen that moment to peer in over the cop's shoulder. Her two words were sufficient to inform Menlo that he had the unparalleled opportunity to interrupt something that might turn out to be fun. His eyes glowed.

"He'll be busy for a while," Menlo grunted, eyeing Kathleen as offensively as possible.

She gave it back to him with interest, and Menlo's face burned briefly red.

Much as he would have enjoyed seeing Farrell tangle with the cop, Spraggue nodded her back outside. "Five minutes. If it's longer than that, go on home and I'll phone."

"You sure?"

"Yeah."

Menlo could have taken out a patent on obscene leers.

"I asked you a question," he said triumphantly, as soon as Farrell's perfume wafted out of the immediate area.

"I'm sure it must have been important."

"What were you doing at the reservoir?"

"What are you doing here? Last time I looked, this was Cambridge, not Boston."

"If you got any complaints, I'll be glad to take you down to the Cambridge Police Station and you can—"

"No, thanks."

"So what were you doing at the reservoir?"

"Running."

The conversation had lurched downhill from there. The calmer Spraggue's manner, the more he seemed to rile Menlo. And Menlo had always had the effect of a persistent buzzing mosquito on Spraggue.

The first time they'd met, with shattering results, Spraggue had been a licensed P.I. working a case. Like the majority of their encounters, it had ended with Spraggue getting hauled off to a cell in the Charles Street Jail, only to be rescued prior to incarceration by a fleet of the best lawyers ever to whip up a writ of habeas corpus. By a conservative estimate, Spraggue figured he'd held up Menlo's appointment to lieutenant by two years. Two years well spent. Maybe he should have stayed a private investigator just for the satisfaction of keeping Menlo off the captain's roll.

Now it seemed that any hint of a trace of a possibility that Spraggue might be back in the private investigation game was enough to bring Menlo roaring over from Boston, enough to make him stretch his authority in order to cart Spraggue in for questioning, enough to make him threaten a material witness jailing. Spraggue failed to feel flattered by the attention.

"What were you doing at the reservoir?"

By the time the question got asked for the fourth time, they were in Menlo's dingy downtown office and the fantasy-fulfilling night with Kathleen had gone up in smoke.

"I suppose this is now an official inquiry?"

"You might say so."

"Get the stenographer in here, then. Make it nice and legal."

"That ain't necessary."

"Oh, but it is. Without one, I do my famous impersonation of a clam."

"Oh, yeah?" Menlo's right hand clenched instinctively into a fist.

"And my lawyer will find it lamentably easy to demonstrate that you did not bring me here with any official purpose in mind, but were just having a slow night and decided to harass an innocent citizen to pass the time."

That brought the steno in. It also got Menlo's feet tapping in the same drunken rhythm they habitually beat when Spraggue's needling pierced the skin. Not for the first time, Spraggue thought that he really ought to measure the interval it took to get the captain's legs shaking. He never clocked it; he continually assumed that each present encounter was the final one—that he'd never have to see Menlo's big, dumb boxer's mug again. But there always seemed to be an encore, one more session with Menlo barking harebrained questions and Spraggue managing not to get hit in the mouth.

"Okay," Menlo had said once the stenographer was situated, "what were you doing at the reservoir on the afternoon of April 16, 1982?"

"Running."

Menlo's questions droned on, augmented by dire warnings concerning the fate of private citizens who persisted in screwing up police investigations. Spraggue quit listening and started imagining horrible tortures for Pete Collatos, who'd gotten him into this mess in the first place. But his mind kept picturing Kathleen . . . Kathleen in Celia's long flowered dress . . . Kathleen shrugging out of her clothes in his dressing room . . . *Damn.* A night that should have been an occasion to remember, to savor, shot to hell.

"Where ya want me to drop ya?" the cabbie asked.

Unwillingly, Spraggue opened his eyes. His fingers closed on a card in his pocket. After all that waste of time, Menlo had actually had the nerve to dole out his card along with the admonition to call with any newly remembered details of the shooting. Spraggue read the embossed face of the card once, ripped it across. "Turn onto Brattle," he said. "Stop in front of Reading International."

Usually he walked to the theater from his house, but today, pressed for time, he'd driven straight in from the reservoir. Found a damn good parking place. A tow zone, true, but he couldn't recall ever seeing a car towed in the Square. Particularly a car with a Cambridge resident sticker on the windshield. If the cops really needed the parking fee, they victimized a car with New York plates. Vengeance for what the Yankees routinely did to the Red Sox.

When he'd located the empty space, smack on Brattle, he'd considered it a good omen. Based on the disaster his evening had turned into, his car had probably been stolen.

He paid off the cabbie and glanced at his watch. No point in calling Kathleen. She'd be deep in dreamless sleep by now—unless she'd invited one of the other actors home as his understudy.

The Porsche was still there.

He drove up Brattle, sped by Fayerweather Street, and only realized after he had passed it that he'd never had any intention of going home.

FOUR

He caught the tail end of the amber light and veered left at the Fresh Pond Parkway. The normally jammed hairpin turns that would spew him out onto Soldiers Field Road were wide open. He rounded them cautiously in spite of an urge for screeching speed; the Buckingham Browne & Nichols School parking lot was a known cop hangout and he'd had a recent overdose of law enforcement.

Flicking on the radio, he got static. Most of the decent FM stations had limited broadcasting hours. Before pushing the WBCN button, he switched to an AM all-news station to see what the media was making of the attack on Donagher.

The WEEI talk show broke for a commercial as soon as he got in tuned in and he hurriedly lowered the volume on an inane, repetitive, advertising jingle. He twisted the knob back up when he recognized the voice on the air.

Frank Bartolo, no doubt born Francesco, was a fixture in Massachusetts politics. His rasping, heavily accented voice was not the perfect instrument for radio, but he'd done his own commercials for school committee, for district attorney, for state representative, and now that he was after a seat in the U.S. Senate, he saw no need to hire spokesmen. Not that he was actively campaigning at the moment. Oh no. He was merely commenting on the disturbing news that someone had taken a potshot at his rival—ultraliberal, free-spending, anti-religion-family-and-apple-pie Senator Donagher—managing to voice his concern in a way that implied a cheap publicity stunt as the likeliest motivation for such a dreadful, albeit understandable, act. Maybe, in his never-ending quest for equal exposure, Bartolo would be forced to run the marathon. Spraggue envisioned the pear-shaped, balding, fiftyish Bartolo panting up Heartbreak Hill and one corner of his mouth turned up in a wry grin. Do him good.

He punched the WBCN button and got blasted by New Wave rock. Late at night, the tamest of radio stations loosened up; WBCN went wild.

He swung into a legal U-turn, then cut a right onto Parsons Street. Because Aunt Mary lived there, he knew every shortcut to Chestnut Hill. For most of the ride, he tried to convince himself that the family mansion, Mary's home, was his destination; never too late to call on Aunt Mary. But he felt drawn to the site of the afternoon's shooting, probably, he realized with a grimace, by Menlo's arrogant command to steer clear.

The area was as dead as the denizens of the Boston College graveyard across the road, pitch dark in contrast to the cemetery's brightly lit boundaries. Was B.C. concerned about the possible desecration of tombstones? Or were courting couples rather than midnight vandals the object of the excess wattage? Did glowing lights instead of college deans now serve in loco parentis at the predominantly Catholic school? Briefly, Spraggue considered the residents of the graveyard; was it true that, once granted tenure, Boston College professors never left the grounds?

The eerie solitude prickled at the back of his neck, made him press the car door gently shut instead of slamming it. He yanked open the trunk and pulled a flashlight out of the toolbox that he considered his "scene of the crime" kit even though he was careful, since his retirement, not to refer to it as such. The flashlight issued a strong clear beam. To save the aged batteries, he clicked it off and waited for his eyes to adjust to darkness.

Only distant high-rise apartment house lights coupled with the occasional honk of a riled automobile reminded him that he was on the edge of a major city, in the middle of an urban sea. The wind sent gooseflesh up his arms. He zipped his jacket, turned up his collar, spat out the last sour taste of police headquarters' vending machine coffee.

When he finally moved, his footsteps echoed, shuffling against the hard ground, the tufted grass.

He located the gnarled elm behind which Donagher had taken refuge through a mixture of memory and dead reckoning. The cops had altered the landmarks; the battered, metal garbage can knocked down and used as a vaulting block to aid in scrambling over the high fence had been righted. It had left its mark: a mound of crumpled, brown paper bags, beer bottles, orange peels. And its unappetizing scent. Spragthe shut his eyes and recreated the scene on the inside of his eyelids until he was certain that he could direct a group of actors in a docu-drama reconstruction of the sniping. He tried to confirm his memory by using the flashlight to check footprints, but cops had plodded over the site, their hard-soled shoes unique in a forest of running sneakers.

He drew an imaginary line from Donagher's tree to the path, inched along it, shining a cone of light at the ground, stooping to shift marble-sized pebbles, examine wormlike twigs.

Then he climbed the fence and began a survey of the trees surrounding the target elm. More likely to find the track of a bullet here, *if* the sniper had been a decent shot . . . *if* he'd used bullets, not blanks.

He was crouched in dense underbrush, poking a knothole with the point of his pocketknife, when he heard the footsteps.

Smothering the flashbeam in the soft earth, he froze. The ground was blanketed with fallen leaves, brittle branches; they would raise a crackling alarm if he moved. He craned his neck and waited, his night-blind eyes fastened on the path.

Some ill-advised insomniac runner? A night-shift cop on casual patrol? An ardent journalist with photographer in tow? Spraggue had never run into any of those obliging criminals who are irresistibly drawn back to the scene of the crime. Neither had any of his cop acquaintances. Still, he stayed crouched out of sight; it was too late to spring back onto the path and declare himself. The footsteps drew nearer. Instead of passing, stopped.

A street lamp, a full moon, a decent complement of stars—even the dimmest of lights might have made identification possible. Spraggue regretted ever using his flashlight; its brightness had ruined his night vision and only time would restore it. He inhaled softly, held the breath for a count of ten, blew it out, listened to the shuffling footsteps, peered steadfastly, unblinkingly, in their direction, as if he could defeat the darkness by the very intensity of his stare.

There. A shadow moved. A beam of startlingly clear yellow light shot out. The intruder had a flashlight of his own. It shined briefly in Spraggue's squinted eyes, focused on the path.

From the whispery noises, from the changes in elevation of the beam's source, the intruder seemed to be echoing Spraggue's earlier movements, searching for a pebble, a button, a bullet.

A cop?

The muscles in Spraggue's calves and thighs, already strained from the afternoon's run, protested his awkward crouch. He rested his right hand, palm flat, on the ground in front of him and shifted his weight forward to the hand. Mistake. His left leg cramped suddenly and he drew a sharp involuntary breath.

The shadow on the path straightened; the flashlight beam hovered perilously near.

"Who's there?" the shadow said in a nervous low voice.

Spraggue turned his flashlight full on the path, using the other beam as a target, aiming at a point six feet high, aiming to blind.

The man wore a dark business suit, appropriate for the chilly April night, but hardly de rigueur for running. He was tall, extremely thin, with hunched shoulders, a gawky neck, and a standout Adam's apple. His wire-rimmed glasses reflected the light for an instant. Then, with an inarticulate cry, he took to his heels, fleeing clockwise around the reservoir, out towards Beacon Street.

Spraggue gave agonized chase, cramped calf muscle and all. Dammit, was he going to spend his entire life racing around this accursed body of water, pursuing futilely, foolishly, those who could, with no effort, outrun him every time? He kept on in dogged anguish, hoping the man in front of him would stumble, trip over some snaky tree root. Maybe he'd be able to outrun a prone opponent.

By the time he arrived, panting, in front of the public swimming pool, he heard the motor roar. The dark car made a screeching illegal U-turn, swung back toward downtown Boston. Spraggue, bent with pain, drenched in sweat, watched it veer out of sight with growing satisfaction.

This driver hadn't had the foresight to smear his license plate with mud. The tiny light over the plate picked out the red letters and numbers on the white metal like neon in the dark. Spraggue repeated the sequence aloud, fumbled in his pocket for a pencil, wrote it on the back of a bank deposit slip.

Tomorrow, he'd present it to Captain Hurley, his old police department buddy and Menlo's chief rival. And then he'd quit involving himself in matters that didn't concern him, go back to concentrating on acting and Kathleen, possibly in reverse order.

But as he trudged back toward his car, after massaging his legs for a good five minutes, he couldn't resist one last peek at the scene of the sniping, one more look for the elusive bullet.

He didn't find it, but he did find where it had been. Two feet from the ground, in the trunk of a tree two yards to the right of the target, a knife had hacked away at the bark and removed something cylindrical in shape. The cut was a good three inches deep in the wounded bark.

Back in the Porsche, he checked the glow of the dashboard clock: 3:10.

Never too late to call on Aunt Mary.

FIVE

Golden lamplight filtered through sheer curtains in the ground floor windows of the Chestnut Hill mansion, evidence of Aunt Mary's wakefulness. Spraggue had once believed that she slept from 5 A.M. till 9 A.M., that for those four hours the ticker-tape machine stayed silent, the computer ceased to hum, the playing cards and crossword puzzles rested idly on the shelves. But he'd shown up at seven thirty one morning, right in the middle of the supposed rest time, and discovered her in the act of smacking a croquet ball around the grounds to the horror of the gardener. A remarkably stodgy man for one so young, said gardener was in grave jeopardy of losing his job.

As he flipped off the ignition, the porch lights blazed and Mary Spraggue Hillman tugged open the heavy oak door. Pierce, the butler, loomed behind her; in spite of her seventy-odd years, he rarely beat her to the door.

She wore an Icelandic wool shawl tossed over a scarlet dressing gown with the flair of an aging patrician gypsy. Etched with countless feathery wrinkles, her skin had stayed taut to her fine bones and retained the pink-and-white coloring of youth. Deep crow's feet at the corners of her eyes and mouth slashed upward, imparting an aura of perpetual good humor. The red warred with the silver in her curly hair.

"Well, dear," she said crisply, her voice splitting the darkness like a homing beacon, "Pierce is delighted that you've arrived. Without intervention, he would certainly have lost yet another hand of gin rummy. Soon he will owe me his salary unto all eternity and I shall have to collect debts from his grandchildren."

"Winning agrees with you; you look lovely." Spraggue mounted the front steps and aimed a kiss at her offered cheek.

"They do say antiques are in vogue this season," she said drily. As they entered the foyer, she stared at him critically and made a noise that in anyone less refined would have been a grunt.

Spraggue lifted one eyebrow inquiringly.

"You have elm leaves in your hair, my dear," she said. "Just bits and pieces of them, really. I am trying to deduce what revelry you could have indulged in that would cause a four-hour delay between the termination of your performance and your arrival at my front door replete with elm leaves. I am far too tactful to inquire, but even at my advanced age, I possess an active imagination. . . . What would you like to drink, and are you at all hungry after your evening's whatever?''

Spraggue let her take his arm and draw him into the library, his favorite room, unchanged since his boyhood, probably unchanged since his great-grandfather, robber-baron Davison Spraggue, had built the massive Georgian structure to the confounding of his enemies and to their secret admiration. The vast room was two stories high with a system of wrought-iron balconies and spiral staircases that enabled one to reach the towering bookshelves that covered three walls. The Oriental rug was a twenty-by-twenty-four-foot Kashan with plenty of parquet border surrounding it. One wall of books was broken up by a huge bay window that overlooked the front lawn as it swept down to the wading pool. The fourth wall was the focal point of the room: over the marble mantelpiece, skillfully lighted, hung the Cézanne landscape that was the pride of the Spraggue Post-Impressionist Collection.

Mary made a beeline for her favorite chair, a green velvet wingback near the bay window. Spraggue sprawled on the matching sofa. Pierce, with a distinct air of relief, began collecting cards off the game table, melding them into a pack.

''See that?'' Mary murmured softly. ''Didn't even ask me if I wanted to play out the hand. Imagine what rotten cards he must have had!'' She shifted her focus abruptly to her nephew. ''You look sleepy,'' she said, as if the very idea of sleep at three in the morning was absurd. ''Coffee to keep you awake or wine to further sedate you?''

''No coffee.''

''Wine, then. If you overindulge, you can sleep it off in the tower room.''

"No."

"Seems a logical plan to me."

"No."

"It *is* your room, in *your* house—"

"Aunt Mary, I don't want breakfast in bed tomorrow. I don't want all my clothes to mysteriously disappear during the night and turn up tomorrow morning washed, pressed, and brushed, with all the missing buttons sewn on. I want to go home and collapse on my unmade bed in my own disarray and wake up and find everything just where I left it."

"I'll explain to Dora that you prefer to—"

"Why not get me drunk first and then try to persuade me to stay?"

Her eyes accepted the challenge. She hesitated for perhaps five seconds, smiled sweetly, and said, "How long has it been since you've tasted any of your very own 1968 Holloway Hills Private Reserve Cabernet?"

He smiled, recalling more than the rich, earthy taste of wine, remembering an entire hectic autumn laced with the heady smell of crushed grapes, the musky scent of Kate Holloway's perfume. "It's long gone," he said. "I doubt we made over a hundred cases that year."

"I received a present today."

"It's not your birthday."

"At my age, one celebrates whenever one can. For instance, I intend to celebrate the receipt of a half case of '68 Private Reserve Cabernet direct from Miss Holloway herself."

"And why is Kate so nice to you and so rotten to me?"

"Sex rears its ugly head. But, alas, I must tell the truth. I was instructed to share the booty with you."

"In a letter I'm not supposed to read?"

"Personal, I believe she termed it."

"Personal about her or personal about me?"

Aunt Mary arched one eyebrow. "Where were you tonight, my dear?"

"You're too polite to ask, remember? Don't you think the Cabernet should be saved for a dinner? What about something lighter for tonight?"

"Perhaps. Of course, Dora did make pâté to go with it—"

"Done," Spraggue said. "Bring on the wine."

Mary nodded in Pierce's direction and he stopped shuffling cards and retreated silently, closing the double doors behind him.

"Now," Mary said with a smile of quiet satisfaction, "I wish to speak to you about real estate."

"That is not the way to keep me awake and alert."

"Both your father and your grandfather found the subject endlessly fascinating."

"I must have been a changeling."

"Nonsense. Look in the mirror and then look at the portrait of your grandfather in the foyer. You're exactly—"

"Only on the outside," Spraggue said.

"It's a good thing for you that I find matters of finance fascinating."

"No argument. Why don't I give you power of attorney and then I won't have to listen?"

"Michael," Mary said firmly, "while I am planning to live forever, as you know, they tell me money can't buy that, and some day you may have to figure this mess out on your own."

"I'm listening," Spraggue said in what he hoped was a suitably chastened tone of voice. He swallowed another yawn and was sure Mary saw him do it.

"Besides," she said, "this may intrigue you. It smacks of illegality."

The doors eased noiselessly open, ushering in Pierce bearing a laden silver tray. A crusty loaf of French bread steamed in a wicker basket lined with white cloth. A cut crystal decanter bounced colored prisms of light off two wineglasses and a blue ceramic bowl. The butler placed the tray on the coffee table, and, dismissed by some imperceptible sign from his employer, left them to fend for themselves.

"For some time," Mary said, between sips of wine, "I have been interested in purchasing a building on Commonwealth Avenue in the Back Bay. 312 is the address. It's located next door to two buildings already owned by the Sprague Foundation. With the third building secured, the entire trio could be modernized, improved—"

"We're not talking condo conversion here, are we?"

"You vetoed that last year. Still the building is attractive."

"If you think it's a good deal, go ahead and—"

"No, Michael. It's complicated. The price of that building is being arbitrarily raised."

"How do you arbitrarily raise the price of a building? A building is worth whatever somebody pays for it."

"Ah. You do learn what I teach you. In this case, the property is being passed back and forth among a series of "straw" owners. No money is actually changing hands, but the figures on deeds are skyrocketing."

"So somebody found out that you're after the property," Sprague said. "You've got a leak in the organization."

"I think the assumption of a gossipy employee is invalidated by the fire."

"The fire?"

"Just a small blaze in the basement of this overpriced edifice. One of our tenants, a dear man in the garden flat, noticed an odd smell and called the fire department before anything drastic occurred. I wouldn't have even known about it if the superintendent of our building hadn't mentioned it."

"So?"

"So now I'm worried that they are not kicking up the price in order to get money out of me. I'm worried that their target may be some insurance company, that they may be planning to burn the building down. I have called the police and the fire department, and both have treated me like a dotty old lady."

"A mistake."

"I have phoned the Registry of Deeds, the Tax Assessor, the Insurance Commissioner. And I have come up against a brick wall; I am utterly stymied. I know no more about this property than I did on the day I first viewed it. I can find no trace of the principal owners; they are not in the phone book nor do they drive cars licensed in Massachusetts—"

"A lot of honest folk prefer to register their cars someplace with less extortionate insurance rates."

"And one of the so-called owners is a firm, a holding company, whose lawyer will not respond to my lawyer's questions."

"Undoubtedly what they pay him for," Spraggue said.

"Would it interest you if I said there was a very good chance that the fire was caused by someone spilling a pool of lighter fluid directly underneath a radiator?"

Spraggue swallowed a bite of bread and pâté, took a long drink. "Mary," he said, "listen to me. I'm a working actor. I do a minimum of five shows a week, sometimes eight. I play five different roles. I know what you're trying to do. You're trying to get me back into investigation work. You never give up, do you?"

"Seldom."

"I know you preferred my former career."

"Call me a busybody old lady. I deserve it. The arson squad intimated as much. But I would like you to bring the situation to the attention of some of your police department cronies; I thought maybe that nice Captain Hurley . . ."

"I'll ask him," Spraggue said. "But that's it. That's all."

"Do you like the pâté, dear?"

"Does that mean business is over?"

"Compliment Dora if you do like the pâté. She's been threatening to leave again. Go somewhere more exciting, somewhere with young people who entertain. Open a restaurant."

"She's been threatening to leave ever since I can remember."

"She'd love to have you move back in. You were always a challenge to her—"

"Forget it."

"If she quits, it will be on your head."

"There's enough on my head. I have a performance tomorrow and you neglected to pass on to me your secret gift of needing next to no sleep."

"It's no gift, believe me."

"Thanks for the food, and when you write Kate, tell her the wine made me think of her in positively indecent ways."

"The tower room awaits you. It's all made up."

"No," Spraggue said. "Thank you, but no. I have a room in a house that belongs to me, bought with money I earned. It ain't the tower room, but it's mine." He'd almost made it back to the car when she leaned out the door and called his name.

What now? he thought.

She hurried down the stairs, leaving the door ajar. "I forgot to tell you about the phone call," she said breathlessly. "It's not important, I suppose. Just odd. I don't even know who it was that called; and yet I can't rid myself of the feeling that I ought to know his voice."

"Whoa," Spraggue said. "One of us seems to be rambling."

"Nonsense. A man called a little after five this afternoon. He did not ask to speak to you. He asked *about* you. Specifically, he asked, and I quote, if you 'were on a case.' I hesitated, asked him again whom he wished to inquire about. There could very well be, and probably is, a Doctor Sprague in the vicinity. I thought the man might be attempting to reach a doctor. But he merely repeated his request and when I didn't answer immediately, he hung up."

"But you thought you recognized the voice?"

"One of those feelings . . . Yes . . . I'm sure I've heard it before."

"Do you remember a friend of mine named Pete Collatos? A cop?"

"With an unmistakable Boston accent? It was not he."

"What about Brian Donagher then?"

"Senator Donagher? He was shot at today, right at the reservoir, if you can imagine such—"

"Did it sound like him?"

"No. Not at all. Why? What's going on? You're not—"

"I am not investigating the Donagher shooting, Aunt Mary. Remember? You want me to call the senator and tell him you're available?"

"Do not tease a harmless old woman."

"Hah," Spraggue said, closing himself into the shell of the Porsche. "I'd be doing the guy a favor."

SIX

Anyone who goes to bed at five in the morning ought to have the sense to take the phone off the hook. That was Spraggue's first coherent thought after the harsh jangling jarred him into a sitting position. He swore as he staggered across the room to the table on which the offending instrument shrilled. Kathleen, he thought, and his mood improved markedly.

He grabbed the receiver, said "Hang on," then carried the phone back to the bed and sat, Indian fashion, lifting his feet off the cold wooden floor. He wrapped the comforter snugly around his body.

When he finally said "Hello," all irritation was gone from his voice.

Instead of returning his salutation, the distinctly male voice on the other end of the line said sarcastically, "So you're out of the business, huh?"

"Pete?"

"Why the hell were you creeping around the Chestnut Hill Reservoir at three in the goddamn morning?"

"What time is it now, Pete?" Spraggue said flatly.

"Eleven. I waited until I thought you'd be up."

"Very considerate."

"You just want to work the case alone, is that it? No partners?"

"Pete, does this have anything to do with a big dark Buick, license plate 365-890? Because I'm planning to call Hurley to get the plate traced."

"No need to bother, Spraggue."

"I'd have to have a better reason to ignore that car than your say-so."

"Well, that's why I'm calling, to invite you over for a chat about the reservoir and the poison-pen letters Donagher's been getting."

"Pete, I meant it when I said I wasn't working the case."

"Dammit, Spraggue, Donagher almost got killed!"

"And I'm sure that the Boston Police have a ring around

38

him so tight he'll have to get a note from Mom to go to the bathroom.''

"Don't bet on it," Collatos said bitterly. "He's an independent cuss; won't put up with any of that. Wants to go out and mingle with the people. Doesn't want the electorate to think he's running scared. When the cops suggested he give the marathon a miss, he blew sky-high. Look, the house is in Brighton, one of those big Victorian jobs on Sparhawk Street—"

"Not interested, Pete."

"Well, I'll bet a certain Captain Menlo would be interested in the fact that your car was parked out by the reservoir at three in the morning."

"Which reminds me, did you happen to mention my name to the dear man yesterday?"

"I wouldn't tell him if his hair was on fire."

"But you'd use him to blackmail me into coming over."

"That's a nasty word, Spraggue. I'm trying to help you out. Get you interesting work, answer some questions for you before you go shooting your mouth off to the cops about some car parked at the reservoir that's got no bearing on—"

"Look, Pete." Spraggue knew that if he didn't interrupt, Collatos would go on forever. "I'll come for fifteen minutes, but that's it."

"I want your opinion of those letters and—"

"And you'll tell me who belongs to the dark Buick."

"55 Sparhawk Street," Collatos said.

The phone clicked.

SEVEN

Spraggue considered alternatives—two of which, ripping the phone's umbilical cord out of the wall and diving back under the down comforter, seemed particularly attractive. Then he sighed, stood up, and resolutely sank to the floor for his customary twenty-five push-ups, only to discover the full extent of the damage inflicted by yesterday's sudden spurt of running. He lay flat on his stomach, trying to convince his calf muscles that they were not too tight to allow him to flex his feet and tuck his toes under. After a brief, painful struggle, he abandoned the push-ups, rolled over, and did twice his usual number of sit-ups to compensate.

He stared at the cracked white ceiling for five minutes, crawled over to the bed, reached for the phone, and brought it down to his level.

The way things were going, he didn't want to ask Pete Collatos for any favors, even one as minor as the name of the appropriate officer to handle Mary's potential arsonist. And mentioning the arsonist to Hurley as a casual aside was no longer an option if there was no reason to call Hurley about the Buick.

He dialed 911, police emergency. The high intermittent beep let him know he was being recorded from the moment the gruff-voiced cop answered on the second ring. He asked to be transferred from the Cambridge Police to the Boston Police, then made it quick.

He used the voice he'd adopted for the jailkeeper in a long ago run of *Inherit the Wind* at the Berkshire Theater Festival. It came to mind for the obvious reason: Jailkeepers reminded one of jail and jail was where he was headed if Menlo uncovered evidence of his late-night prowl around the reservoir. It also seemed a safe bet for nonrecognition. Less than two hundred people had seen the play, and not even the nastiest critic would recall the slightly Southern, high, breathy tones he'd taken such pains to perfect.

"That fire at 312 Commonwealth Avenue was set," he said.

"Who is this? State your full name and address."

"Do yourself a favor. Check out the insurance on that place." Spraggue hung up, ignoring a second plea for his name. TV cops would already have had the call traced, a prowl car on the way to his front door. With the real-life Boston Police, the question was whether they'd even bother to check out the tip.

Hauling himself to his feet, leaving the phone on the floor, he tried to stretch the ache out of his muscles. No soap. He went downstairs, padding barefoot into the living room.

Spraggue's apartment, the top two floors of a Fayerweather Street triple-decker, wasn't exactly furnished. Its barren quality was a direct response to the finished perfection of the Chestnut Hill mansion. He'd bought the place on his return from England, for its proximity to Harvard, determined never to live in old Davison Spraggue's museum again. That had been the easy part. Convincing Mary that she ought to remain in the family mausoleum had been the tricky half of the deal. She'd finally acquiesced when he'd threatened to donate his patrimony to the Commonwealth of Massachusetts for use as a museum. All he'd taken from the house he'd grown up in was one chair, a brown suede monster comfortable enough to sleep in at a pinch, one Oriental rug, and two paintings.

At the time, he'd thought he would enjoy furnishing and decorating his own place. He still thought so. He never got around to it.

He'd bought a bed and stuck it at one end of the big sky-lit room that was intended as the third floor living room. He'd ordered plain white shades for the multitude of windows, but never gotten as far as curtains. The built-in chests of drawers in the closets seemed sufficient for storage. One of the appropriated artworks, a signed Picasso sketch, hung on a wall visible from the bed.

The remainder of the decor consisted mainly of plants, showered on him by Mary, watered sporadically. Their health, their glorious green profusion, made him suspect that Mrs. Wales, the lady who cleaned his apartment in exchange for a steep reduction in her first floor rent, augmented his haphazard care.

The old brown chair was the only item of furniture in the living room, unless you counted cushions. He'd bought a few pieces for the dining room at an auction: an old trestle table, eight ladderback chairs in need of recaning. The second painting hung in the dining room: a Van Gogh still life swirled in glorious golds and reds that made up for the room's lack of window or fireplace.

He went into the kitchen to scramble eggs. No barren quality there. Two walls were entirely covered by pegboard, and the pegboard bristled with every conceivable cooking gadget invented, from garlic presses and egg slicers to meat mallets, pastry brushes, and wine pulls, from the very helpful to the ludicrous. Most were gifts. He owned six egg timers, ranging from serviceable to mildly cute to positively obscene. He never used egg timers.

He washed the eggs down with black coffee, the beans ground in one of three gift coffee grinders. He ground by handcrank this morning, shuddering at the thought of the noisy sleek electric grinder.

He dialed Kathleen from the kitchen wall phone, scraping up bits of egg on the last crust of toast, chewing hastily as the phone rang. She snatched up the receiver as if she'd been waiting for the call. Once he identified himself, all the eagerness faded. She thought she might be coming down with a cold. She was absolutely exhausted. She would definitely be busy after tonight's show. Possibly busy for the rest of her life.

Farrell didn't take well to being stood up. It had probably never happened to her before. Getting semi-arrested didn't seem a good enough excuse to her. Her tone intimated that he should have shot the man dead who threatened last night's rendezvous. Spraggue wondered whether the judge at his murder trial would consider Menlo's interference in his tryst with Kathleen grounds for justifiable homicide. That would depend on the judge's age, he supposed. And his eyesight. And his memory.

He hung up, dressed, hobbled down to the car.

Sparhawk Street was a three-block section of faded elegance trapped between St. Elizabeth's Hospital and Market Street in the Brighton section of Boston. For a politician, it was an unusual address; the transient-liberal-student enclave rarely managed to elect one of its own to City Council, much less the U.S. Senate. But Donagher, with his marathon-earned fame, had a name-recognition advantage that had outweighed the clannishness of North End Italians and Southie Irish when he first ran for city-wide office, that even now ignored town boundaries and made him as popular in the rural Berkshires as he was inside the Route 128 industrial belt.

The huge old homes were in various states of disrepair, making it impossible to guess whether the area was on the way up toward respectable gentrification or down toward seedy poverty. One staid colonial had the faded air of a rooming house. A pillared porch boasted a Greek-lettered banner: a college fraternity house. Noisy neighbors.

They weren't very loud on a Saturday afternoon. Probably still asleep, hung over from the revels of Friday night. Spraggue sympathized; he felt a bit hung over himself, from the stale air of the police station, Mary's wine, and the shattered expectations of the night. He didn't feel like chatting with Collatos. He didn't feel like analyzing crazed death threats.

Parking was allowed on one side of Sparhawk Street, which left one-and-a-half lanes for two-way traffic, less if you counted the half lane devoted to the propagation of potholes. Spraggue was driving cautiously, scanning the houses for addresses, when he noticed the plain dark car parked halfway down the street. Two men dozed in the front seat, one with a newspaper spread partially over his face.

Spraggue kept his foot pressed firmly on the accelerator and breezed right past the house that must have been Donagher's, a neatly painted blue Victorian. About twenty feet before Sparhawk came to an end at Cambridge Street, a narrow road opened on the left: Murdock Street. Spraggue took the turn, then the next left: Mapleton. He checked for other unmarked cars, maybe a stationary utility van. The street seemed clear, so he pulled sharply to the right and parked.

He strolled back along Mapleton, hands shoved in his pockets, until he could plainly see, through the carefully tended back garden of a white colonial, the light blue paint he'd noted on 55 Sparhawk. A house the size of Donagher's would have more than one entrance, that was certain. How vigilant the police? How nosy the neighbors?

As if in response to his question, a woman walked swiftly down the narrow concrete-slab walkway that led into the yard of the white colonial. She matched the pale sunshine. Her long, fine golden hair was brushed tight to her skull.

Her beige raincoat was cinched at her waist with a matching belt. She wore dark stockings and tiny high-heeled shoes. Stopping for a moment to shove a wide-brimmed khaki rainhat over her hair, she shot one careful glance to her right, one to her left. She seemed not to notice Spraggue. He caught only a glimpse of a delicate pastel face, like the face of a Dresden China shepherdess after the painter had set a final wash of gray over all his brighter tones.

The woman turned abruptly and sped off toward Market Street, leaving Spraggue to wonder how she could move so quickly on her tiny tap-tapping heels.

He waited until she was out of sight, then hurried up the walkway. It took a surprising turn behind a stand of budding trees and led, not to the presumed garage of number whatever Mapleton, but directly to the back porch of Donagher's blue Victorian. Spraggue stared speculatively after the pastel woman. Had she come from Donagher's house?

Collatos was at the back door before he could push the buzzer, a broad grin splitting his swarthy face. "Cops out front," he said casually as they shook hands.

"You could have mentioned them when you called."

"I knew you'd spot them. Even had a bet on it with Murray. You just won me five bucks."

"Murray?"

"Come on in, Spraggue. I feel well-disposed toward you."

"Nice place" was all Spraggue said as they moved down a hallway with a glistening wooden floor into a lace-curtained front room furnished in stolid New England unimaginativeness accented with a few not inexpensive antiques.

"Donagher lived here long?" he asked, taking Collatos up on his invitation to sit on the chintz sofa.

"Maybe twelve, fifteen years. I think ever since he got married."

"Big place."

"It's more than just his house. It's staff headquarters, campaign headquarters. They've got rooms fixed up for people to stay over and they're always full. I moved in when I took the bodyguard job. Donagher's campaign manager lives here. One of his speech writers."

"Is the senator here much?"

"Oh, yeah. Especially lately, with the marathon coming up and the election. Brian's a real home and family man so he's a regular commuter between Washington and Boston."

"Odd that the whole family hasn't packed up and moved to Washington."

"Coffee?" Collatos asked.

"Black."

Spraggue left the uncomfortable couch as soon as Collatos went off in search of refreshment. He circled the room, pulled back one edge of a curtain cautiously. The unmarked car was in place. An envelope on the polished wooden mantel caught his eye, a packet full of amateur photographs. He shook them out in his hand: Donagher; two towheaded boys, maybe ten and fourteen years old; the pastel woman. The perfect political family. Except that the smile on the pastel woman looked tight, forced.

He heard Collatos' footsteps and shoved the prints back in their packet, placed the envelope back on the mantel. He wondered if Donagher's wife made a practice of leaving the house by the back door, scurrying down a neighbor's driveway, wearing a concealing hat. Maybe she was avoiding the patrol car out front. Spraggue kicked himself for not heeding his first impulse and following her. Then he kicked himself again for the thought. Follow Donagher's wife. What the hell for? He clenched his teeth and warned himself off.

When Collatos returned with the coffee, Spraggue was seated decorously on the couch, tapping his foot against a square of drab, but expensive rug.

"Want a doughnut?" Collatos asked. "Did you know that politicians live on doughnuts? We got glazed, plain, jelly, sugarcoated—"

"Who spotted me at the reservoir last night?" Spraggue asked, refusing the doughnut with a shake of his head.

Collatos took his time selecting a particularly gooey lump of dough that oozed red jam when bitten. "Want to meet him?" he asked.

"Why not?"

The man with the wire-rimmed glasses started talking as soon as Collatos ushered him into the room. He was last night's apparition all right, wearing a gray suit, instead of a dark one. His tall, skinny silhouette, his stick-out Adam's apple, left no doubt about it.

"Pleased to meet you," he said, offering a gawky handshake. "You scared the hell out of me last night. I almost called the cops right then. If Pete hadn't been awake when I got home, if he hadn't realized who you were—"

"And how did you manage that?" Spraggue asked Collatos.

"Murray saw your car. A goddam silver Porsche, and I'm not supposed to know who it is?"

Spraggue turned to the man called Murray. "Just what game were you playing at the reservoir last night?"

"He sounds like a cop," Murray said, and Spraggue remembered how many times Menlo had asked him similar questions during their unfriendly session downtown.

"Murray is Senator Donagher's campaign manager," Collatos said hurriedly, as if his title explained the man's presence at the reservoir. "Murray Eichenhorn—Michael Spraggue. Sit down and drink some coffee, Murray, and don't antagonize the man, please."

"Hey." Eichenhorn sent Spraggue a disarming smile that would have worked better if it hadn't been practiced as much. "Look, I don't mean to be difficult. I didn't get much

47

sleep last night. I was tied up all day in meetings. The Donagher campaign's really starting to rev up. And then I got word that some nutcase tried to shoot my man. I almost had a heart attack myself. But I was booked solid; I couldn't get over to the reservoir. Insomnia and curiosity sent me out on a wild-goose chase in the middle of the night, that's all."

"What were you looking for?"

"Sure you're not a cop?" Eichenhorn's smile faded, reasserted itself. "Sorry. I just wanted to see the place. Brian had described it to me. I wanted to see how close I'd come to looking for a new job."

"Campaign manager . . . You coordinate Donagher's publicity?"

"No crime in that. I handle all his media contacts, hire and fire his speech writers, make sure he wears a tie at the Ritz-Carlton and a hard hat on a construction site—"

"Faking incidents for publicity purposes may not be on the statute books but—"

Eichenhorn's face reddened like an embarrassed adolescent's. "Forget it," he said. "I want Donagher to blitz this election. I want a landslide. He takes over sixty-five percent of the vote here in Massachusetts and Donagher's on his way to the White House. I'd do just about anything to ensure that he wins big. That's my job. But I'm no dope. I'm no prankster. I'm not about to try some absolutely harebrained stunt like shooting bullets into a crowd—"

"You wanted to see if they were real bullets, didn't you?"

"Yes."

"Because you suspected somebody of pulling a stunt. Who?"

The campaign manager pressed his thin lips together, stared blankly at the window as if he could see beyond the closed curtains. "I don't suspect anyone," he said. "I went because I'm having a hard time convincing myself that this

48

business is real, that whoever wrote those letters means what he says. I thought maybe if I saw it for myself, saw real bulletholes, I might be able to believe it.''

''Believe it. They're real.''

''Donagher's leading in all the preelection polls. He doesn't need any cheap stupid stunts. This is the worst kind of thing that could happen, especially now, before the race. Kooks encourage each other. Some misfit reads about somebody taking a potshot at a senator and heads over to his local gun shop. It makes me sick. . . .''

Sprague studied the campaign manager's face, let his eyes fall to the man's lap, noticed his white-knuckled hands, nails bitten to the quick.

''Take a look at the letters?'' Collatos said to break the uncomfortable silence.

''That was the deal. A look. Anything I find, I give you. Gratis.''

Collatos grinned. ''And that should keep Menlo away from your door.''

EIGHT

Donagher's death threats were no hastily scribbled scratches penciled on the backs of discarded envelopes; they were works of craftsmanship.

Collatos presented him with a battered shoebox containing the poison pen's collected works. Murray hadn't lingered; he had appointments booked on top of appointments, for himself and for the senator, coordinating the loyal troops with the election looming near. He'd shaken Spraggue's hand in parting and floored him by asking whether he had any intention of ever running for political office.

"You'd be great," he'd said earnestly. "That old New England background. The money wouldn't hurt. Good image. Be sure to contact me if you—"

"It wouldn't bother you if I were a fascist?"

"Are you?"

"A communist? A Democrat? A Republican?"

"The only labels I care about are *winner* and *loser*," Donagher's campaign manager had said with no hint of a smile to soften the brutal formula into a joke. Then he'd glanced at his watch, frowned, and left the room, slamming the door with unnecessary force behind him.

"Fingerprints?" Spraggue asked, setting the shoe-box down on the desk in the small alcove near the fireplace.

"I checked them," Collatos said. "The cops checked them. Negative."

"The cops? I thought—"

"Yesterday. We had to show them yesterday, after the sniping. I insisted on it. Donagher's practically not speaking to me. Says I scared his wife."

Scared. The pastel woman hadn't looked frightened of anything beyond discovery of her clandestine exit, Spraggue thought.

"The police made copies," Collatos said.

"Okay. Now leave me alone with them."

Collatos had obediently disappeared, and Spraggue had enjoyed his absence.

Each note had been constructed by cutting separate words out of newspapers, lining them up precisely across the diagonal of an eight by eleven sheet of heavy cream-colored bond, fastening them in place with liberal dollops of rubber cement. None was signed, but the method itself was a signature of sorts. All had been created by the same hand.

The choicer obscenities were inked in; the *Globe* and the *Herald* declined to print such words, generally substituting a welter of dots, dashes, and exclamation points. Here, the anonymous correspondent had shown a curious blend of careful planning and lack of foresight. He'd printed his obscenities in squared-off block letters, using a ruled line to keep his remarks straight, painstakingly erasing the line afterward. But he'd obviously cemented his newsprint words into place before adding the obscenities; the last few letters of *motherfucker* were jammed into their allotted space. The rest of the document was meticulously neat, if not overwhelmingly original.

Words cut out of newspapers . . . untraceable. A million papers sold daily in the metro Boston area. Of course, a real nut might just keep the paper as a souvenir; if the cops happened to ring the right doorbell, the one-in-a-million doorbell, there the evidence would sit, in plain sight. Fat chance. Spraggue concentrated on the printing.

Printing was harder to identify than typing. If the messages had been typed, he could have come up with the make of the machine, with some guess about the proficiency of the typist. But printing, especially this squared-off block printing . . . Hell, nobody wrote like that normally. It wasn't the elongated style of a draftsman's hand. It was similar in all the notes, so identical that Spraggue wondered if all six notes had been prepared at one time, mailed separately.

No misspelling. No fingerprints. No return address.

Moreover, no personal knowledge of Donagher. The notes screamed about political issues, the tired battles fought in the newspapers for years: abortion, busing, school funding, property taxes. They pushed the ordinary buttons, sang the usual songs. They were unique only in their vehemence, their obscenity, their ultimate threat.

"So?" Collatos said hopefully when he reentered the room half an hour later.

"Written by a retired schoolteacher with a slight limp and a passion for chocolate-covered raisins."

"Come on."

"The only remarkable thing about these masterpieces is the amount of time they represent. You ever sit down with the morning paper and try to compose a note out of the front page? Look how meticulously the damn words have been snipped out: careful little cuts with a sharp scissors. Whoever it is has a good eye. He, or she, left a similar border around all the words, except where he, or she, had to amputate a large word to make a smaller one."

"Huh?"

Spragge's finger jabbed at the sample he held up. "Look at the word *die* in this one. Chopped off right after the *e*. It's the first part of *diet* or *dietician* or *diethylbarbituric* for all I know. It's about the only shortcut our correspondent took."

"A crazy shut-in with nothing better to do?"

"Got me. The thing is that the time taken doesn't square with the message delivered. If somebody out there is really gunning for Donagher—and this kind of note says serious— you'd think there would be a personal grudge. But there's nothing like that. None of the 'I know what you did with my wife' stuff that ought to be here."

"What about political assassination? It could be some jerk who's aching to off somebody in the public eye. Get his name in the papers like John Hinckley or what's-his-name Chapman."

"Did they write notes?"

"No," Collatos said reluctantly.

"Right. They left journals, but they gave no warning. If

52

these were written by somebody seeking publicity, why didn't he send them to the newspapers, especially after Donagher ignored the first ones?''

"I don't know."

"These letters have nothing to do with the shooting at the reservoir. That's my gut reaction, Collatos. The two don't mix. Look at these things; they're political documents. They could have been put together just because the right words happened to be available in the morning paper. Look at this one on abortion:

> THE KILLING OF THE UNBORN IS MURDER!
> DEATH TO THE GODDAM SENATOR WHO
> SUPPORTS THE GODDAM ABORTIONISTS WITH
> TAX DOLLARS!

All the words could have come from one article. The *goddams* were added later. Somebody stuck in nasty words to make the notes seem fierce. Well, they'd have to be a whole lot fiercer to alarm me. Nobody's going to shoot Donagher because property taxes are too high. Or they happen to disagree with his position on capital punishment—''

"That doesn't get me very far."

"What did you expect? Let me see the envelopes."

Spraggue said this last bit as if he were relenting, giving in to Collatos' urging. That was acting. He wanted to see the envelopes. He was hooked.

They broke the pattern. They were typewritten. Each one on a different typewriter.

"Whoever it is," Spraggue said, eyebrow arched, "works in an office large enough to have five typewriters."

"Six," said Collatos. "Six notes, six envelopes. And all different."

"You only gave me five."

"Dammit." Collatos counted the sheaf of envelopes twice, searched the floor, peered under chairs and sofa. "There were six of them when I gave them to the police to copy—"

"All with the same address. The cops probably thought they wouldn't do any harm by helping themselves—"

"They never do," Collatos muttered.

"So speaks an ex-member of the force."

"Who'll deny it if he's ever quoted," finished Collatos. "What do you think of the envelopes?"

"More of the same. Too clever, too complicated. Who's going to bother to use five typewriters?"

"Six."

"Six. And your phantom letter writer is either an indifferent typist or a bad typist trying hard or a good typist faking it. That covers the population, doesn't it?"

"Helpful."

"When did they first start coming?"

"About a month, five weeks back. One a week, always on Wednesday. Two this week."

"So whose typewriter have you checked?" Spraggue asked. "Donagher's? That guy, Murray, probably has one. What about Donagher's wife? And he's got a teenaged kid—"

"Come on—"

"Come on, yourself. You're not dim. Who'd you check?"

"Everybody in the house," Collatos admitted sheepishly. "Murray, Lila—that's Mrs. D—Donagher, both his Washington office and here, and I like the guy. I even tried to get into Bartolo's headquarters, see if—"

"You try City Hall yet? The State House?"

"I'd like to."

"Pete, I think it's pretty hopeless from that angle. Too many typewriters in the hands of too many creeps."

"So what do you think I should do?"

"Stop worrying. Donagher was probably right when he said the sniping was a random incident. Even if it wasn't, he might not have been the target. Maybe that hairy Vietnam vet is screwing his neighbor's wife. Maybe one of your ex-cop buddies is after you."

"I wasn't there. I was talking with you, remember? Isn't there any angle I can take off on? I'm going crazy doing nothing."

"Just stick with Donagher until the election and—"

"And?"

"Nothing. No rabbits out of my hat."

"If anything else should come to you—"

"Sure. And in the meantime, maybe you could talk Donagher out of running the marathon."

"Yeah," Collatos said gloomily. "And maybe I could talk him out of breathing."

"The cops provide good security the day of the race. Thousands of them line the course. They've had celebrity runners before. Cabinet members, movie stars . . ."

"Think about it, Spraggue. If somebody wants to kill Donagher, what an opportunity . . ."

"If Donagher were going to be the front-runner, yes. Then I'd make damn sure I had somebody covering the rooftops along the route. A sniper could take down the front-runner anytime, maybe even the guy coming in second or third. Where do you figure Donagher's going to wind up?"

"Hell, he'll be damned pleased to hit the top hundred. He hasn't run seriously in five years. And back when he came in second, in '62, two hours and twenty-three minutes took home the laurel wreath. The women are running that now."

"Then I'd tell Donagher not to tie a helium baloon to his wrist, not to wear a bright red campaign poster on his chest. Put him in with a bunch of other guys in running shorts and I doubt our sniper could single out a senator in the midst of ten thousand runners."

"You think so?"

"I do."

"I talked to the cops and they're going to put some sharp-shooters on the roofs, starting in Cleveland Circle. Cops and crowds are so thick after that . . . It's before—"

"The spectators are jammed in all along the route."

"You going to be there?"

The elaborate casualness of the question set off warning bells. "Why?"

"I've been checking the route and I was wondering . . ."

Spraggue sighed. "What?"

"The top of Heartbreak Hill. If I were a sniper, that's where I'd pick."

"Why?"

"There's that moment when the runners come up the hill; they're silhouetted against the background one by one. And Boston College has all those towers around . . ."

"You want me to watch the race from Heartbreak Hill?"

"Would you?"

"You want me to be your water boy?"

"Nah. The senator has gofers stationed all along the roads for that. Just be there, Spraggue, Okay?"

They shook hands on the deal.

NINE

Kathleen, alas, after that missed connection on Friday night, had definitely lost interest. By Sunday's *As You Like It* matinee, Spraggue had married her twenty-seven times on stage—and still no consummation. He had to admit he was losing interest himself. He found Kathleen more charming as Celia than as Kathleen, wished the attractive dark-haired actress playing Rosalind looked a little less like Kate Holloway, or, alternately, that she were not married.

When he left the theater, face scrubbed and sore, a man was waiting by the stage door. Not a cop. His gray wool suit had cost a month of policeman's pay; his blue silk shirt, possibly a week. His fingers played nervously with the knot in his soberly elegant tie. If they hadn't moved, Spraggue might have mistaken the man for a store-window dummy.

His blankly handsome face lit up as Spraggue tried to pass, and he stuck out his right hand in anticipation of a handshake.

"Ed Heineman, TV-4," was how he introduced himself.

Spraggue suppressed the desire to ask whether the initials stood for transvestite or television. There was the faintest trace of stubble on the man's chin, which ruled out the first possibility, and there was the immediate sense of familiarity, which supported the second. Not that he recalled seeing Heineman on the midget screen; he had seen Heineman clones, boy-men for whom the words *clean-cut* and *fresh-faced* had been invented.

The planes in the man's face were stronger than his handshake. He had brownish blond hair, razor cut, gleaming with studied casualness—and possibly hairspray. Spraggue returned the handshake, gripping a little harder than necessary.

Heineman removed a small notebook from his pocket, a leatherbound notebook so slim it hadn't disrupted the line of his suit. He flipped it open to a clean page, slipped a stub of pencil from a band of leather near the binding, and said with a faintly Southern drawl, "What have you come up with on the Donagher business?"

Spraggue had learned the poker face early in life, at a time when the comings and goings of the Spraggue family had been fodder for gossip columnists and intrusive insensitive photographers, mastering it in all its icy perfection at his parents' funeral. It settled over his features as he peered around him. The Square was crowded with pedestrian traffic. A lot of passersby wore running shoes. The out-of-towners in for the marathon liked to catch a glimpse of Harvard. He couldn't see anyone holding a TV camera. They didn't make them small enough to be imperceptible. Not yet.

He said, "Why don't we go somewhere and talk about it?"

"Where?"

"The Harvest Bar is noisy, but it's close."

"Fine."

The red-haired waitress knew Heineman by name. She fussed over him, wiping the already spotless butcherblock table with a damp rag until it sparkled, turning on a full-voltage smile, so powerful it drew the glances of other patrons, who, with extreme casualness, indicated to their

58

companions that a presence, a celebrity, was in the very same room!

Heineman made conversation while Spraggue ordered a glass of wine. How much he'd enjoyed the production of *As You Like It*, mostly.

"Do you have any identification?" Spraggue asked.

"Ed Heineman," the man said, stunned. "The waitress knows me. Everyone—I guess you haven't seen the weekend news lately."

"You must have a card or something."

The man went fishing in his hip pocket, eager to dispel the idea of possible fraud. He opened an impeccable card case, displayed Edward Heineman's driver's license embellished with Edward Heineman's photo. Even the Registry of Motor Vehicles hadn't been able to take a bad picture of the man. Spraggue feigned nearsightedness to get the card case into his own hands, clumsily dropped it, and spent a moment shuffling through the plastic sleeves to get back to the license before handing it back.

"So what is this about?" Spraggue said, sipping his glass of Burgundy. Heineman drank Scotch on the rocks.

"The Donagher death threats."

"Why talk to me about that?"

Heineman stared at his drink. "A tip."

"You checked this tip out with the senator?"

"Might have."

"I can't very well comment on something I know nothing about. Not for the record." Spraggue signaled for the waitress, asked her to bring the check.

"Off the record," Heineman said.

"Off the reccord, what did you expect to get?"

"The story from your angle."

"Which is?"

"You were in on that disturbance at the reservoir. Did Donagher hire you after that? Or," he said, when Spraggue didn't respond, didn't even raise an eyebrow, "are you investigating something else for the senator, something of a more personal nature?"

"You've got some inaccurate information, Mr. Heineman."

"Ed," the man said ingratiatingly.

Spraggue ignored him, waiting for the check.

"Look," Heineman said, "I know you've been to Donagher's house. The police—"

"Are they your source?"

"I'm not divulging any sources."

"Fine with me. I'm not divulging any answers."

The waitress edged her way through the crowd to their table while Heineman got flustered. "Let me pay for your drink at least," he said angrily. "I'm not doing this well. I just want a story. I don't know what you've heard about me. This is a tough town to break into. I got this tip and it seems hot; it involves a lot of well-known names. This is a slow news day. I'm just following up on a possible lead the way any reporter would. I know I've got a lot to prove in this town, partly because of, well, what I look like, and partly because of where I work. TV newspeople aren't exactly respected around here. I'd give my eyeteeth to break a major story within six weeks of arriving, spit in the face of those damn holy print people—"

The man was starting to look positively human. His face was getting red, as if his tie had suddenly tightened up and turned into a noose.

"Is this an indication of your usual reportorial finesse?" Spraggue asked, watching the Scotch waver in its glass as Heineman banged his hand on the tabletop.

"Dammit, no," the reporter said. "I'm usually . . . I mean, I'm damn good at my job."

"Yes?"

"I should never have done this," Heineman muttered. He

snatched the check off the table, knocking the bar glass to the floor in a shower of golden liquid and broken glass. It missed the elegant tie, the blue shirt, the gray suit, and soaked a paunchy gentleman at the next table. Heineman marched off to the bar, paid the check, and left without a backward glance. He didn't even smile at the waitress, who looked crushed by his indifference. A murmur from the crowd followed him out the door.

There were two telephones in an alcove near the entrance, one in working order. Spragge waited for a woman in tight jeans to finish relating a tale of automotive repair woes. He fed a dime into the machine, dialed, and got an answer after five rings.

"Let me talk to her, Pierce," he said.

"Could you possibly call back after seven?"

"Don't give me that. She's playing some game and doesn't want to be disturbed. Disturb her."

"Well . . ." Pierce sounded hesitant.

"Yell at her."

The sound that came over the receiver managed to be shocked and refined at the same time. A man behind Spragge coughed, just a gentle reminder that there was only one usable public phone and it was highly sought after.

"I am not playing games." Mary's voice came over so strongly that he held the receiver away from his ear. "I was meditating; and you have interrupted me. I will never reach a higher plane of existence if you—"

"Do you remember a little conversation we had about threats on some politician's life?"

"I am far from senile."

"You didn't happen to give out the information that I was interested in the case? To a newsman?"

"How could I, not being privy to that information?"

"Someone did."

"Will you be on the six o'clock news, dear? Which station?"

"Aunt Mary—"

"I admit that I have selfishly enjoyed occasional snooping at your behest."

"And that you would like to see the formation of a firm of private investigators with Spraggue and Hillman on the front door in gold leaf."

"My dear, it is late in life for me to consider taking up a new profession and I would insist that the door say Hillman and Spraggue."

"I thought so."

"But I did not abet the media."

"An Edward Heineman from Channel 4 thinks I'm up to my neck in Donagher's troubles."

"Channel 4. That's the new weekend boy, the one who—"

"Yes."

"What you just heard over the phone was my mind clicking into gear. And it is past due, Michael. Past due. I told you I'd never sleep from thinking about it—"

"What?"

"It was something in the conjunction of the phone call and the news. But I couldn't come up with it."

"Mary, tell me the important part first and then fill in the blanks."

"Edward Heineman was the man who telephoned and asked if you were 'on the case.' "

"Are you sure?"

"Of that voice? Of course."

"Thanks."

That answered one question.

Spraggue ordered another glass of wine at the bar, mulled over the other questions as he drank. Like who tipped Heineman off? Was Heineman really working a story? If he was, why didn't he have a camera crew along?

And most important: Why did Heineman carry in his card case the dog-eared photo of a woman who was a dead ringer for the blonde who'd left Donagher's by the back door?

TEN

Sunday evening's *As You Like It* passed like a dream, all disconnected sequences, interminable waits, and sudden urgencies. Tired, Spraggue found himself settling into the predictable rhythm of a show performed too often; he had to struggle against frozen pat responses, find new actions, new activities.

Two curtain calls, each with a modest swell of applause when he bowed. Home. The silence pressed the walls of his apartment inward until he took refuge in the radio and half a bottle of Beaulieu Cabernet. It took time, hours sometimes, for his body to come down from the high of performance, descend to the calm of sleep.

The phone jangled. At first it was part of his dream, instantly, senselessly incorporated. But its shrill insistence stilled the dream and he sat up in bed.

He cursed the moment when he'd deliberately arranged the furniture so that he'd have to leave the comfort of the bed in order to answer the phone. This had occurred while he was still a private investigator and apt to get calls of some importance in the middle of the night. The furniture-rearrangement binge had postdated a 2 A.M. phone call, a conversation during which, according to the other party, he'd agreed to some extremely illegal activities. The next morning, with no memory of the call, he'd gone out and almost gotten himself killed.

He swung long legs out of their blanket cocoon. Tomorrow he'd move the end table and the telephone back. Get rid of the "scene of the crime" kit. Maybe then he'd be more convincing when he denied being a private eye. Maybe even Menlo would believe him. Even Aunt Mary.

The phone rang on. Spragague made it over to the table in the dark, fumbled with the receiver, picked it up fully expecting a wrong number, possibly a frat house ordering pizza. Or Aunt Mary forgetting that lesser mortals slept.

"Spragague?" The voice was sloppy drunk; if it hadn't called out his name, he'd have hung up after roasting some punk's ears with choice curses.

"Who is this?"

"It's me. Your old dumb buddy, Collatos. You expecting somebody else, pal?"

The voice was slurred, unsteady.

"What the hell do you want now? It's late."

"Hey, hey, that's no way to talk to a guy. Listen. I gotta tidbit for you. But you gotta give me your word not to repeat this."

"What?" Spragague closed his eyes, shook his head, and regretted responding to Collatos' bait at the reservoir.

"It's a little secret, jus' a secret."

"If you've got something to say, say it. This is no time for games, Collatos."

"Sorry, sorry," Collatos sing-songed. "Sorry I bothered you. It's just that I figured it out. That's all. Figured it out and not to worry . . . Oh, hello," Collatos said suddenly. He drew out the last word in a muffled humorous drawl. It

64

sounded as if he'd turned his face completely away from the receiver.

"I hope you enjoy running with a hangover," Spraggue said impatiently. "Good night."

"So, Joe," Collatos said abruptly, speaking directly into the phone again. "Like I said, I'm planning to come in under two-forty, maybe even a two-thirty if Donagher presses. He can still turn on the speed."

"What's this *Joe* shit?" Spraggue said. "Is somebody listening in?"

"Yeah, that's right, Joe. Look, I've got to get off the phone."

"Did you find out something or not? Should I bother checking out Heartbreak Hill tomorrow?"

"Hey, Joey, I'll be in touch. The news'll keep. How about we see each other after the race? In the Pru garage? I'll be the one with the sore feet."

"Okay. Is it something to do with the letters? Do you know who wrote the letters?"

But Collatos had already hung up.

Spraggue flicked the plunger once, twice; a dial tone hummed in his ear.

ELEVEN

Marathon morning was glorious: sixty degrees, low humidity, capped by a bright and cloudless azure sky. A perfect day for spectators, it rated no more than two out of ten on the runners' weather scale. For runners, a cool, overcast drizzle of a day was ideal. A brisk wind had the Channel 4 commentators squawking like anxious hens; if the runners had too much tail-wind advantage, a record run would not be official. The overkill number of network personalities had no weightier matters to discuss and therefore chatted about wind velocity with a vengeance, shunting the viewers off to hastily established "Weather Centrals," where earnestly grinning gentlemen displayed colored maps and said, in at least ten different ways, that they weren't sure, but maybe the wind would die down.

Sprague had made the pilgrimage out to Hopkinton to view the start of the race three times: once with his parents, when he was a child and they were bound up in the race in some ceremonial capacity; once when he'd driven a friend out to the chaos of the starting line; once as a competitor. He grimaced at the memory.

He'd been a teenager—an impossibly young Harvard freshman, an unregistered entrant who'd never run more than an occasional ten miles with the cross-country team. He'd stumbled, panting, off the course just past Wellesley College, collapsing ignominiously behind the shelter of a merciful pine tree. He'd run out of steam before then, should have abandoned the race at least a mile earlier. But how could he quit at Wellesley, with all those coeds cheering him on?

He'd always meant to race again. Life had interfered. Instead of running the marathon the next year, he'd run away—all the way to England and the Royal Academy of Dramatic Art. . . .

He sighed and stared at the TV screen. All that was ancient history, long before the race became a media event, back when the field of runners was still a manageable size. The Boston Athletic Association struggled valiantly every year to pare the field down to three thousand, shortening the qualifying times. But they had no control over the renegades who waited until the official starters were off and then hurled themselves into the race.

Edward Heineman didn't seem to be among Channel 4's on-the-scene crew. Nor was he manning the station desk. Spraggue switched channels.

The Channel 5 helicopter flashed an aerial shot: The ground around the raised white spire of Hopkinton Church lurched and settled, as if the church had been built on a sprawling anthill. An earthbound camera operator scanned the first row of runners, the ranked world-class runners, the Rodgers and the Salazars, the Waitzes and Teskes, tensed for action. These runners would have the chance to sprint when the starting pistol sounded. They'd be off with the shot, letting the second rank, the second row, race forward. Further back, blocks away, blocks behind, the runners were packed in like mannequins en route to department stores. It was impossible to tell which arm belonged to which runner.

The helicopter shot was a classic; it could have been this year's or last year's, or a relic saved from the early sixties. April 19 meant the marathon at Hopkinton, just as December 25 meant Christmas. The town of Hopkinton, always referred to on this occasion as "the sleepy little town of Hopkinton," awoke once a year to play host to the multitudes, providing gym floor space to rest on, town green space to stretch in, and every available bathroom in town.

Spraggue surveyed the crush of runners; there weren't more than ten, maybe twenty, with the remotest chance of victory. But ten thousand eager faces attested to the lure of the race. Every exhausted combatant who crossed the finish line, who conquered 26 miles and 385 yards of unyielding pavement, won the marathon.

Maybe next year.

11:45 A.M.—time for the first race of the marathon to begin, the wheelchair competition. The twenty chairbound athletes spun away from the starting line, determination propelling muscular arms.

Spraggue realized that he was watching the tube with more than random curiosity, that he was searching for a particular runner. If he'd been manning a camera, he would have treated the audience to a view of Senator Donagher.

The Channel 5 reporter was roving through the crowd near the starting line, interviewing marathon celebrities: Johnny (The Elder) Kelley, who'd run in over fifty Boston Marathons: Tom Brown, whose family had been responsible for firing the starting pistol since the beginning of time. Steeped in tradition was the Boston race.

Pete Collatos must be somewhere in that stifling crowd, a sea of runners ahead of him, an ocean behind. Spraggue remembered so clearly his own teenage terror of falling at the start, of being crushed under heedless racing feet.

There—a miniature Brian Donagher peered out of the TV screen, pacing, half jogging, smiling tightly, nervously. Pete Collatos, his shadow, showing no effects of the previous night's debauch, grinned uncomfortably, straight at the camera. The reporter didn't mention the upcoming election; his station might have to grant Bartolo equal time if he gave Donagher any opportunity to spout campaign slogans. And there could have been no "equal" time. The draw of the sports hero being what it was, it was only a matter of years before the entire Senate was filled with ex-football heroes. Marathon fame gave Donagher an unfair advantage. Bartolo, if he were watching, must have been fuming.

Five minutes to twelve. The runners were all poised to prove their prerace predictions. The contest would be marred by the absence of several elite runners. Patti Catalano was injured and out of the running, a disappointment for those who liked to cheer on the hometown favorite. Toshihiko Seko, last year's winner, wasn't defending his title. Spraggue wondered if Seko's no-show status had anything to do with the perennial dispute over fees. The BAA prided itself on not paying expense money; the draw of the race was enough, they maintained. But with so many other races boasting commercial sponsors, playing under-the-table prize money in defiance of AAU rules, how much longer could venerable Boston hold out? How much longer could the world expect marathon runners to remain amateurs considering the incredible salaries paid to other athletes?

The aerial camera panned the throng of runners. All the way up the provincial main street of Hopkinton, the line stretched—runners twenty, thirty abreast. Sleek professionals with concentrated faces. Weekend joggers, muscles tensed. Some wore sweat suits. Some brief shorts. There were runners with funny hats, white cotton gloves. Runners with exotic faces. Men. Women. Teenagers. The Cowman, who always ran the race with a horned headdress weighing him down. And an incredible variety of T-shirts.

The T-shirts were crucial. The fans keyed in on them during the race, yelling "Come on Detroit Track Club! Hey, Motown, you can do it! You're almost there, Detroit! Six more miles, Detroit! You've got it, Detroit! Run, Detroit! Go!" Or Memphis or Seattle, or Argentina, Canada, Sweden . . .

Spraggue tried to remember the code used for the official numbers. *W* for women; that was easy. *M* for masters, the older runners. *V* and *F* were also age-linked, he thought, but he wasn't sure. Why didn't any of the commentators think to explain that instead of blathering on about the wind?

The starter raised the gun. The front-liners got down into the approved starting crouch. Even the commentators grew silent as the starter prepared to press the trigger.

When it finally fired, the gun gave off a disappointing pop. In the front row, they ran. In the tenth row, they jogged. In the twentieth row, they marched slowly forward. Two city blocks back, nothing. No discernible motion.

Some, out of impatience more than necessity, began to jog in place. And then, with astonishing suddenness, the logjam gave. The screen was filled with bobbing heads—up and down, up and down. Like a flood pouring into the sea, the runners streamed forth out of Hopkinton. It took twenty minutes for the parade to pass the starting line. The commentators wisely held their tongues. The stream of humanity needed no discussion.

Back in the bad old days before running had become a popular pastime, the on-scene reporters had generally greeted the gun with: "Well, folks, it's Patriot's Day and the saps are running!"

The camera watched the runners speed off past the spire of Hopkinton Church, head out on the open road to Framingham. The fleetest would cross the Prudential Center finish line in downtown Boston some two hours and ten minutes after the starting gun sounded. The rest would falter across all day. No trophy was given for the final finisher. Spragge had heard tales of runners staggering across the no-longer-there line well after dark.

He hoped he wouldn't have to wait that long for Pete.

Fifteen minutes after the final dawdling runner had crossed the starting line, Spragge left his apartment.

The signals from Collatos had been confusing and contradictory. Since no clarifying phone call had come from Donagher's bodyguard, Spragge had determined to fulfill both requests; he'd observe the race from the top of Heartbreak Hill, and he'd meet Pete after the race in the Prudential Center garage. It could be done, either by a judicious choice of driving routes or by the use of public transportation. Only tourists got trapped on Patriot's Day.

One hour and twenty-five minutes before the fastest runner would crest Heartbreak Hill, he was on his way, driving over to Boston College. Early, but not too early. The hills would be crowded, teeming with spectators who desired nothing more than to cheer their favorites on.

He parked on one of the twisty side streets off Beacon Street and trudged up the hill to Commonwealth Avenue.

Heartbreak Hill was a misnomer. The stretch of the race known as Heartbreak was actually three hills, three gentle inclines in a three mile section of a downhill course from Hopkinton down to the sea. It was their geographical placement in the race that was the killer. They struck after twenty miles, when most of the runners were just starting to "hit the wall," that physical and psychological barrier of pain that every marathoner knows and dreads.

A crowd was already forming in front of St. Ignatius Church, a knot of police and observers. Crowd control was a touchy issue along the twenty-six mile course. Some cities had complained this year about the expense of providing policemen to line the route; Pete Collatos wasn't the only cop laid off as a result of the supposedly tax-saving Proposition 2½. Kenmore Square, in Boston proper, was the worst place for the runners, close enough to the finish line to attract hundreds of watchers and blessed with Fenway Park. With considerable foresight, the Red Sox always scheduled an 11:00 A.M. game. Just as the biggest glut of runners raced through, the game would end and thirty thousand screaming fans would be loosed into the general melee. Last year the crowd had closed the runners off to a single lane. Everyone said that the spurious women's 1980 champion must have jumped into the race during the Kenmore Square confusion; things had gotten so jumbled, so out of control, that the Goodyear blimp might have joined the race unobserved. During the final frenzied mile, ropes, plywood boards, and mounted police had to be used to keep back the cheering hordes.

Conscientiously, Spraggue kept his promise to Collatos. He had a chat with a robed priest on the doorstep of St. Ignatius, an idle, pass-the-time-of-day talk that yielded information: The bell tower was certainly locked today of all days. Wouldn't it be a shame now if some youngsters got to thinking the tower would be a good place to view the race and one of them fell through the rotten boards up there? Spraggue nodded his head in earnest agreement and moved on, looking up at the rooftops, almost colliding with passersby. He had to force himself to do the job, so unlikely did the appearance of a melodramatic killer seem on such a festive afternoon under bright revealing sunshine.

He'd brought along a radio to keep track of the race. Without one, standing for over an hour at one particular point on a twenty-six mile race course could be limiting. He alternated between WEEI and WBZ, switching to see who had the best coverage. Because he had the radio, other enthusiasts hovered near.

"Is Billy leading?" That was the most often asked question, Bill Rodgers being the local hero. "Where are they now?"

The latter query, once the runners got as close as Framingham, was unnecessary. You only had to look up to spot the helicopters. Spraggue counted five and hoped they all had qualified pilots, accustomed to flying in close formation. A small biplane trailed an ad for a local Chevy dealer. Ah, the joys of amateur athletics! No matter how the BAA tried to keep the crass world of big bucks from intruding on their marathon, every world-class runner would traipse by studded with advertising slogans. Bill Rodgers was a personal advertisement for his own line of running togs.

"Who's leading?"

Spraggue pressed his ear to the radio. "Ron Tabb. Not much chance to win, but he always goes out strong."

"Where's Salazar? Where's Rodgers?"

The radio was starting to be a pain.

When the first wheelchair racer made it by, biceps straining, face crimson, everyone forgot about the radio and

72

cheered. The helicopters were hovering almost overhead now; the wheelchair contestants heralded the runners to follow.

The first runner always had an escort. He was preceded by the press bus, flanked by motorcycle cops, followed by a police car. It was a wonder that the man could run, so hampered was he by a cloud of carbon monoxide—spewing vehicles.

A swelling roar of approval shook the spectators. Not one, but two runners hove into view, impeded by the motorized cavalcade. A close race! The crowd loved an all out dead heat finish even better than they loved the spectacle of their own Bill Rodgers running the hills in splendid isolation. Eyes strained to catch the numbers as the runners, scarcely a meter apart, flashed by. Papers rustled as viewers checked their programs. Beardsley and Salazar! Salazar was expected, but where was Rodgers? Who was this Beardsley? Spraggue listened to the radio and watched the crowd.

He found himself enjoying the crowd as much as the race, maybe more.

In the immediate vicinity of the church, there must have been at least ten individuals clutching water bottles. Spraggue wondered how many of them were there by appointment, waiting for a specific runner, how many were there to hand out the precious fluid to the generally needy. A tall blond guy with a blue T-shirt, a terry sweat jacket, and ropey muscles looked like he ought to be out there running. Except for the tape on his ankle. He limped a few steps out and offered his water bottle and words of encouragement to a dark foreign-looking man with a huge mustache.

Off to his right, a group of Boston College students waited to cheer on a classmate, passed the time barbecuing hamburgers on a portable hibachi, drinking endless cans of beer from a huge cooler. They carefully piled each empty beer can on a ten-can-base pyramid, creating a roadside shrine to Budweiser. The picnic smell provoked in Spraggue an exquisite hunger.

Now that little guy with the pink face standing under the streetlamp, he might be the flunky Donagher had stationed nearby with water. . . .

As the crowd went crazy, shrieking, singing, climbing trees for a better view, the world class runners passed—the sleek thoroughbreds, the thin whippets, the models for the rest. TV cameras perched on the top of the hill transmitted every detail cross-country.

The talk turned to records. Were they on a record pace? Could there be a record with this blasting sunshine, this heat, this dryness? A tiny dark woman, a doctor or nurse, said authoritatively that on a day like this, each runner would need ten ounces of fluid every fifteen minutes, not to mention salt.

In other races, once the winners went by, the crowd diminished, the excitement dulled. Not so in the Boston Marathon. The crowd grew steadily, many of the new arrivals bearing signs and banners. WE LOVE YOU, 345. GO, BOBBY! TULANE TRACK CLUB. Family and friends congregated, waiting for their own winners. The Hill was a place where encouragement was needed.

The runners came thick and fast now, each raised fist eliciting a cheer, each new face cause for celebration. The question asked now was, where's the first woman?

Not until 1972 had women been allowed in the marathon. Before then, the athletic union, in its wisdom, had decided that women weren't made for endurance sports; the most a woman could be expected to run was 100 meters. Not that women hadn't run the marathon before '72. As far back as '51, a Canadian woman had sneaked by the ruling board. And Cambridge's Sarah Mae Berman had been in the thick of things for years. Roberta Gibb had run in '66, shocked by the AAU's dictum that ''women are not physically able to

run long distances and furthermore, they are not allowed."
But they were all unofficial contestants, right up until the infamous K. Switzer—*K* for Kathy, unbeknownst to the male
guardians of gender purity—had run with an official number, a number that was almost forcibly ripped off her chest
by the outraged race director.

Now the women were in to stay, breaking two-thirty,
passing a lot of the men. No one seemed upset by it. It gave
the crowd something extra to cheer about when Charlotte
Teske went by with her motorcycle escort, something more
to wonder about. Where was the supposedly front-running
Grete Waitz?

First wheelchair, first man, first woman. Still the crowd
stayed, waiting for family, for friends, for all the winners to
pass by: the conquerors of middle-aged spread, middle-aged
torpor, vanquishers of cigarettes and emphysema. And always the crowd waited for Johnny Kelley, forever young.

A cheer rang out, louder than any since Charlotte Teske
had passed. Brian Donagher crested the hill, Pete Collatos at
his side. Sweating, winded, Donagher thrust both hands in
the air. The crowd lifted him on. Exhausted, he glowed.

"Hey, Brian!" The call came from a woman Spraggue
had noted briefly when he'd considered who in the crowd
was likely to play Sir Galahad to a thirsting stranger—a tall
woman with creamy, pale skin, wearing a long skirt, more
formally dressed than the other spectators. She bounded out
of the crowd, took a few running steps, waved a blue-tinted
plastic water bottle in Donagher's direction and hollered, "I
voted for you in every election!"

Donagher, who'd been glancing around as though expecting someone or something, flashed her a grin, and, to
the delight of the crowd, altered his course to accept her
offering. The woman's heavily lipsticked mouth opened
and closed as she strained to keep up with Donagher's
slightly slackened pace. Those near her laughed, but

Spraggue was too distant to hear the words she addressed adoringly to the senator. Spraggue studied the panto-mime; the woman urged Donagher to take the water bottle and run with it, not to bother about returning the bottle to its rightful owner.

"Finish in under three hours and I'll vote for you again!" the woman said loudly. She had a deep friendly voice with the faintest trace of an Irish brogue.

Donagher sped on. Spraggue saw him squeeze at the straw-topped bottle before the profusely sweating Collatos held out a hand for it. They shared the water as they ran. A shout went up: "Donagher! Donagher! Donagher!"

Then the two were out of sight and the cameras that had followed the celebrity runner since he came up the hill, panned back to catch the next human wave.

The finish line. That was the next challenge: getting there. Viewing the crowd, Spraggue feared that he'd been overly sanguine about mobility on Patriot's Day. He took stock.

The car was temptingly close. But once in the car, once downtown, he'd need a place to park—and those, on Marathon Day, were impossible to find. The garages were jammed, closed for the most part. The out-of-town tourists, fed up and amazed that a city would have no provision for parking, would have taken up all the favored tow zones. He didn't believe in blocking fire hydrants or snatching slots reserved for the handicapped. He could park at the police station on Berkeley Street. . . . No, Menlo might hear of it and haul him in again. . . .

There was nothing for it but a combination of running and public transportation.

The mass of people heading toward the finish line would dash over to Lake Street and the Boston College line. So Spraggue went in the other direction, downhill to

Beacon Street and the last stop on the Cleveland Circle line.

He didn't jog, he raced. The exuberance of the runners was contagious and he put all his pent up energy into the run, making the two miles in well under fifteen minutes, delighted with himself.

And, wonder of wonders, a trolley! There was one stopped dead at the end of the line, the last few stragglers hopping aboard! Spraggue turned on a last burst of speed and made it onto the steamy car before the double door banged shut.

The trolley was stuffed, jammed to suffocation. Spraggue considered the alternatives and decided that a few inches of cattle car would do, as long as it got him downtown to the finish line. He found fifty cents in his pocket, then had to scramble around to locate another quarter. The fares went up so quickly and erratically on the Green Line, you never knew what to shove in the box. And they didn't accept dollar bills.

After a two-minute wait, the car lurched forward. It immediately halted, for no other purpose than to tumble the standing passengers around, then pitched forward again, swaying uncertainly down the track.

From the right-hand windows, the passengers could see the runners as they veered onto Beacon Street. It was an advertisement for good health: Get out there and run and you won't have to endure the stench and unsteadiness of the Green Line!

The runners, though they were by no means the fleetest, traveled faster than the trolley. Unlike their elite predecessors, they were feeling it, slogging along on automatic pilot, with blistered feet and frozen faces, barely able to respond to the crowd's encouragement. In infrequent gaps in the row of spectators, one could see a runner sitting on the curb, pouring water over his head. One man had his shoes off and two attendants splashed water on his bleeding feet.

He hoped the trolley wouldn't tilt with all the passengers bunched up to one side, trying to see out the filthy windows.

Spraggue heard the siren as they passed Washington Street, craned his neck to see where it came from. A fire on Marathon Day could be a disaster, if blaze and engines were separated by the line of runners.

No fire. Collatos could have told him that by the siren, but Spraggue had to wait until he saw the ambulance. It raced up the wrong side of Beacon Street and must have come to a halt nearby because the siren kept blaring in his ears. The train rumbled on for a few hundred feet more, screeched to a stop.

Spraggue, near the front of the car, could see that this was no ordinary traffic-light delay. The police car was pulled across the tracks, blue lights flashing. The MBTA driver gave a deep sigh and leaned back in his seat, shrugging his shoulders and issuing a general curse. The passengers on board groaned as one.

Spraggue asked the driver to open the door. Even if he had to walk the rest of the way in, he was determined to get to the finish line. He started to run, but then he saw the ambulance and the circle of policemen, and curiosity made him delay.

He joined the outer edge of the circle in time to see the man lifted and placed on the stretcher. He could hear the hum of the crowd: Why didn't these runners prepare for the damn race? Some of these jerks couldn't run around the block, much less—

As they lifted the stretcher, he recognized its occupant: Donagher, prone, white-faced, and unconscious. Spraggue froze. Stopped thinking. Almost stopped breathing. Where the hell was Collatos?

78

"What happened?" He asked the question of the crowd in general. No one knew. Of course there hadn't been any shooting. Just collapsed. Must be the heat. He pressed the radio to his ear, but the commentator rattled on about the wind and the amazing two-second win by Alberto Salazar over Dick Beardsley.

"Where will they take him?" Spraggue hollered to a white-shirted ambulance attendant.

"Red Cross at Coolidge Corner," a woman shouted back. "I think."

Spraggue started to run. Coolidge Corner couldn't be more than a mile away. His feet moved faster than his thoughts. They were stuck on overwhelming relief, relief that there had been no sniper, nothing but a little heat stroke, a setback in the campaign but no tragedy. He wondered where Pete Collatos was. Had the two men agreed that if one went down, the other would finish the race? Hell of a way to bodyguard.

His aching legs told him he must have covered at least three quarters of a mile, when he saw the same silent circle, heard the same siren.

The body on the ground wore Collatos' number. The faces in the circle were grim. Two men, one a perspiring runner, the other a samaritan from the crowd, performed CPR in a regular, hopeless rhythm. A third man grasped Collatos' wrist. He mumbled to himself, shook his head, glanced anxiously about for help.

The red and white ambulance, marked Massachusetts Bay Para/Medical, skidded as it came to a halt. A man and a woman in tan uniforms jumped out, leaving the doors flung wide. The woman took in the situation at a glance, opened the rear door, removed a strecher. One of the CPR administrators yielded to the tan-uniformed man. In seconds, Collatos was on the stretcher, wheeled to the mouth of the ambulance, swallowed. The woman rigged an IV as the vehicle sped off. The civilian who'd given CPR sat on the curb, looked ready to vomit. The runner who'd given aid patted him on the shoulder, rejoined the race.

Spraggue, his heart pounding as if he'd run the full course, his mouth as dry as if he'd eaten sand, stripped off his T-shirt and used it to pick up the blue-tinted plastic water bottle that lay next to a drain near the curb, where it must have fallen from Collatos' shaking hand. He turned and took a few running steps back toward Heartbreak Hill, stopped.

The tall woman who had handed Donagher the bottle would be gone; he could feel it in his bones.

TWELVE

On the day of Pete Collatos' funeral, spring took a giant step backward into February.

The tulips dotting the grounds of the New Calvary Cemetery in Mattapan lay flat against the earth, their petals defeated by the chill gusty wind. A field of glistening black umbrellas, useless against the slanting downpour, blossomed instead, under a dour gray sky.

Media representatives were there en masse, shielding their cameras and their waterlogged spiral notebooks. They'd been there all along.

FIRST MARATHON CASUALTY IN 86 YEARS! the intial headline had screamed. SENATOR'S ILLNESS LINKED TO MARATHON DEATH had followed. And then, with the question mark accented in heavy black ink: AMPHETAMINE POISONING CAUSE OF DEATH? And so on. Continued on page 18. And photographs . . . endless photographs. Of a squinting Collatos, proudly displaying his gold detective's shield. Of Donagher, attempting a weak smile in his hospital bed. Nothing too petty or too personal to escape the heavy-handed public embrace.

By the day of the funeral, the headlines had moved on. The mysterious marathon death was relegated to the Metro pages, where the columns of print contracted, grew more speculative, finally disappeared. Juicier items: murders, rapes, airline crashes, coups d'état—all the ugliness of life that is passed off as the day's news, conspired to erase the reality of Collatos' death.

What media coverage remained ensured a large turnout at the funeral. People who would have stayed away entirely or slipped off after the Mass at St. Columbkille's, followed the solemn cortege down Market Street, lured by the TV cameras.

Donagher, Spraggue thought, with grudging admiration, would have come, illness or no, TV cameras or no. The politician stood, head bowed, immobile, at the graveside. He'd lost weight in the past week; his clothes hung on him. Not surprisingly; he'd been admitted to Beth Israel Hospital with a temperature of 105 degrees and blood pressure registering 250 over 140. Four days he'd been hospitalized.

Behind the senator, his pastel wife, Lila, and Murray Eichenhorn, his campaign manager, held a whispered conversation. Eichenhorn kept jerking his head around, searching the crowd, nervously shifting his weight from one foot to the other. Spraggue wondered if the man envisioned another attack on Donagher, was terrified that he might be in the line of fire. A sniper would have had to be suicidal to take a shot at Donagher here, with half the funeral company wearing the dress blues of the Boston Police.

Candidate Frank Bartolo would never have ventured out to the cemetery to freeze in the rain if it weren't for the TV cameras. Spraggue had seen him conversing with Governor Edwards after the Mass, noted the governor's vehement nods and jabbing pointed fingers as he explained to his protégé the wisdom of denying Donagher a monopoly of the six o'clock news. The governor had attended the Mass to bestow his charismatic presence on the less than assertive Bartolo, to ensure that the cameras recorded the fact that the influential governor and former State Representative Bartolo were inseparable. He'd managed to turn the church ceremony into a tasteless parody of a wedding: pews on the right for supporters of Donagher, pews on the left for the bridegroom, Frank Bartolo, the governor's puppet.

Spraggue stared at Bartolo, memorizing the jowly face, five o'clock shadow already visible at noon, the sleek-fitting black suit that almost disguised a paunch. Governor's man. Safe vote for the conservative status quo. Or was he? Once elected to the Senate's lofty heights, would Bartolo develop unexpected beliefs of his own to shock his benefactor? Did the governor have the goods on Bartolo, something related to those shady Mafia connections the *Boston Globe* seemed so certain of, something that would keep Bartolo in line, blackmail him into coming across with the key vote in the tight situation?

Spraggue stood to one side, removed from the main body of mourners, not eager to be identified with one political faction or another, missing Pete Collatos. Not the brightest of men, not the best of friends. Hell, until this Donagher business started, he'd seen Collatos what? Twice in two years? But the knowledge of never again, the finality of sodden earth clunking against the iron casket, brought a lump to his throat and made him look away.

By conservative estimate, Spraggue thought, he must have died some fifty times on stage, more if one counted the multiple comic deaths of Mortimer in *The Fantastiks*. On stage, he'd watched so many friends die, played Horatio to so many doomed Hamlets. . . . But Collatos wouldn't be resurrected for tomorrow's matinee.

Aunt Mary, beside him, lightly touched his fingers. Sympathy seemed to flow from her hand to his, leaving him curiously comforted. She'd held his hand throughout that eternally long funeral after his parents had died in that fiery car crash, while he'd still thought it the "tragic senseless accident" the newspapers gloated in retelling: a fable for our time, illustrating that ever popular theme that money cannot, after all, buy happiness—or eternal life. It was summer then, but the sky had been just as leaden. Aunt Mary's hand seemed so frail, so cold, that he pulled her closer under his umbrella, put his arm around her shoulders. His other hand, clutching the wavering umbrella, felt as if it were welded to the handle.

No one held, comforted, or warmed the funeral's chief mourner, Pete's sister, Sharon. Donagher had tried, been rebuffed. Sharon Collatos . . . No, the last name was no longer Collatos. She had married; Spraggue remembered that, but he couldn't recall her married name. Nor could he see a likely husband in the crowd. Did the man work Saturdays? Was he out of town? Wasn't there a friend, a neighbor, a cousin, an aunt, to take the black-clad woman's arm?

He watched her while the somber priest hastily read the final words, knowing that the chill rain disposed no one to linger. Her black suit was either borrowed or purchased in haste. Or else she, like Donagher, had lost too much weight too rapidly. Borrowed, more likely; she hadn't the coloring to wear black. Her skin and hair were too dark to set it off. Her shapeless raincoat could have been a man's. Her hair was scraped back off her forehead and forced into a bun at the nape of her neck, blurred with a black lace veil. Her face was a mask that one tear would have cracked and shattered.

She reminded him of Medea, not the Medea of the final curtain, but the just betrayed Medea, pondering that most horrible act of vengeance.

What had each of these people meant to Collatos; what had he meant to them? Spraggue scanned the crowd for some young attractive woman; had Collatos dated a special girl? When had his parents died? Who was here to say fare-well to a friend? Who was present to record his political loy-alties on camera, to have his face splayed across the evening news?

Shutting his eyes, Spraggue methodically relaxed, un-clenching the jaw that was always the first to tense, shrug-ging the shoulders that were the next to go. Usually, the relaxation ceremony was reserved for preperformance jit-ters.

The whole damned ritual reminded him of a performance, an empty piece of theater that had nothing to do with Pete Collatos, alive or dead.

The priest finished droning and Medea took center stage. She hurled a bouquet of blood red roses at the coffin, an an-gry heave, not a gentle toss. Some cry, some involuntary grunt escaped her lips, and she looked away, blinking hard. Still no tears, no crack in the mask. Donagher took her arm, but she wouldn't move away from the yawning hole. It took Donagher's wife to lead her off. The pastel woman seemed so frail, but her tiny tug prevailed.

The mourners should have melted gratefully back into their cars, escaped the gray storm and the gloomy land-scape, the gaping hole filled with new death, the final sound of earth shoveled down on the coffin. But the TV cameras stayed. So, instead of bolting, the cops and politicians that made up the bulk of the herd lingered, gathered in hopeful photogenic groupings, crowded to press Donagher's hand, express their horror at his narrow escape. And that, that last play for the attention of the cameras, turned Spraggue's sorrow into anger.

He left Mary standing by the car, entered the crowd near Captain Hurley, intending to ask a few, just a few of the questions he'd been longing to ask, at least to set up a later appointment, to find out what the hell the Boston Police were doing to ensure that whoever had killed Collatos wouldn't go undiscovered, unpunished.

Two things got in his way.

The first was a smiling old man who stumbled, trod on Spraggue's toe, and forgot to mumble an apology. A retired cop in faded dress blues, with a crinkled red face, the old fellow seemed to be treating the funeral like a grand occasion, a chance to get out of the house and socialize, to feel useful and young again, instead of simply enduring the tedious hours until night, when he could legitimately try for the sleep that wouldn't come anymore.

The old man neatly buttonholed Donagher's campaign manager, backed him up against a budding maple. Spraggue would have passed them by, with perhaps a sympathetic smile at the obviously trapped Eichenhorn, if the red-faced cop hadn't spoken with such drunken loudness.

"So, Marty," the old man sang out, and his melodic brogue pinned down his native origin as easily as his face, "It's a treat for these old eyes to see you after so long, doing so fine, too."

Donagher's campaign manager stared at the man in blank incomprehension for ten or fifteen seconds. Then he turned paper white and grabbed the old cop by the sleeve of his aged uniform.

A tight, fake smile stretched across Eichenhorn's mouth, but his eyes darted left and right, as if he were checking out the people in immediate earshot. He muttered something in the old man's ear.

The old cop hooted a laugh that wound up in a coughing fit. "Surely, there's no harm—" he began, but the rest of his words were cut off as Eichenhorn quickly draped an arm across his shoulder and led him off under a stand of oak trees.

Intrigued, Spraggue started to follow, wondering why a man named Murray would react so oddly to being called Marty. A cold voice stopped him, spun him around.

"You," the Greek Medea said. "You. I want to talk to you."

THIRTEEN

Her voice was low, husky with unshed tears, but its intensity burned across ten feet of muddy ground like a laser beam. A glance at her frozen eyes told him that this was not a request to be fobbed off with the excuse of a waiting aunt, a matinee still to be performed.

The Medea woman motioned him toward an isolated stand of rhododendrons, using the merest nod of her head. He tried to shield her with his umbrella. She stalked off without noticing. Weary of keeping the umbrella upright in the gale, he folded it and followed her, rain pelting his face.

Everything about the woman was so terribly controlled, Spraggue thought as he trailed behind her . . . her carefully balanced walk, like a drunkard's in a police lineup, her marionette gestures, her unanimated voice, her painted face. . . . She was smaller than her drawn-up posture made her seem. She had a short, sturdy body, more accustomed to jeans and T-shirts than black suits, stockings, and high heels. She stumbled as she turned to check on his progress and he sped up. One chink in that awesome armor would collapse the entire facade. He'd never be able to reassemble the pieces on his own.

She turned and faced him, swallowed with effort. Spraggue tried to find in her granite visage some trace of a laughing windswept girl in a photograph that had been a fixture on Pete's desk. Not a gorgeous girl, not a knock-out—but a woman with such a genuine smile, such deep secret eyes, that Pete had finally hidden the photo in a drawer. Too many cops asked for his sister's phone number, he had complained. He'd wanted better than that for baby sister.

This woman was older than the teenager in the photo, older in ways that had nothing to do with passing years. Her eyes were sunken in dark shadows. Spraggue regretted that he hadn't asked for the phone number of the laughing girl; then, she'd seemed too young, too innocent, too burdened with the baggage of being a friend's treasured sister. Now she seemed too old. He wondered if the sparkle would ever reappear in her empty eyes.

"So," she said. "You're Spraggue." Her voice lowered the temperature five degrees.

"Your brother must have described me."

"Pete . . . didn't . . . We rarely spoke. . . . I asked someone."

Spraggue wanted to ask why, but said nothing. She would explain; she wouldn't have made the painful effort to talk to him unless she had a reason. He was prepared for something, but not for what came.

Sharon Collatos' lower lip trembled momentarily, then stiffened. Her breathing was so shallow and quick, he was afraid she might faint.

"What are you going to do about it?" she said.

If volume had been substituted for intensity, her words would have deafened the remaining mourners. But her tone was just above a whisper and more powerful, more urgent for that.

"Your partner's dead, so what are you going to do about it? Almost a week and have I seen you at the police station? Have I seen you at Pete's apartment? What are you doing?

Spraggue considered options: Either melting into a puddle at her feet or turning into a pillar of salt seemed preferable to saying, "I was no partner of your brother's; where did you get that screwy idea?" Particularly since he had a pretty strong inkling that the screwy idea had come from a source that could no longer be impeached. Damn Pete Collatos.

Pete's sister took his silence for shame.

"You know what the police told me?" she said. "Nothing. That they have no single clue, that unless a miracle occurs, my brother's killer will never be found. That the case will stay open, so I shouldn't worry my little head. Maybe in ten years or so, they'll get a break. Then they sent me to see the medical examiner—"

Spraggue shuddered; he'd been there, too. He hoped the M.E. had been a trifle more politic with this grieving woman.

"A man in a white coat said to me, 'isn't it an *interesting case*? Like with guinea pigs, with rats, with mice. He says

88

maybe it isn't even a murder case, just an assault. I ask him how that can be when my brother, my only relative in this world, is lying cold in his coffin. And you know what he said?''

"Look, Mrs. . . .'' Dammit, why couldn't he remember that name?

"Miss Collatos,'' she said coldly.

Oh, Christ, yes. Pete had mentioned separation or divorce. "Miss Collatos, I have a car here. We could sit in it and talk. There's no need for you to get pneumonia.'' Or me, he thought.

She stared up, noticing the rain as an external phenomenon for the first time, as bewildered as if she had thought that the rain was her own personal misery, unseen, unfelt by others.

While thus confused, she allowed Spraggue to take her arm and lead her to the warm interior of Mary's Mercedes. Pierce was in the driver's seat, Aunt Mary beside him. Spraggue made quick introductions, stopped the flow of Mary's sympathetic chatter with a glance, spoke to Sharon Collatos.

"The medical examiner probably told you that the amount of amphetamine in your brother was about twenty milligrams, that ten milligrams is the highest recommended therapeutic dose, that toxic effects begin at fifteen, but that it's highly unusual for twenty milligrams of speed to kill a man.''

"Pete's dead.''

"But the senator isn't. So then they told you that there might have been some precondition in your brother, an aneurism, say, or an idiosyncratic reaction to amphetamine . . .''

She nodded. "And that's what they told the police. And all those fancy words had one effect: The police aren't really looking for my brother's killer.''

Aunt Mary turned, knelt on the front seat and took the woman's hand in hers. "She's freezing, poor thing. Pierce, don't we have a blanket or something in the trunk?"

What they had seemed to be a fur lap robe more suited to a sleigh ride than a stationary auto on an April day. Sharon burrowed into it, gratefully, and for a minute, Spraggue was certain the mask would break, but she shuddered and went on.

"I can hear the defense attorney now. Just a prank that went wrong, Your Honor. How was I to know a little bit of speed would kill a man? I just thought it would make the senator run faster. All a mistake, Your Honor. Then the judge taps that devil woman on the back of the hand, says 'naughty girl,' and that's the end of it. Except that Pete is dead. And from what he told me about the business you were working on together, about those anonymous notes, I know he didn't die because of some crazy prank. I know that someone intended to kill Senator Donagher . . . to—"

She ran down suddenly, like a clock, overwound and dying.

"Spraggue," she said in a painful monotone, "Mr. Spraggue. My brother always called you just by the one name. . . . I was not a good sister to my brother; we weren't as close as we should have been. I said to myself, there's time for that. There are other things I have to do now, more important things. There'll always be time for Pete. And someone took that time away from me."

Aunt Mary opened the car door, got out into the downpour, entered the back seat, and put her arm around Sharon's quivering shoulders. Sharon turned her head away, closed her eyes to blink back tears, but she let Mary's hand stay. What, Spraggue wondered, staring at Sharon Collatos' too white face, made him think of that other woman, the one on Heartbreak Hill, the one who'd handed Senator Donagher a supposedly harmless bottle of water. . . ?

"From what Pete told me about you," Sharon said, "I'm sure that it isn't the way it looks. You wouldn't just let them pull a cover-up, pretend that it was all an accident, unrelated to his work. But with all the publicity . . . You know nobody wants this to be a murder. The politicians hate the idea; they think assassinations come in threes and that somehow, by ignoring the first one, by denying it, they can prevent other crazies from copying whoever killed Pete. And the marathon people, they don't want their happy little race involved in any scandal. So please don't be insulted, but I had to ask . . ."

And then she said it again: "What are you going to do about it?"

FOURTEEN

The question buzzed in his ear like an annoying fly through a hectic sold-out matinee, a hurried overcooked dinner, and on into the night. As he smeared his face with greasepaint for his evening role as one of the two interchangeable comic doctors in *The Caucasian Chalk Circle*, he repeated it to himself. What am I going to do about it?

Partners . . . Damn Collatos for using that word, that pat emotion-charged word. Partners: Spade and Archer; Nick and Nora. You risk your neck to save a partner. Even if you hated him, you don't let him die unavenged. Partners. He swore and rubbed at a wayward smudge of eye shadow, stared at himself critically under the arc of makeup lights, swore again, and glanced down at the numbered tube of Max Factor base on the table in front of him. Wrong color—way too light. He'd make his entrance looking like an escaped extra from *Night of the Living Dead*.

Goddammit! he told himself sternly, concentrate!

Partners.

He was still cursing the word two and a half hours later as he sponged the makeup off his face, dressed in his street clothes, and marched out the stage door, heading for the police station.

He half hoped that his best, indeed his only, civil contact on the homicide squad would be out. Captain Frederick Hurley, had he known Spraggue was on his way up, would have gladly arranged the favor.

Hurley owed Spraggue. An ace cop with a steel-trap mind, Hurley had been interred in Records, shifted there as a tribute to his remarkable memory, unhappy as hell with the inactivity. He'd been dead-ended at his desk until his old acquaintance Spraggue invited him to a murder at a local theater. Spraggue had even set up the denouement of the case in such a way that Hurley, rather than Chief Investigating Officer Hank Menlo, had reaped the rewards. The ensuing publicity sped Hurley out of Records and back onto Homicide, and helped not a little in his later promotion to captain. So Hurley owed.

Hurley probably wouldn't feel like paying off the debt on a case as politically charged as this one.

Halfway up the stone steps of the Berkeley Street Police Station, Spraggue executed a neat turnaround, and crossed the street to an all-night drugstore where he purchased two large coffees, black, and two glazed doughnuts that still had a little give to them when squeezed. He counted out two dollars and twenty-five cents under the glare of fluorescent bulbs. If Hurley was in his office, exercising the penchant for night work that kept him away from a disintegrating marriage, the offering might grease the opening moments of a tricky encounter. If Hurley was out, the lost investment was certainly of the bearable kind. A minor loss compared to, say, the loss the Spraggue Foundation would have to shoulder should Aunt Mary's suspicions prove correct and the fire department have to be called out to quell a blaze of suspicious origin at that building on Commonwealth Avenue.

The graying sergeant at the beat-up desk to the left of the door was a familiar old-timer. He answered Spraggue's wink, dispensed with the badge, phone call, and escort routine. Good. If Hurley didn't know of his arrival, he wouldn't have a chance to play hide-and-seek in someone else's office.

Spraggue crossed the linoleum floor to the elevator, punched the top button.

As the aging cage made lurching progress toward the sixth floor, he idly envisioned Sharon Collatos with a smile turning up the corners of her wide mouth. . . .

He waved the white coffee-and-doughnut sack aloft like a flag of surrender as he tapped on the fingerprint-smeared glass panel of Hurley's door.

The slouching figure in the chair, telephone clamped to one ear, fingers twirling a cigarette butt, swung around in his swivel chair at the noise, grimaced, and motioned the bearer of gifts inside. Spraggue twisted the knob and entered the claustrophobic closet Hurley called home.

The captain was speaking to his wife and, from one end of the conversation, Spraggue could tell that all was not billing and cooing. Hurley held the receiver distastefully away from his ear and issued imprecations to the heavens with his shaggy eyebrows.

"Trouble?" Spraggue asked, when the frown lingered after Hurley hung up.

"Same old theme song: When you got to be a captain, I thought you'd work civilized hours. Now, can I help it if I like night work? Why be a cop in the daylight? What the hell kind of asshole crook works nine to five?"

"Housebreakers."

"Exactly. Boring crooks work in the daytime. What's in the bag?"

Spraggue drew out the coffee cups and set the doughnuts on a hastily cleared square of Hurley's ancient desk.

"Think I don't know a bribe when I see one?" The captain sipped the hot liquid gratefully, tapped the Styrofoam cup. "How much you think this fucking cup of coffee is going to get you?"

"Well—"

"Wait until I turn on this tape recorder," Hurley said. "The D.A. told me to tape all potentially compromising conversations."

"I heard Boston cops were hard up, but I had no idea you could buy them so cheap."

Hurley laughed and bit into his doughnut. "Hard as a bullet," he observed. "I'm not as broke as a lot of my fellow officers. I don't come across for stale doughnuts."

"Pete Collatos," Spraggue said.

"Shit." Hurley slammed the top drawer of his desk shut so hard that the desk rattled and coffee spilled over two files and a newspaper clipping. "What's old Caesar say to Brutus when he sticks the knife in? *Et tu*, Brutus?"

"Something like that."

"What I really needed right now was one more person to ask me why the hell I'm not out solving that lousy case. What about the twenty other unsolved murders we got on the books? This Collatos business is barely a week old."

"But if a case isn't broken within twenty-four hours—"

"I know. I fucking taught you that. The more time goes

by, the less chance of closing a case. What do you think I ought to be doing? Exactly?''

"What are you doing?"

"Number one: I'm not in charge. Number two: I understand they've got a twenty-four-hour guard on Donagher.''

"So if the murderer tries again, you'll get him."

"Maybe. Maybe not. If somebody wants to kill you, make out a will. That's what I tell guys who come in here wanting bodyguards. I say, sure, we'll protect you, but don't invest in any long-playing records.''

"Clever."

"Look, Spraggue, nothing we can do to bring Collatos back. I liked that kid. I did. He was a pain. He overdramatized. He was shitty on routine. But he was fun to shoot the bull with, you know?''

Spraggue nodded. "How's your file on anonymous letter writers?''

"I know what you're thinking, Spraggue, and believe me, we're ahead of you. We've been over those letters, and the only way we're going to trace them is if the guy starts writing again and puts his return address on the back of the envelope.''

"'Great.''

"By the way," Hurley said, elaborately unconcerned, "a guy came in to ask me about you the other day, before this Donagher business broke. Guy named Heineman. Mean anything to you?''

"No."

"Hah. You wouldn't tell me if he were your long lost brother. Your automatic reaction to talking to a cop: say nothing.''

Even better than saying nothing, Spraggue thought, was changing the subject.

He said, "Have the doctors come up with anything new on the autopsy report?"

Hurley snorted, took a sip of coffee as if he wanted to wash a bad taste out of his mouth. "You remember that article in the *Globe* last year, the one that said that if you want to commit a murder, come to Boston to do it? They had a point. The M.E. is now trying to find out whether Collatos was on drugs."

"You're kidding."

"They're trying to prove he took something before the race, that he was dosing up on speed anyway, and that his first hit, combined with the stuff he drank during the race, was enough to kill him."

"Doesn't that smack of blaming the victim? Just a little?"

"Look, Spraggue, at least they're still trying to make sense out of it. That won't last long. They'll have to move on to someone else soon, seal up all those little jars, file them in cold storage and that will be that."

"And you? You going to file it away in one of these coffee-stained folders and forget it? He was a cop."

"You come here to bribe me or just to rile me? What have I got to go on?"

"You could start with the woman who gave Donagher the water."

"Thanks a lot. You know, she hasn't bothered to waltz her ass by and explain why that water was dosed with dextroamphetamine. She's heard all about it on the news, read all about it in the *Herald*, and yet she hasn't come in. So from that, we can draw the inference that this woman was no innocent bystander. Or that she was an innocent bystander, but now she's scared. Or she doesn't read the *Herald* or watch the news—"

"Dammit, you've got a good description—"

"Christ! Descriptions! It's hard enough to describe a

man, but a woman! Suppose she had a wig on, dyed her hair? She could have been my sister, for Chrissake, with different clothes and hair and makeup. None of the eyewitnesses gave us the same details—"

"I saw her."

"You mean nobody's taken your statement yet?"

"Nope."

"Shit."

"Who's in charge of the investigation?" Spraggue asked quietly.

"You've already guessed. Menlo. And he wouldn't ask you for a dime to call the fire department if his house was burning down. Look, before you go, why don't I get your statement, and if I think it's any good, I'll send you down to the police artist who's trying to do a composite."

"Sure."

"And while you're at it, tell me exactly why you're here, so when Menlo asks me, I can lie to him. If you don't, I might guess the truth and just blurt it out to the bastard."

Spraggue took his time chewing stale doughnut, finally had to help it down with a sip of coffee. "I'm asking myself the same question," he said finally. "Why am I here?"

"Are you working for Donagher?"

"No."

"For Collatos' sister? Anybody? Because your license is sadly out of date and Menlo could crucify you."

"Let's say I'm investigating on my own. No client."

"Okay. If he asks, I'll tell Menlo you got lost and came up to ask me the way home."

"Tell him I'm interested in a suspected arson at 312 Commonwealth Avenue."

"Are you?"

"My aunt is. She owns the place next door."

Hurley made some marks on a file card. "I'll see what I can find out."

"Thanks."

"Is that what you really came here for? Is this bit about Collatos a blind?"

"Tell me, is your artist better than a TV camera?"

"Huh?"

"Heineman. Wasn't that the name you mentioned? He's a newscaster on Channel 4. TV cameras follow Donagher. They were trained on him when he came up Heartbreak Hill, when he ran over and took the bottle from that woman. Have you put out a call for pictures? Have you gotten tapes from all the stations?"

"I told you, I'm not handling the investigation."

"Could you find out?"

"I guess so."

Spraggue smiled.

"Now," Hurley said, "let's get a steno in here and hear what the lady looked like."

Spraggue did his best.

Closing his eyes, isolating himself from the reality of the hard chair beneath him, the stale cigarette smell of Hurley's domain, he envisioned the chaotic marathon scene. He played it like an acting exercise, starting with himself, recreating his mood, recalling the clothes he'd been wearing with such clarity that he could feel them against his body. Then he moved outside himself, using senses developed by years of training. What had he felt? The baking sunshine, the dry breeze. Smelled? The nearby barbecue, the piney tang of a cone-shaped tree. Touched? Heard? The drone of distant automobiles, the bright chatter of friends, the rushing swelling cheers. Always he worked from the general to the specific, and when he had dressed his inner stage with sound and smell, he opened an inner eye and saw.

The man with the bandaged ankle . . . the college students . . . the small unshaven man . . . and across the road, twenty feet away, the tall woman. All this took only seconds; it was the work of a professional actor, craft rather than talent.

He spoke in a monotone, without opening his eyes, giving an oral picture of a woman he'd hardly taken note of at the time, painting her clothes, her speech, her way of walking, until Hurley sarcastically asked if he didn't want to throw in her name as long as he was at it.

But the woman's face was an unfocused blur. The police artist's sketch could have been any one of a hundred thousand women. And even as he spoke, Spraggue grew increasingly uneasy, aware of a twinge of doubt somewhere just beneath conscious thought. He picked at it, pulled at it, but the idea stayed in shadow, an itching scab just out of reach.

It gave him a bad night, and in the morning, he couldn't remember his dreams.

FIFTEEN

Squinting against dazzling sunshine, Spraggue raced up the stone steps of the Senate office building. In spite of haste, split-second timing, and plain good luck, he was late for his 10:00 A.M. appointment with Senator Donagher.

It was Monday, the working actor's Saturday and Sunday rolled into one. No performance tomorrow, that was what he'd remembered in the middle of the night; that thought had triggered his 4:00 A.M. phone call to his ever wakeful aunt, and that phone call had set gears spinning in relentless motion, wheels that had rotated him to Washington, D.C.

The morning had been bedlam.

Mary had returned his call before dawn; the phone's shrill wail had jerked him into unwilling semiconsciousness. The urgent buzz of the front door sounded while he was still showering. His aunt had said she'd send a driver; he'd been surprised that she'd chosen Pierce. Drive, he certainly did. Spraggue shuddered at the memory of the frenzied race to the airport; he doubted any Boston cabbie could have beaten that twenty-two-minute rush-hour charge.

Then the airplane, the Spraggue Foundation Learjet, ready to lift off as soon as seatbelts were fastened on the black leather swivel loungechairs. Again surprise; Pierce was prepared to come along for the ride. Mary had sent not merely a chauffeur, but a spy. Even now, Pierce trailed a scant two steps behind him, with the appropriate room number neatly typed on a three-by-five card.

A woman opened the door when Pierce knocked, so quickly that she must have been standing right behind it, an attractive middle-aged woman who seemed to be doing her best to hide behind a drab shapeless suit and fade-into-the-background posture. Donagher was framed within a second, interior doorway, seated at an ornate desk, scanning a thick document, using one pointing finger to mark his place.

The woman began a practiced lament: The senator was extraordinarily busy and his time was strictly limited; she really had no idea how anyone had managed to wangle an appointment on such short notice, but it would be very discourteous if . . . She would have gone on had the resourceful Pierce not charmed her out of the room.

Dear Aunt Mary . . . She'd been pulling political strings so long she knew where all the loose ends were located, which one to tweak first for the desired effect. Like who to call if you needed to see your senator on a moment's notice. Money talked in Massachusetts politics, a lot more clearly than a private detective's expired plastic-coated photostat.

Donagher dog-eared the corner of the document, closed it with a bang, and emerged from behind the desk offering a handshake. He was wearing a pale blue shirt and the pants to a pin-striped three-piece suit. The vest hung off the corner of a rocking chair, wiping the marble floor. The suit jacket was crumpled on a brocade divan. After checking to make sure the heavy oak door to the hallway was firmly shut, he studied his wristwatch, and said, "So what's all this about? How can I help you?"

"Questions."

"About the upcoming campaign or about Collatos? I got some conflicting signals."

Mary would have given them, using the lure of a campaign contribution to keep him on the hook. "About Collatos," Spraggue said.

Donagher gestured Spraggue onto the divan, pointed at the tallest pile of documents on his cluttered desk. "See this? This is the draft of a report for the Subcommittee on Energy Research and Development. The pile next to it is for the Subcommittee on Advocacy and the Future of Small Business. The Committee on Foreign Relations has just taken a half-hour recess to study one of the most convoluted amendments to a simple proposal that I've ever had the pleasure of viewing. I ought to tell you I don't have the time, but I won't. Just keep it brief and direct . . . and, well, I guess it can't be any more painful than it already is . . ."

"Three questions."

"They could have been handled over the phone."

"No, they couldn't."

"You're the judge of that." Donagher made an effort to relax. He lifted one foot and flexed it slowly. With his suit, he should have been wearing highly polished wing tips instead of soft slippers. Spraggue spotted the correct shoes under a corner of the desk, wondered if the senator's toes were balloons of blisters from the marathon. "Go ahead," the senator said.

"Okay. I assume you were with Collatos the night before the race."

"He was with me. Wherever I went, he went. He stuck like glue after that day at the reservoir."

"At twelve thirty, the night before the race, where were you?"

Donagher closed his eyes and blew out a deep breath. Tiny wrinkles stood out in his forehead like wavy river lines on an old map. "The night before the marathon is the spaghetti dinner. I decided not to go to the traditional blowout at the Prudential Center because of the crowds. I listened to the cops that far. If I'd listened to them and not run the race, Pete might . . ."

"There's no point in playing that game," Spraggue said, after a pause. "If, might, maybe . . ."

"I know, I just . . ." The senator's right hand went to the back of his neck, massaged knotted muscles. "I decided to throw an alternative to the Pru's spaghetti supper at my home, a small party. A few friends, a few runners. Some of the folks who'd been to the real feed came over later."

"Who?"

"Why?" Donagher countered.

102

"Does it make a difference?"

"I didn't invite anyone who had the remotest desire to kill me. And I don't want people getting the idea that accepting an invitation to my house is the same as accepting an invitation to be grilled by the police."

"You're refusing to give me a list of names?"

"Until I know why you want them."

"Well, then, try another question. Did you overhear Pete making a phone call at about twelve thirty the night before the marathon?"

Donagher considered, frowned, shook his head no. "Is that all you want to ask the people who were there that night?"

"Yes."

"Important?"

"Probably not."

"Well, most of them were gone by twelve thirty, but I'll tell Murray to give you a list. I understand you, or rather, your aunt, requested a meeting with my campaign manager. May I ask why?"

Instead of answering Spraggue said, "I still have another question."

"This'll make three."

"I saw you come up Heartbreak Hill—"

Donagher pointed down at his painful feet. "I was almost gone. Thinking of quitting. The crowd kept me alive."

"You were looking into the crowd for someone. Who?"

"I, uh, no . . . I don't recall looking for anyone in particular."

"I saw you."

The senator gave a sheepish laugh. "What you saw was Senator Donagher peering around for the TV cameras. That, I admit. I wasn't so far gone that I couldn't recognize a good broadcast opportunity. It's a sin of vanity. If I see a camera, I try to look as if I'm not going to fall down. I may even at-

103

tempt a smile. At the top of Heartbreak, smiling is not easy."

"I got the impression that you were looking for someone with a water flask."

Donagher's smile froze. "I can't help the impression you got."

"Most leading runners have people stationed along the route."

"I am no longer a leading runner. I did have a few friends waiting along the first half of the course. I do most of my drinking early in a race."

"Relax."

"I was not looking for that woman. I don't know that woman. I—"

"You're not listening. I never said you knew her. I said you took water from her because someone else wasn't there."

As he spoke, Spraggue stood and crossed the marble tiles over to the desk. He picked up a silver-framed photograph, blew dust off its face.

"These your kids?"

"Tommy—I should say Tom, he's almost fifteen—and Joey. He's still a baby. Ten."

"They ever wait along the course for you? With water?"

"You're wrong, that's all I can say."

"What about your wife? That would have made a good broadcast opportunity. Doesn't she usually wait along the course with a water bottle?"

"Look, there's no 'usually' about it; I haven't run a marathon in six years. She may have given me water during an occasional race; I think she did. But that was years ago. This time she decided she'd rather see the race from the finish line."

"Okay."

"You've had your three questions. Is that all?"

"Enough. Thanks for your time."

"Wait," Donagher said. "I'd like to ask a question. I've answered three, certainly you can answer one. I've been meaning to ask it ever since this horrible business happened. Even before. Pete . . . Pete asked me to hire you, but . . . I didn't think it was necessary. I didn't take the threats seriously. But now . . . I've checked with the Boston Police and you seem to have a decent reputation. Will you work for me? Find out who killed Collatos? Who's trying to kill me?"

"No."

"No?" Donagher pulled his chair back and sank into it. His face collapsed along with his body, making him look his age.

"I'm sorry," Spraggue said, "I've already got a client."

SIXTEEN

"I can give you fifteen minutes at the absolute most," Aunt Mary said sternly some four hours later, when he'd finally bulled his way past Pierce and two fierce secretaries.

Today her bright red shawl livened up a conservative well-cut gray suit. Her bedroom had been converted for the day into its office mode; the peach-colored alcove containing the peach-satin-covered bed was curtained off. The click of computer keyboards, the muffled beat of footsteps, the clang of telephones punctuated her conversation. She stared meaningfully at her chunky gold watch.

"You want me to begin when the second hand hits the twelve?" he inquired.

"Darling," she said, indicating a desk filled to overflowing with papers, flickering computer terminal, a bank of telephones flashing angry red lights, "the market is in a bit of an uproar—"

"How long would it take you to lift fingerprints off a wineglass?"

She considered the question, eyes narrowed, pointed chin tilted to one side. "Crystal?"

"Yeah."

"Whose?"

"Oh, forget it," Spraggue said easily. "You probably don't have the time."

"By removing me from this desk at this time, you could conceivably lose fifty thousand dollars."

"Or gain it. The stock market is a colossal crap shoot; you told me that yourself."

"True." She nodded at one of her assistants, a fortyish woman with graying hair and a wide smile. "Helen, if Consolidated hits twenty-six, sell short, ten thousand shares, and buy Xenon no higher than eighteen and a quarter. I have been lured from my duties by a major stockholder. Hold all calls."

"That," she said, as her nephew accompanied her down the stairs to the library, "was blackmail, pure and simple. You knew I couldn't resist. Did you pick up this bit of crystal in Washington? Was it a profitable trip?"

"Possibly."

"I hope you do indeed possess a mysterious glass with unknown fingerprints on it. Otherwise I shall brain you in the hallway with a hatstand and the police will never pin it on me."

"Don't worry. I've got it. Where's your fingerprinting paraphernalia?"

She padded across the room and rang the bell on Davison Spraggue's mahogany desk. "I haven't the faintest. It's been ages since I've even thought about it. Soon the man from Sotheby's will be after me to auction it off as an antique, not that I would ever part with anything that provoked such pleasant memories. But Pierce will know."

He did, which surprised Spraggue no more than it did Mary. Spraggue sometimes thought that if he asked Pierce for the red rubber ball he'd played with at age ten, the butler would instantly whip it out of a pocket. Pierce didn't have the fingerprint kit on him, but he did a quick turn, left the room, and returned with it tucked under his arm in less than three minutes—unflustered, walking at his accustomed, dignified pace.

"Thank you," Aunt Mary said. "I sometimes am overcome by the desire to ask you how you do that, whether you have a complete inventory of the house written down and stowed away somewhere. Item: one fingerprint kit; location: third shelf, north hall closet. Item: one faded teddy bear; location: second shelf, south guest-room closet. No," she held up one hand as Pierce opened his mouth. "No, I really don't want to know. I prefer to imagine."

Pierce nodded and took his leave.

"He's got it all memorized," Spraggue said. "He doesn't need a list."

Parts of Aunt Mary's fingerprinting kit would have given the collector pause. The original black bag, very like a doctor's, had been issued to her during World War II, when she had served in the OSS. She'd kept it up to date by strategic additions, culminating in a frenzy of purchases when her nephew had first become a private eye. Just in case she was ever called on to help, she'd explained hopefully.

She spread yesterday afternoon's edition of the *Globe* over the maroon leather blotter in the center of the desk.

"The glass, please," she said.

"Coming up." Sprague retrieved a parcel wrapped in a pink napkin from beneath the folds of his overcoat and presented it to his aunt.

"And don't get your prints all over it," she added.

"Yes, Mum."

"Sorry."

"You should be. Here I've brought you a nice toy to play with and you insult me."

"I only apologize once. While I play with the toy, you can tell me all about it."

"All about what?"

"I perceive from the napery that the glass comes from one of my favorite establishments."

"How discerning of you."

"Knowing you were in Washington, knowing your fatal weakness for bouillabaisse, seeing a goblet wrapped in a distinctive pink linen napkin, the conclusion that you lunched at Le Provencal is unavoidable. Don't even try to deny it."

As she spoke, Mary laid out her tools: a jar of fine grayish powder, several delicate brushes, a few larger ones, glazed white paper, an insufflator, a camera with different lenses and a metal holding contraption to position it above the desk, tongs, magnifying lenses.

"I hope I'm not hunting senatorial fingerprints," she said.

"No. And the staff at Le Provencal sends its collective love."

"They should have sent bouillabaisse. Go on."

"After I saw Donagher, I took his campaign manager to lunch. I got him drunk and asked him who was out for his boss' hide."

"And?"

"He thinks it's political."

"Politicians think everything's political."

"This is how he put it: A lot of people hate Donagher's politics, call him anything from a bleeding-heart liberal to a communist sympathizer, but the man's opinions haven't shifted lately—"

"The only thing that's changed is that someone's trying to kill him."

"Right. So Eichenhorn, the campaign manager, ties it to the upcoming election. He says that now's the time for the conservative political action committees to take Donagher out, because if Donagher wins sixty percent of the vote in Massachusetts, he's going to be a presidential contender. And a popular one."

"Do PACs hire assassins?"

"Well, Eichenhorn thinks the whole shebang was a screw-up, stage managed either by Bartolo with help from the mob or our own Governor Edwards with aid from same."

"A screw-up?"

"Yeah. He thinks somebody just wanted Donagher to look bad, to drop out of the marathon without finishing. Eliminate Collatos' death from the picture and what have we got? Donagher down on the ground, gasping. You saw the wire service photos: Donagher loaded into an ambulance; senator stuck in ice bath. Those photos sure didn't make Donagher look like any presidential contender. If it hadn't been for Pete's death, nobody would have checked to see if Donagher had been poisoned, there wouldn't have been any outpouring of sympathy for Donagher. People would have seen him as a failure, not a victim. End result: Somebody neutralizes all the favorable publicity Donagher gets from running the marathon."

"Ah . . ." Mary said softly. "There's a nice clear thumb, a man's right thumb and three fairly good fingers. I hope it isn't you, dear."

"Pretty sure it isn't."

Mary pulled a stamp pad from the desk's center top drawer. "All the same, would you mind? The right thumb should be sufficient."

Spraggue grimaced, surrendered, rubbed ink on his thumb, pressed it against one of the sheets of glazed paper.

"Then this Eichenhorn doesn't think you're up against a killer?" Mary asked.

"He thinks some pol hired himself a dirty trickster, à la the Democrats' infamous Dick Tuck."

"Do you think his theory holds water?"

"I don't know. I tried to sound him out on Donagher's personal life, but he clammed up. According to him, Donagher's a candidate for immediate sainthood."

"So few saints in political life, these days," Mary said.

"And Donagher's not one of them. He lied to me. And he did a pretty good job."

"Isn't that a requirement of elective office?"

"He was expecting someone to be at the top of Heartbreak with a water bottle—"

"Then he had an arrangement with that woman?"

"No. I don't mean he was looking for *her*. He took the bottle from her because he got stood up. Whoever he was expecting didn't show. He's protecting somebody—and I'll bet it's his wife."

"Not exactly the perfect political wife, is she?"

"What do you mean?"

"Chronic alcoholism is not an election plus, so I've heard."

"Where do you dig up all this dirt? Is Pierce a gossip?"

"I keep my ear to the ground."

"The ground right over the sewer?" He peered over his

aunt's shoulder as she gently blew excess powder from the surface of the glass. "How's it going?"

"Fine. The fingers have not lost their cunning, although the eyes are rather on the way out, I'm afraid. Still, they suffice to tell me that these prints are not yours. Now, do you want me to lift them, so that you can present them to your Captain Hurley without telling him from whence they came?"

"That was the general idea."

"Ahhhhh. There." She brandished a white four-by-six card on which she had fastened the plastic tape that held the prints. "Beautiful, if I do say so myself."

"Lovely." Spragque pressed his lips together, then said in a faraway voice, "One more thing. Do you have a VCR?"

"Videocassette recorder. I have two. One VHS; one Beta."

"Do you have a standing order for every gadget that comes out on the market?"

"Just about."

"Do you mind if I play a cassette I recorded at home?"

"Not if it's good."

"It's last Sunday's eleven o'clock news."

"What a depressing thought."

"The Channel 4 news."

"Ed Heineman?"

"The man does interest me," Spragque admitted. "He keeps Lila Donagher's picture in his wallet."

SEVENTEEN

Ed Heineman had a voice Spraggue wouldn't have minded appropriating: effortlessly mellow for a man of his limited age and experience, with unusually low pitch and pleasing timbre. Ten years ago, some speaking coach would have hauled the upstart aside and hurriedly eliminated any vestige of his Southern upbringing. Today, in the anything-goes TV-radio world, accents were considered homey and attractive, no longer the kiss of death.

He watched the tape for the fourteenth time moving his lips along with Heineman's. The videocassette recording was easier to work with than an audio tape alone; he could not only hear the deviations from Standard American Speech, he could see the shape of the newscaster's lips on his curiously open *A*, his unconventional *E*. After a while he just listened to it, lying flat on the Oriental rug in the library, staring at the grape-leaf molding of the ceiling two stories over his head. Mary had long since returned to her bedroom office. The walls and doors of the mansion were so thick they muffled even the sounds of her clacking machinery. He might have been alone in the vast house.

He scooped up the notebook lying at his side, scratched out a symbol, made another in its place, and nodded with satisfaction. Phonetics had been a compulsory part of his classical actor's training, at RADA, where professors thought nothing of ordering up Hamlet's soliloquys in anything from Northumbrian to Liverpudlian to Texan. Spragge thought Heineman might hail from Georgia, but he wasn't sure. He wasn't any Henry Higgins; his goal wasn't identification, but mimicry. Short-term mimicry at that.

Transcribing Heineman's words into the International Phonetic Alphabet was an exercise in frustration. Just as he would start to congratulate himself on how well he remembered his lessons, he'd come across a sound for which he recalled no symbol, have to flick off the tape, and search through an old copy of Kenyan and Knott's *Pronouncing Dictionary of the English Language*. When he at length completed the transcription, skipping a few words he knew he'd have no occasion to use, words like *government*, which Heineman pronounced guvment, and *Iran*, which he pronounced airun, it was two in the morning and only the beginning.

There was no sense in perfecting a general Ed Heineman; that would take days, and he only needed a persuasive two-minute Heineman. So, first, he constructed the message, a single thought conveyed in three variants. Which one he actually delivered would depend on who answered the phone. He wrote them out, deliberately choosing as many words as possible directly from the evening news, it being more difficult to extrapolate from an accent than to copy one. Nowhere in his prepared text did he actually lie. The lie was in his voice, not in what he said. If someone answering the phone were to mistake him for Ed Heineman . . . well, he could hardly be held accountable for that.

He jackknifed into a sitting position and carefully recited ten words, common everyday words in which Heineman's pronunciation differed from the norm—lowering his pitch to the level of Heineman's, breathing where Heineman would have breathed. The man, in his newscasts, had a jerky pattern of delivery. Talking to him in the bar, Spragge had noticed a similar quality in his off-camera speech, an easy

113

gimmick to copy. That and the slightly Southern pronunciation should carry the deception. He practiced his lines nonstop until Aunt Mary appeared, cheerful and rested, to announce that it was 5 A.M. and would he like croissants for breakfast?

He succumbed, ate three freshly baked pastries smeared with apricot jam, but foreswore Dora's excellent coffee. He drove back to Cambridge, set the alarm clock to allow a scant four hours sleep, threw himself fully dressed across the bed. When he woke, he showered, shaved, and changed, rehearsed in front of a mirror. At the last minute, he decided not to make the call from his house. Who knew what tracing devices the cops might have rigged on Donagher's line? He set off on foot for Harvard Square.

The morning air was cool and bracing, more like nippy autumn than gentle spring, but it hadn't fooled the swelling buds on the oak trees. The heavy tree limbs were speckled with tiny verdant spots of color, like a pointillist painter's dots: lush, vivid green from a distance, sparse, separate buds from close at hand. Keyed up with a rush of pre-audition adrenalin that compensated for too little sleep, he repeated his lines into the breeze as he walked down Brattle Street, hardly aware of the great houses on either side of what had once been called Tory Row.

The first real phone booth he encountered was on Church Street. The others he'd passed had been ugly, modern stands, blue poles with phones perched on top and no provision for privacy. Behind Sage's, where that old French restaurant had been and the new building was now, were actual booths.

He placed a ragged-edged three-by-five card, his speech written painstakingly in the letters and symbols of IPA, on the shelf reserved for the ripped-out Yellow Pages. The dangling metal cord that should have bound the phone book to the booth got in his way and he used his right hand to

114

wrestle it under the shelf, dialing with his left hand and cradling the phone between his shoulder and chin. He dialed the number Collatos had given him two weeks earlier, tapped his fingers through six long rings, hoped the right someone would answer the phone.

A woman's voice, low and sweet.

"Həloʊ" was all he said. It was one of Heineman's most distinctive words: He said həloʊ, not hɛlo. He was sloppy with his vowels.

"Ed?" the woman murmured, alarmed. Spraggue exulted; she'd got it in one.

He'd taken time selecting a likely setting. Where would Lila Donagher agree to meet Ed Heineman? Someplace that offered privacy, someplace she wasn't known. Not a park, not an open space, where she could simply walk away when he, not Heineman, approached. He wanted her seated, with food in front of her, in a place where a hasty departure would cause a scene.

The Harvest Café.

It was always crowded; the central bar was the focal point of Cambridge's young, affluent dating crowd. It boasted alcoves and tall plants and one booth, in particular, that was almost invisible from the door. Heineman was known there, probably lunched there; it was credible. And the food was good, entailing no gastronomic sacrifice.

"a nid tʌ tɔk tʌ yu," he said. "Urgently. Tomorrow. Lunch at the Harvest Café. One thirty. Ask for Mr. H's table."

"Someone might see us." The protest came out in a harsh whisper.

"Trust me," Spraggue said. "It's important."

When he hung up, there was a clatter of change and his dime was refunded into the compartment at the bottom right of the pay phone. He stared at it, a dingy gray circle resting on his palm, stuffed it back into the phone. Ma Bell deserved it.

EIGHTEEN

He won the complicity of the Harvest's headwaiter with an early arrival and an improbable romantic tale solidified by a sizable tip. The arrangements completed, he waited outdoors at a white, painted wrought-iron table on a chilly semi-enclosed patio still off-limits for the season. Pigeons foraged underfoot.

It wouldn't do for Lila to approach a seated Spraggue. She might have seen him going into the Sparhawk Street house; if so she'd back off, aware that a trap had been baited. He planned to wait until the headwaiter had relieved her of her coat, anchored her to the table with a drink. Then he might have a chance to get out enough words to convince her to stay.

She was late. He heard her heels tap-tapping on the concrete blocks of the path that passed the patio and froze, but she didn't glance his way. Instead of giving her the stature she lacked, her high heels accented the wobbly thinness of her ankles, made her seem more childish instead of more adult. She wore the same raincoat she'd worn the morning he'd read the anonymous letters, belt cinched tight, collar raised. Her corn-silk hair, her slightly receding chin, her wide-set blue eyes all made her look as dangerous as a waif in an orphanage, as murderous as Alice in Wonderland.

Before she passed out of sight, she fumbled in a maroon leather shoulder bag for a small leather case. From it, she removed a pair of glasses. Not attention-grabbing dark sunglasses, but rose-tinted aviator frames that subtly shortened her nose and broadened her face. She donned them with the practiced gesture of a woman schooled in pretense and yanked open the Harvest's front door.

Spraggue watched white paint flake off wrought iron.

She would be settling into the booth at the back of the front right-hand section of the restaurant, the part called Ben's Café. The waiter, following instructions, would have urged her into the seat facing away from the door. She wouldn't object to the table or the choice of seat. No one disturbed that table except the staff. Only the kitchen lay beyond it; the telephones and restrooms were elsewhere.

Curtain time. The black-vested waiter elaborately mouthed his readiness.

He'd succeeded in parting her from her raincoat. She wore a mannish pale blue shirt tucked neatly into a slim navy skirt. A schoolgirl outfit. A thin gold chain gleamed around her neck. She sipped at a glass half full of amber liquid and ice cubes.

"Hi," Spraggue said easily as he slid into the booth.

She was startled. Her arm jerked and she hastily slammed her drink back on the table. "I'm sorry, but—" Her cheeks reddened. She thought it was a pickup. Then she stared up at him and her eyes narrowed even as her blush deepened.

"I wanted to talk to you—"

"I'm sorry." She had the habit of apology. "I have to—" She half stood, remembered her missing raincoat, tried in vain to catch the waiter's eye.

"Michael Spraggue." He held out his hand, but she didn't take it. "You already knew that."

She sucked in a deep breath. "I don't mean to be rude, but I'm waiting for someone, and—"

He let his voice descend to Heineman's pitch. "I'm

sorry," he said in Heineman's drawl. "I didn't know any other way to get to see you."

While she stared at him with her mouth slightly open and her cheeks burning scarlet, he nodded to the waiter who hovered just out of Mrs. Donagher's sight. Eager to play his role in smoothing over this lovers' quarrel, the waiter set steaming bowls of soup in front of them.

"It's great stuff," Spraggue said encouragingly. "And I'd hate to eat it alone."

She swiveled her head and peered suspiciously at the other diners.

"It would make quite a scene if you walked out now," he said.

"It would? Or you would?"

"I might call out your name. Who knows? I might faint."

A corner of her mouth twitched. She measured the distance to the door with her eyes, then said, "What do you want?"

"Sit down. People are getting curious."

"I asked you what you were after."

"A bowl of soup. A quiet lunch. The answers to some questions."

"Such as?"

"Eat your soup. And smile a little. The waiter's getting anxious."

"What did you tell him?"

"Better you shouldn't know."

"I know who you are, Mr. Spraggue."

He raised an eyebrow, spooned soup.

"I know that you used to be a professional busybody of sorts and that you gave it up. I've seen you on stage at the Harvard Rep. If I'd recalled your histrionic abilities, I would have handled 'Ed's' phone call differently."

"How differently?"

"I would have hung up." She made an attempt at the

118

soup, put her spoon down with a clatter against the china bowl. Spraggue started at the noise, looked up. For a moment he thought she would brave the thirty feet to the door and the threatened scene, but to his amazement, a slow smile spread across her face. "And then," she said, after a long pause and in a manner nicely calculated to flatter, "I would have missed what promises to be an interesting afternoon."

He wished he could snatch the rose-tinted glasses off her nose, divine in those blue eyes a reason for her sudden change in tactics. Not that the blue eyes were focused on him. No, she had a way of looking over him, behind him, through him—never at him. He was saved from immediate reply by the timely arrival of a bottle of Chateau St. Jean Chardonnay. The waiter, delighted by their apparent rapport, tried some clumsy banter; it fell flat.

"So," she said confidingly, when the silence after the waiter's departure had stretched to the breaking point, "I suppose my husband hired you to do this."

She might as well have dispensed with the question altogether and given the traditional *en garde* to begin the fencing match.

"To do what?"

"Let's not be naïve. To set me up."

"You don't think he has any right to be curious about you and Heineman?"

"I hope you are not one of those people who believes that when a married woman agrees to lunch with a man other than her husband, there is something sordid going on."

"I hardly believe in anything. Keeps me from being shocked."

"So often the simplest explanation is the best. Once things start getting complicated—" She shook her head gravely, stared down at the tabletop, tilted her bowl slightly, and ate the dregs of her soup.

"Would you call this a complicated situation?"

"Only because I tried to keep it simple."

"I don't understand."

"I wanted to avoid just the misunderstanding that seems to be taking place."

"In your husband's mind?"

"I don't think my husband would have hired you to check on any extramarital outings I might be arranging—not on his own. He knows me too well, knows I wouldn't fool around on principle." She attempted a smile. "And knows I don't have the time. But he might have been convinced to do it by one of his aides, if said aide thought I might be up to something that would screw the precious campaign. One of his aides might have hired you himself, in which case that aide is going to be out the door so fast once Brian finds out—" She bit at her lower lip as if that were the only way she could stop the angry words pouring out of her mouth. She tried to make her voice light and inconsequential again.

"I'll soothe your fears," she said, with a touch of sarcasm. "Eddie Heineman and I went to high school together. We did have a passionate affair; it took place half a lifetime ago and was consummated by hand-holding in the library."

She was doing it again; looking at everything but him. Spraggue wanted to reach over and lift her chin, frame her delicate face with his hands, and force her to meet his gaze.

Instead, he hazarded a guess, said, "Why did you tell your old friend Ed that he might want to talk to me?"

"Ed didn't tell you . . ." Her sentence didn't end. It ran out of steam.

"Tell me what?"

She took her time answering and when she finally replied it was to his first question, not his second. "I was trying to help him out. He's new here. I mean, we went to school together years ago, in Lynn, but his people were from the South and they moved on. Didn't like it, the cold and the
120

snobby Yankees. He wants to make a name for himself, so when all the reporters were going crazy about that horrible business at the reservoir and then you came over to the house, I thought, well, I thought I'd give Ed the inside track. . . ."

Plausible, but it didn't fit with the rest of the conversation, with her forced flirty tone, her searching manner. If she'd assumed then that her husband had hired him for protection, why was she now assuming that the senator had hired him to 'set her up'? Set her up for what? The short end of a divorce settlement?

"You could have given him a bigger break, an exclusive interview with your husband."

"No."

"They don't get along?"

"It's not like that. It's not some stupid rivalry, for heaven's sake. They haven't even met."

"Your dear old friend and your husband?"

"They're just separate parts of my life. I knew Ed before I met Brian. They have nothing in common. Politically, they're on opposite poles. Ed's as conservative as they come . . . and . . ."

"Yes?"

"And how would it look if people knew Ed and I were friends? If he supported Brian on the air, the audience would say that he was biased because of me."

"But he doesn't support your husband, does he?"

"He tries for a balanced viewpoint," she said, no inflection in her voice.

"Maybe," Spraggue said, "he's biased against your husband because of you."

"That's exactly the kind of thing people would say."

Conversation waned when the main course, bluefish with ginger sauce, was served. From Lila's enthusiastic inroads on the fish, he diagnosed her silence as hunger rather than reticence, and soon she started talking again.

"I hope I've curbed your suspicions about my fidelity. It was childish, I suppose, not to want Brian to know about Ed."

"Romantic."

"Let's not use that word. Brian will have to know, I assume."

"It depends."

"On? Are you working directly for Brian or did Murray Eichenhorn pay the freight?"

"I still have a few more questions."

"Oh."

She handled silence well. She swallowed another sip of Chardonnay.

He monitored her alcohol consumption. Much as he had wanted a drink in front of her when he'd joined her, he'd been uneasy about ordering liquor for a woman his aunt had labeled a chronic alcoholic. He'd warned the waiter to give her a wide choice: Would she care for a drink, a cup of coffee, a glass of juice? She'd selected a Scotch on the rocks, taken an interest in the wine. . . . Could a chronic alcoholic drink socially? Had Mary gotten some inaccurate gossip?

"I wanted to know about Pete Collatos," he said quietly.

"Pete? Does Brian think I fool around with every man in town? Do you have a list of names to interrogate me about?"

"Just tell me about Pete."

"He's dead."

"That's all you've got to say?"

"Look, what is this? I've explained about Ed. More than I should have. What does Brian want? I know he doesn't want a divorce. Good God, not now. Not with a Senate race in the offing. There's no reason for him to—"

122

The bluefish had been grilled over charcoal, crisp and hot on the outside, moist and buttery within. The sauce was piquant enough to cut the oiliness.

Mrs. Donagher tilted her knife and fork across her plate, carefully, one inch apart, their handles touching the white tablecloth. She said: "I think I've behaved like a fool."

"What?"

"Never mind. I was talking to myself. I should do more of that, less talking to other people. You never said my husband hired you. You never did."

"Right."

"You never said anyone from his office hired you. And I went ahead and talked to you—Are you working for some gossipy newspaper?"

"No."

"Who else would care about my friendship with some local reporter?"

"I'll be honest with you—"

"That'll be a change."

"I haven't lied."

"Go on."

"I'm more interested in Pete Collatos than I am in Ed Heineman."

"Dead is dead. There's nothing you can do about Pete."

"You're not a seeker after justice?"

"Justice is so seldom tempered with mercy these days."

"How much mercy does the person who murdered Pete Collatos deserve?"

"Isn't *murder* a strong word?" she said. "There are other explanations besides murder."

"But dead is dead, regardless of the explanation."

"Yes." Her eyes darted everywhere, looking at everything but him. Her hands played with packets of sugar, twisted her wedding band, picked at bitten fingernails.

"What if the man or woman responsible for Pete's death were of, let's say, diminished responsibility?"

"A crazy person?" For once, she sounded defiant, as if she expected to be accused.

"Or a child," he said. Donagher had reacted to the suggestion that one of his boys might have been the absent water giver. Would Lila do the same?

"A child?" she repeated, almost inaudibly.

"Yes."

She stared hard at the table, poked a forkful of fish around her plate. "A child wouldn't have access to amphetamines."

"A teenager might."

"What are you getting at?" she said. She abandoned all pretense of eating. Her knife slid off the edge of the table and fell with a soft plop on the carpeting, but she didn't seem to notice.

"I spoke to your husband the day before yesterday."

"He's in Washington."

"He's protecting someone."

She twisted the gold chain around her neck.

"Someone close to him, someone he cares about . . . maybe his older son."

The color left her cheeks so rapidly he felt guilty at using the son to make the mother talk. "What did he say that made you think of Tommy?" she said. Her tongue moistened dry lips.

"It's just a conclusion I jumped to, based on some ideas that the police will probably hit on sooner or later."

"Like?"

"Like who was your husband looking for when he came up Heartbreak Hill? When the police review videotapes of the race, that will be as clear to them as it is to me. I saw him."

She said nothing.

"Like who would your husband lie to protect? Who would have access to amphetamines? Who might contemplate a 'joke' using speed? Who might feel a little left out in the thick of the campaign, a little in need of attention—"

"Tommy doesn't take drugs. He goes to a Catholic school, a very strict school."

"I never said he took drugs. And he needn't have bought them in school. If you're the right age, you can be approached in broad daylight in the middle of Boston Common. He's the right age; too young to be an undercover cop, too old to go running to his folks with the tale."

The waiter cleared their dishes.

"Coffee?"

"Yes."

They didn't exchange a single word waiting for the coffee. When it came, Mrs. Donagher raised the steaming cup immediately to her lips, burned her tongue, set the cup down quickly with a rattle of china.

"Have you mentioned this theory of yours to anyone?" she said after a while.

"Not yet. I thought I'd get your reaction first."

She sipped from her water glass, tentatively tried the coffee again, didn't speak until she'd drained the cup. "There's no need to spread that tale any further. It isn't true."

"You'll have to convince me."

"Oh, hell," she said, "I was the one who was supposed to hand Brian his stupid water at the top of Heartbreak Hill."

NINETEEN

Usually he left his dressing room door ajar. He liked to hear the actors clatter down the stairs, relished their overblown, dramatic words of greeting. The colorful clothing his colleagues selected as the badge of their profession, the costumes they chose for the street, intrigued and often delighted him. One plump character actor was a font of information on the latest Hollywood casting poop; one aging ingenue had a sister who kept her up-to-date on New York auditions. The sense of belonging that the acting company provided, albeit temporarily, in his life was a gift he ordinarily treasured.

"And imagine," he heard the ingenue say, "after he'd called her back to read three times and made her do all those nasty improvs, then he had the nerve to . . ."

He shut the door. It wasn't heavy, not the noise-blocking oak slabs of the Chestnut Hill mansion, but it blurred the piercing sopranos, the preening tenors, the rush of tap water, into a faraway hum that could be easily ignored.

Automatically, his fingers aligned the evening's makeup on the table in front of him. *As You Like It* tonight. From Oliver to anonymous courtier back to Oliver . . . One beard, two different base coats, three camel's hair brushes . . . Four changes of character in a single day, counting his impersonation of Edward Heineman, newscaster.

The skilled actor, by relentless study or special talent, could make every word, each economical gesture, a truthful image. Lila Donagher hadn't the gift. She couldn't answer to the ages of her children without worrying her lower lip with her teeth. Every other word she uttered sounded false, a trait the most accomplished liar might envy.

If she spoke the truth, she was the one Donagher was protecting. She had offered her tale only under pressure, and seemed genuinely afraid that her son would be blamed if she failed to own up.

It was tawdry; it was vulgar: The morning of the marathon the senator and his wife had indulged in a domestic quarrel. He had been guilty of some husbandly assuming, namely that Lila would tow the kids to the race in order to demonstrate to the press what a loving family man Donagher was. There she would stand at the top of Heartbreak Hill, the last of the senator's faithful crew of cup-bearers, well within scope of the TV cameras, and present him with his water flask and, perhaps, a photogenic wifely kiss. The kids would flash toothpaste-perfect smiles on cue.

And, Lila had said defiantly, maybe she would have done it, except that he had neglected to ask. He knew how she hated campaigning, knew how much she resented the invasion of her privacy. And, in spite of that, her participation in an event she dreaded had been guaranteed without her consent. She had been understandably furious.

While representatives of the press had lurked outside Donagher's front door, waiting for the first glimpse of the senator in his running shorts, hushed angry words had been exchanged inside. Why didn't Donagher get another one of his aides to hand him water on the hilltop? While he was at it, why didn't he get one of them to go to church with him, sleep with him, bear his kids? And Lila, who Spraggue suspected never got the last word in an argument with her more loquacious husband, had given up talking, smiled and nodded politely, and decided not to show up. She hadn't told her husband of her planned truancy.

127

She had gone to visit Ed Heineman instead.

Ed Heineman, a man who might have an interest in giving Lila Donagher an alibi . . . A man who might be in need of an alibi himself . . .

Someone knocked on Spraggue's door and swung it open before he had a chance to say keep out.

He'd seen Kathleen Farrell since their never consummated Friday night date, acted opposite her both before and after Collatos' death. But now he realized that it had been a long time since he'd really looked.

She was certainly theatrical, a red cape swirled across her shoulders, blonde hair windswept into a tangle of curls. She leaned over and left the imprint of her lips on his forehead. He twisted to look up at her, changed tactics, and stared into the mirror instead. Her hands came to rest on his shoulders.

"You've become a stranger," she said, with a teasing pout.

"It's been a tough week."

"We could improve it."

Spraggue tried to generate enthusiasm. She waited, shook her head sadly.

"You puzzle me," she said.

He didn't answer.

"Hot and then cold. First, the come on, then you back off so far I'm not sure we're acting on the same stage."

"I have a one-track mind."

"And for a while it was on me, but . . ."

"It may get back on the track yet."

"But you wouldn't want to push it?"

Her eyes were almost the same shade as Sharon Collatos' eyes. What, he wondered, would Sharon's eyes be like when she smiled, when they melted into pools of chocolate velvet glittered with pinpoint pricks of light . . .

"I'm preoccupied," he said. "This Collatos business."

"You told me you hadn't seen the guy for two years before you met him at the reservoir."

"Yeah, but . . ."

"Yeah, but what? Dead people are more important than live people?"

"I have to finish my makeup. Ten minutes to curtain and you're not even started."

Her face was ready for makeup, just washed and glowing, dusted with tiny pores and a sprinkle of freckles across the bridge of her nose.

"It wouldn't do me any good to invite you out after the show?" she said.

"Tonight?"

"No, next year. Of course, tonight. I assume you're busy?"

"Not necessarily," he said slowly, seduced by the scent of soap, the light hands on his shoulders.

"The Harvest serves until . . ." she began.

"Not the Harvest." He hoped the place wouldn't always remind him of Ed Heineman's embarrassed half grin, of Lila Donagher's hand-wringing confidences.

"My place?"

"You are direct."

"I am."

"Okay," he said.

"Don't sound so enthusiastic. I may change my mind," she said on the way out.

So may I, he wanted to call after her.

After the first scene, he got safely into *As You Like It*. Escape from reality, that's what the audience sought; escape from self, that's what the actor got. Contentedly, he let Michael Spraggue go, let his problems stay behind in the dressing room, less important, momentarily, than the torment of a belittled brother, the plight of a banished duke.

He hadn't locked his concerns away tightly enough; they surfaced in the oddest way.

He viewed Act Four, scene one, from behind the false proscenium, stage right, watched it closely because of all the *As You Lie It* Act Fours he had enjoyed or suffered through, this one pleased him most by its staging. He'd seen better acting, notably at The Old Vic, but this director, unlike most American directors, trusted his actors with Shakespeare. The American approach to Shakespeare was to jazz it up. Convinced that American audiences had no true love of the music of Shakespeare's language, that American actors were incapable of handling the magic words, most directors moved their actors with a vengeance, cartwheels during soliloquys, no less. But Howard Desmond let Jaques do 'The Seven Ages of Man' simply, seated on a bench, not waggling so much as a finger for emphasis. He let Rosalind and Orlando court each other with the ancient words, not with modern skittish movement.

"Men have died from time to time, and worms have eaten them, but not for love."

Comforting thought.

"Come sister," the actress playing Rosalind took Kathleen's hand in great good humor, "you shall be the priest and marry us."

How must it have looked in Shakespeare's day, when the woman playing the man was actually played by a boy? He tried to see the scene with the eyes of a Globe groundling circa 1600. Somewhere inside himself he could hear a bell resonate, a warning klaxon, but nothing more.

Onstage, during Act Four, scene three, he paused so long before a line, that Kathleen peered up at him, startled.

Maybe it was the sight of Rosalind swooning at the bloodied handkerchief. He stared at her as she fell. Did something in that fall remind him of Collatos' unseen fall? The thought would not surface. And he couldn't urge it upward, not there, on stage. He fought to keep his concentration on his role, his next action, his next line, until the feeling faded.

It came back stronger in the last act, when he kissed Kathleen, placed his rough cheek against her smooth one, studied her face with the delight of a lover in the beloved.

Her heavy creamy makeup . . . so different from the clear, translucent skin he'd noticed earlier in the mirror. What was there about a heavy, creamy complexion that tugged so naggingly at one corner of his mind?

He was grateful he had no more lines to muff, nothing left to do but dance in the final wedding.

Kathleen steered him through the moves.

They took a cab to the place she'd leased for the duration of the Harvard Rep's season, a flat in a gray, paint-peeling two-family, close to Cambridge, but with a Somerville address that knocked down the rent. She sat in the middle of the back seat, her thigh a scant inch from his, her hand lightly caressing the fabric of his pants, teasingly near, never quite close enough. When he groaned and reached for her, she laughed and slid across the seat, her skirt artfully hiked, her long, bare legs tilted away from him, slightly, consciously spread. The cabbie spent a lot of time staring in the rearview mirror. Her honey-colored hair brushed against Sprague's right shoulder, releasing a cloud of scent that reminded him of other women in other cabs, and flipped his stomach over with desire. The ride seemed long enough to take them across state lines, the cab oppressively hot, the journey up the shadowed walk to her door a half-mile trek through a steamy, fragrant jungle.

She didn't seem to notice the dusty wooden floors, the sprung, faded sofa and chairs, the dingy, bleeding wallpaper. She hadn't brought him home for the ambiance.

The bed was unmade, yellowed sheets tumbled on the saggy mattress.

She stripped with all the lights on, pleased with and conscious of the effect. She was stunning, willing, practiced. He couldn't help contrasting her lush body, her pornographer's-idea-of-a-woman's body, with Kate Holloway's spare, sculptured beauty.

When he told her he'd expected to discover that her blonde hair was dyed, she giggled and confessed that it was—all over.

She faked an early orgasm; he was almost certain of it, and pushed harder into her, determined to get past accomplished actress into woman. But she wriggled and postured as if she were staring up past his shoulder into some invisible ceiling mirror, rating her own performance, making love to her own spectacular body, using him as some incidental instrument.

When they were finished, hot and breathless and sheet-entangled, she stretched diagonally across the bed, smiling in seeming contentment. Maybe there wasn't any more; maybe the surface was all.

She still had a trace of greasepaint in her hair. It smelled as sweet and phoney as cotton candy.

The realization hit him so suddenly that his entire body shook, with the kind of tremor that sometimes woke him sweating in the night.

"I have to leave," he said, sliding out from under Kathleen's encompassing, sleep-heavy arm.

"Huh?" She opened her eyes into narrow slits. "What the hell's going on?"

He pulled on his pants while he spoke, reached for his shoes. "I can't explain now."

"You're crazy," she said.

In the cab on the way to the police station, he wondered if he was.

Where had the woman who'd given Donagher that water bottle scraped off her makeup? Where had she transformed herself from a tall, big-footed, big-boned woman, with a too creamy skin, a too long skirt, and a too low voice, into the man Spraggue was certain she'd become?

TWENTY

"A man."

Spraggue nodded wordlessly. It was the third time Hurley had repeated the two words since he had first swiveled around to glare at his unannounced, uninvited guest. The captain snuffed out a cigarette in what must have been an ashtray. From the cracked leather chair on the far side of the desk, it was invisible, hidden by overflowing wire in-and-out baskets, a Styrofoam cup collection, a crooked stack of Manila file folders, the dusty phone, and the remains of what smelled like an aging chicken salad sandwich. The first time Hurley had echoed the words, he'd punctuated them with shouted incredulous laughter. The second time, with indignant denial. The third time, his voice was just a mutter, followed by a regretful sigh.

"I was across the street from him, remember? Describing him . . . her . . . to the artist made me uneasy, made me wonder. Then at the theater, during the performance— Shakespeare, you know, girls dressed up as boys—it hit me. A woman, a tall broad-shouldered woman with big feet, a pale creamy sort of complexion, the kind you can get from a tube of grease paint, heavy enough to cover a just shaved beard."

"Why do I get all the fucking weirdos?" Hurley inquired of the cracked ceiling.

"So haul out your mug-shot books and let me paw through them. You've got more male felons than female, I trust? I'll bet you even have a file on female impersonators who've been picked up for the odd misdemeanor over the years, and one on transvestites, and male prostitutes and—"

"We don't have to look in the mug books, Spraggue," Hurley said heavily. "Damn, but I wish we'd picked up on this sooner."

"On what?" Spraggue's stomach took a dive.

"We can just look in the damned morgue; we've had the stiff there a week." Hurley pressed a buzzer hidden under the sprawl of papers on his desk and a blue-uniformed officer opened the door. "Get me the file on JoJo Stearns," the captain barked. The officer nodded, banged the door.

"The ID came in two, three days ago. It takes time to lift fingerprints, match 'em up with the vaunted FBI computer that has more down time than a hooker. Small-time hood death, that's what we labeled it. The kind of death that, unless you find somebody actually standing over the body, smoking pistol in hand, you don't solve until ten years later when some snitch gets burned and wants his prison sentence reduced. Then he says, hey remember JoJo? You still want to know who did JoJo? You get me out of here on a misdemeanor, or you get me Concord instead of Walpole, or you get me one-to-five instead of six-to-ten, and I'll give you my brother-in-law."

"JoJo Stearns," Spraggue repeated.

"He was a very pretty man, in his 'before' photos," Hurley said. "I can understand your not making him as a guy right off. He must have surprised a lot of people in a lot of johns in a lot of bars across this city."

"He's got a record? Vice stuff?"

Hurley shook his head.

134

"Well?"

"I don't know—" Hurley began. He jumped at the thunderous knock on his glass-paned door. The uniformed man entered with a thick Manila file folder. "Just break the door down next time you want to get my attention, Brownlee." The officer smirked and went out. "Jeez, we're hiring real scumbags," Hurley said. "Want to be a cop?"

"Hah."

"That's just it. You don't want to be a cop, but you want me to give you information only cops are entitled to. That's what I was going to say when old shit-for-brains interrupted."

"Hurley, if I hadn't brought my boy-girl revelation right to you, would you have any inkling that this stiff was the one who gave the water bottle to Donagher?"

"*Might* be the one."

"A man dressed as a woman gives a senator a poisoned drink. The senator's bodyguard dies. A man known to dress as a woman on a great many occasions, a man who matches my description of the water donor, turns up in the morgue—when? the very next day? You want to call it coincidence? You get that many guys dressed up as girls in the morgue?"

"Coincidences happen."

"Sure they do."

Hurley played with a pencil. He didn't open the folder.

"So did JoJo die of natural causes?" Spraggue asked. "You didn't say."

"We thought at first it was an accident."

"Why?"

"Came in through the fire department," Hurley said.

"You always this loose-lipped?"

"Shit, man. This isn't my case."

"Collatos liked you. You said you liked him."

"I don't think he particularly cares, right now."

"I care," Spraggue said.

"The fireboys had another one of their typical fires of suspicious origin on Tuesday night. Slummy. Not exactly front page stuff. In case you haven't noticed, two hundred twenty-five buildings in Boston have gone up in flames since last January: Dorchester, the South End, Roxbury, Jamaica Plain. Even Back Bay, where your aunt's got her property. Most of the buildings are abandoned housing stock, old warehouses. This was a three-story wooden place on Tremont, boarded up, thought to be abandoned. It was, except for JoJo."

"He didn't live there?"

"JoJo didn't live anywhere. He sat on one barstool until he found a home for the night and then he went back to another barstool until he found a home for the next night. Can you believe it? A broad with a pecker? You can never tell what'll turn some creeps on."

"Was the fire set?"

"Definitely. And the method was one the fireboys have come to know if not to love. This arson shit is getting me down."

"It got Pete down, too. When he was working—" Spraggue stopped talking and his eyes narrowed.

"I'm way ahead of you, for once," Hurley said. "Arson Squad. Collatos was working liaison with the Arson Task Force and the Arson Squad. Right? And somebody who just might have killed him gets burned up in a fire that sure as hell looks like arson."

"Could it have been an accidental death? Could JoJo have been camped out in that particular house on the wrong night?"

"It wasn't the sort of place our JoJo usually hung out. Not the sort of place to take a trick."

"Then," Spraggue said slowly, "Donagher could have

nothing to do with this. Those threatening notes may really mean as little as I thought . . .''

Hurley opened the file and stared at it, but Spraggue knew he wasn't reading. The captain made a show of reluctance before saying, "JoJo had connections to people who've been investigated for arson, people who are still under investigation . . ."

"Are you saying someone was after *Pete* because of something to do with his Arson Squad work?"

"Senator Donagher didn't die. Collatos did."

"Donagher was the one who was given the bottle."

"But, of course, his bodyguard would taste it. Probably share it; that's what a couple of runners racing together would normally do. We all assumed Senator Donagher was the target, because of the incident at the reservoir, because of the letters, because it seems more reasonable somehow to shoot at a United States senator than a retired cop. But Donagher doesn't have a—what-do-you-call-it? idiosyncrasy with speed. Collatos did. He could have mentioned the fact. He was a talker."

Spraggue ran a hand over his forehead. It came away flecked with grease paint.

Hurley went on. "What doesn't make sense is that Collatos wasn't a threat anymore, wasn't a cop. He was off the arson squad detail . . ."

"He could have known something."

"He was a blabbermouth; if he'd known anything, half the cops in the country would have known."

"Unless he didn't know he knew it . . . didn't know it was worth knowing."

"Come again?"

"Or maybe he'd made a deal with someone . . ."

"No way," Hurley said, slamming his hand down on the desk hard enough to threaten an avalanche of paperwork. "Collatos was as honest as I am. Goddammit, the minute a cop dies in smelly circumstances, people start talking corruption. Blame the victim. If you're going to go after Pete, I'm not—"

"Whoa," Spraggue said. "I was just thinking out loud. Remind me not to do that in front of a cop."

"Sorry."

"Has anyone gone through the files Pete would have had access to when he was working with the firemen?"

"Somebody will."

"What about his apartment? Who looked through that?"

"Menlo."

"Then you might say it hasn't been touched."

"If you plan on going in there, you're going to have to talk to the sister."

"Then the seal is off the door?"

"Did I say that?" Hurley said. "I must be getting careless in my old age."

TWENTY-ONE

He did try to phone Sharon Collatos, made three futile attempts: one as soon as his alarm chirped at 9 A.M.; one after he'd showered, shaved, and dressed; one while boiling water dripped through the filter paper into the coffee pot. He dialed information and checked the number. It was correct.

Before leaving the house, he placed his set of picklocks in the pocket of his windbreaker.

Pete Collatos lived near the Boston-Brookline border, in a

section of the city associated with college kids, not cops. He'd probably chosen the narrow five-story brick building for its proximity to B.U. coeds. Cops he got to see every day.

Stepping down off the Green Line train at the St. Mary's Street stop, Spraggue had a vision of Collatos out to fascinate the sociology majors with his tales of gritty street life. Ah, Pete would have been an object of interest in these self-aggrandizing eighties. Not like the sixties, when a cop on a college campus couldn't get laid.

On Buswell Street, students tossed a yellow Frisbee down the center of the narrow road. Abandon all cars, ye who enter here. Punk rock blared from a fourth floor window. The Frisbee fell at his feet and he flung it back, feeling old.

Pete had thrown a party to celebrate his first and only promotion as a cop. Spraggue remembered the night, the crowd of boisterous strangers crammed into a fifth floor walk-up. He still had the address scrawled across a page in his black Harvard Coop book for the academic year '79–'80.

The building had a security system, but the tenants didn't abide by it. Spraggue pressed the button for apartment 2A. No one home. Same at 3A. 4B buzzed him in without bothering to use the voice-over speaker. He waited a minute in the hallway to see if 4B appeared, readied his apology: Excuse me, meant to push 4A. 4B didn't seem to care who he'd let in; a Jehovah's witness, an insurance salesman, or the Boston Strangler would just have to trudge on up the four flights and introduce himself.

The lock on Collatos' door was child's play. He could have left his picklocks at home and used a credit card. The light in the hallway was so dim that his fingers found the scratches on the lock before he saw them. Had Collatos been a burglary target? Or had the cops made a mess of a simple B&E? Surely Menlo would have roused the superintendent to let them into Pete's locked apartment.

At the long ago party, the essential bareness of the place had been camouflaged by the crowd. Sunlight, flooding through curtainless squares of window, was less merciful. It picked out the worn places on the drab rug, washed the color out of the faded print sofa.

Spraggue closed the door and leaned against it. Floors and ceilings in these older buildings were generally sound-proof; walls notoriously thin. He slipped off his shoes to ensure quiet movement, smoothed thin plastic gloves over his hands.

He walked the periphery of the apartment: five stingy rooms. One living room, tiny kitchen attached by an arching doorway. A narrow hallway opened off another living room wall, leading to one adequate bedroom, one study that barely had room for a desk, and a bathroom big enough to turn around in.

He began with the living room, feeling under the cushions of the sprung couch. He found a dime, two pennies, stale popcorn. He leafed through every dusty book on a board-and-brick bookcase, adventure yarns, police procedurals, "How to Pass the Boston Police Sergeant's Exam." Collatos had dog-eared the corners of paperbacks, used respectful bookmarks for hardbacks. Spraggue didn't think that insight would get him anywhere.

The police had already searched. Cushions on two mismatched chairs were askew. The top drawer of a desk against the far wall hung open. Muddy footprints crisscrossed the yellowed kitchen linoleum.

He learned that Collatos ate Rice Krispies for breakfast, probably with half-and-half; no milk in the refrigerator. Of course, some cop could have spilled it down the drain, his nose offended by the odor. But the same cop would have tossed the reeking cream. He shut the refrigerator. Just a half-empty carton of chocolate chip ice cream in the freezer. Ice cubes.

He tried not to think while his fingers automatically probed the pockets of the coats hanging in the front closet. He recited his lines from the evening's show—*Caucasian Chalk Circle*, he was almost sure. Still, the task depressed the hell out of him. Why did he have to know that Pete kept a forlorn pile of single socks at the back of an otherwise empty drawer, that he should have done his laundry more often? Why should he discover that Pete never resoled his shoes, or threw them out? That he owned no pajamas? Two sets of sheets. That he drank Rolling Rock beer and left the cans in the corners of the living room, especially next to the armchair that faced the black-and-white TV.

In the bottom corner of the lower left-hand drawer of the bureau in the bedroom, he found a cache of sorts: condoms, body oils. Why not in the bathroom? Had Pete not wanted the occasional stay-the-night ladyfriend to open the medicine chest and find him so prepared?

The creak of floorboards in the small study off the hallway startled him. Old buildings had noises of their own. He shrugged and continued stripping Pete's bed. Didn't anybody hide things under mattresses anymore?

The sharp thud from the study was no creaky floorboard. Spraggue froze, dropped the pillow back on the bed. He picked up a cracked glass ashtray, hefted it for throwing weight. The outraged ghost of Pete Collatos wouldn't make so much noise.

He tiptoed to the door of the study. Empty.

There was a closet next to an old-fashioned rocking chair. The chair teetered slowly, back and forth. A rickety aluminum table sat next to the chair. It held an ashtray, a box of tissues, a Rolling Rock can and the telephone. The receiver dangled the floor.

"Come on out," Spraggue said.

Silence.

"Come on."

"Get away," the woman's voice said weakly. "Get away. I have a gun in here. I mean it. I'll shoot."

"Sure you do," Spraggue said, recognizing the voice. "A howitzer or an M-16?"

He yanked open the closet door. Sharon Collatos would have fallen to the ground if he hadn't caught her. He dropped the ashtray and it shattered on the floor.

TWENTY-TWO

"How long have you been here?" he asked.

She huddled on the faded couch, smoothing a black skirt that might have been the same one she'd worn to the funeral. She stared down at her hands to make sure they'd stopped shaking, steeled her voice and whispered, "I have every right to be here." Her voice cracked when she tried to make it louder. "What are you doing here?"

"What you asked me to do. At the funeral."

"I'm sorry about that. I was . . . I had no business . . . Pete's death isn't your responsibility."

"Is it yours?"

Black eyeliner had run down her cheeks in inky stripes. She put her hands to her eyes and smudged them into gray circles, puffy with lack of sleep. Her right stocking had a run up the side. Her wrinkled gray sweater . . . Hadn't she worn that under her black suit jacket at the funeral?

142

"Have you been here since Pete's funeral?" Hadn't the woman any friends, any family, one good neighbor?

"I guess . . . I don't know . . ."

"Christ! That was Sunday. This is Wednesday. Where did you sleep? The bed wasn't touched. Have you eaten since Sunday?"

No answer, just that blank paralyzed stare. When she'd fallen out of the closet, mouth open in a soundless scream, her face had registered terror. He thought he'd seen recognition, even relief when he'd cradled her shaken body, half lifted, half dragged her into the living room. Now, nothing.

"Come on." He walked her into the kitchen, sat her down on a plastic-covered dinette chair. He started to open the refrigerator, remembered the contents and stopped. He filled the kettle with water. Blue flame sputtered into a ring on the stove's front burner. There had been soup cans in the wooden cupboard over the stove. He rejected Campbell's Clam Chowder: no milk. Cream of Mushroom might be tolerable with water.

"Don't bother." she said weakly.

Pete kept booze in a cabinet under the laminated blue countertop. Sprague tilted a dollop of vermouth into the soup. Sherry would have been better. Pete didn't have any coffee, but there were tea bags stuffed into a tin canister.

Sharon Collatos used her left hand to prop up her forehead. With her right hand, she traced circles on the tabletop. Dark, tangled hair fell forward and hid her face. She didn't look up when he put a spoon down next to her. He poured bubbling soup into a chipped bowl.

"Eat it," he said.

"When I heard the door open, I hid. I thought you were Pete's killer. I hoped you were just a thief."

"A soup thief. I leave the cans. Eat." He busied himself

143

with teabags, didn't turn back to her until he heard the clink of silverware on crockery.

"There's another bowlful after you finish that," he said. "Please, you eat it."

"I've been eating regularly, thank you."

"Thank you," she said in a small voice.

"Where did you sleep?" he asked. "I can see you didn't eat, so I can't be blamed for not noticing the fresh potato peelings in the garbage. But if you slept here, I should have been able to—"

"I dozed off in one of the chairs. . . ."

One he'd thought the cops had messed up.

He peeled off his plastic gloves. "I guess I don't have to keep my presence here a secret anymore."

She shook her head and spooned soup. When the bowl was empty, Spraggue refilled it over her protests.

"When I take the trouble to open a can, I expect it to get eaten," he said severely. "Did you come to clear up Pete's things?"

Tears welled in her eyes.

He fetched the box of tissues from the study. By the time he returned to the table, the tears were gone and the stony look was back. He didn't know which he preferred.

"Drink your tea," he said.

Her blind obedience showed her exhaustion.

"I tried to call you," he said. "I wouldn't have broken in if I'd been able to reach you. . . ."

She made a gesture as if to say it was all right, a feeble wave of a hand that would never have satisfied the Medea of the funeral.

"Did your brother talk to you about his work?"

She opened her mouth as if to say something, changed her mind and rested her head on her hand again. Her eyes closed. Her eyelashes were unexpectedly long, so lush and soft-looking that Spraggue felt an urge to touch them, to

144

smooth his thumbs gently over her eyes, down her still damp cheeks.

"Did your brother have a safe? Someplace he kept things that were important to him?"

Still no answer.

"Lie down on the couch and try to sleep while I finish looking around."

"I can't . . . I can't sleep here. . . . I keep hearing things."

"Just sit there. Wait for me. Then I'll take you home."

He had to walk her back to the couch. He made another cup of tea and set it near her on a scratched oak end table. He wondered if her wobbly walk was due entirely to exhaustion, grief, and starvation—whether she'd taken any drugs.

"Call me if you want anything. I'll be in the study."

He started at the left wall, with the books lined up across the back of Collatos' desk, held each one by the spine, and shook it over the threadbare beige rug. Each file drawer came out of the desk. Bottoms and sides were checked for taped hideaways, contents dumped and searched. Five years of telephone bills. Tax returns. Warranties for the vacuum cleaner Pete had rarely used, the cheap stereo.

Footsteps. She stood in the doorway, one hand clutching each side of the doorframe, smudged eyes dominating her pale face. He held out his arms only to steady her, drew her close to keep her from falling, smoothed her dark hair. She pressed against him like a moth drawn to flame, and he found himself kissing a soft mouth that hardened, kissed back with hungry, shocking urgency, parted.

She stiffened as suddenly as she had melted, pulled back, rubbing one hand across her mouth as if she could scrub the kisses away.

"What am I doing?" she said. "Oh my God, what am I

145

doing?" She turned away, her face reddening with embarrassment.

They were panting like two exhausted runners. She was so small without her shoes; her head came barely past his shoulder.

"I'm sorry," he said, because it was the only thing he could think of to break the taut silence. He tried to put a hand on her shaking shoulder, but she flinched.

She backed toward the door, eyes averted. "I meant to . . . I came in to tell you. . . . There are papers in the closet. Way back under a pile of coats."

"Thank you," he said, after a pause, with a formality that reassured her. He waved his arm at the section of the room still to be examined. "This is going to take me a while. So relax. Lie down. Wash your face. Take a shower if you want to. You've got time."

"I'd like that." She ducked her head and one corner of her mouth tilted. He caught a brief, tentative flash of the gentle, laughing girl in Pete's desktop photo. He wanted her more than he'd ever wanted Kathleen Farrell.

"Just don't come in here wrapped in any skimpy towel," he muttered under his breath. "Please."

She left without speaking and Spraggue sat in the rocking chair to let the heat dissipate. He didn't break the pattern of his search to check the closet. One thing at a time, left to right, top to bottom. He stood on the chair to feel around the central lighting fixture. In the bathroom, the shower pulsated. He rubbed his dusty hands down the side of his jeans and remembered the sound of the bolt clicking home after she'd closed the bathroom door, wondered if she regretted turning the lock as much as he regretted her doing it. There was an MBTA map thumbtacked on the wall. He took it down, turned it over. The beige wall was yellow where it had been.

He kept to pattern in the closet, started with the shelf behind the clothes rod. Folded up holey undershirts, a battered blue police hat, a pair of black shoes with a puncture wound in the right sole. Not many clothes in this closet, a few mothball-smelling suits, semi-retired. A pile of games: aged Monopoly, newer Parcheesi, Avalon Hill war games. The closet was deeper than it seemed, slanting outward at the back. He coughed and had to come back out into the study to catch his breath.

The pile of old clothes was in the right-hand corner, behind two cardboard boxes. He tossed the clothes out into the room, raising dust clouds. There was no dust on the two armloads of Manila files.

They were police files, xeroxed copies of material that should never have left the stationhouse. Old files, dating back twelve, fourteen years, in no seeming order.

The bolt on the bathroom door made a noise like a shot. She came out along with a cloud of fragrant steam, fully dressed, back in her gray sweater and black skirt. Her hair was twisted up in a navy towel. Her eyes were puffy, red, but the raccoon rings of darkness had been washed away. Her legs were bare and her clothes fitted with a slight difference. Spraggue speculated that she'd abandoned her undergarments, shrinking at the act of putting her newly clean body back into its three-day prison of mourning and dirt. He kept such speculation carefully off his face.

The only makeup she'd had with her must have been lipstick. She'd applied it too generously, as if to compensate for her pallor, rubbed some of it into her cheeks. He thought she looked terrific, smudges gone from her dark eyes, damp tendrils of dark hair escaping from the towel and framing her face.

She held up a tiny brown bottle.

"What's this?"

"Where did you find it?"

"The medicine cabinet's empty, except for this."

He took it from her. Her hand drew back when he touched her as if an electric shock had passed between them. He turned the bottle carefully in his hand until he could read the yellowed label. It was torn across top and bottom, obscuring date, Rx number, and doctor's name.

40 Parnate 10 mg, it said. *Take two to four tablets daily.*

TWENTY-THREE

They spent another hour filling cardboard boxes from the Beacon Supermarket with the odds and ends of Pete Collatos' short life—photographs, books, records, out-of-date calendars—and carting them down to Sharon Collatos' rusty brown Dodge Dart. She refused his offer of escort, drove off toward Park Drive and Route 2 on her way home to suburban Chelmsford—back stiff, head high, crumpling Spraggue's card between her hand and the steering wheel.

He took a dilapidated cab back to Cambridge, deposited two boxes of yellowing files in the middle of the kitchen floor. Then, mindful of Pete's early, unexpected demise, he burned three old letters, carefully stowed a few more—from Kate, faintly perfumed—at the back of a bottom desk drawer. He hoped that whoever got to read them would enjoy them as much as he had.

He patted his windbreaker pocket to make sure the brown bottle was still there.

It was late afternoon by the time he left the house and the lowering clouds were busy fulfilling their promise. The rain was steady and gentle, redolent of early spring. He walked bareheaded along Brattle to Harvard Square, boarded the Dudley bus, and rode as far as Auditorium station, then strolled up Boylston Street toward Berkeley, people-gazing, window-shopping. He stopped briefly at the Paperback Booksmith, winked at the solemn Lord and Taylor mannequins. A bewhiskered bum and a bag lady shared a brown-bagged bottle on the front steps of the Boston Public Library. A dumpy, elderly couple held hands across a table in Ciro and Sal's window and flashed smiles of blinding contentment.

Hurley spoiled his mood.

Hurley hadn't sniffed any budding daffodils. His weary, red-rimmed eyes hadn't taken in anything but the cracked dull green walls of his office.

"I'm busy," he announced as soon as he saw Spraggue in the doorway. He smacked the file he'd been reading flat on his desk for emphasis, instinctively covered its open pages with his big knobby hands. "What do you want?"

"I'm fine," Spraggue said. "And how are you?"

Hurley shoved his chair back from his desk with a sigh of pure disgust. "You see Menlo on your way up?"

"God forbid."

"I'll bet he saw you. The last time you paid me a visit, he spent damn near an hour cross-examining me. I'm glad the bastard isn't on internal affairs. He'd have me up for treason or something, just for talking to you. And babbling to you about one of his cases . . . that would really burn him."

"After I tell you what I came to tell you, maybe they'll toss him off the Collatos case. You'll get it."

In spite of himself, Hurley was interested. He laughed,

shrugged it off, but Spraggue could see it in the sudden sharpness of his glance at the closed door.

"Just what I need." The captain gestured at his cluttered desktop. "Another case. The fifty-seven I've already got are sprouting paperwork like wings."

Spraggue swung a metal folding chair away from a stack by the wall, snapped it open, and sat down. It teetered on three long legs and a short one. He knew Hurley would easily part with two teeth, if not his right arm, for any dirt on Menlo.

Hurley stalled. "If you're going to tell me that Menlo stole the antique silver from the Collatos place, don't bother. The bastard's been accused before. He covers his ass."

The medicine container Sharon Collatos had said she'd found in the bathroom couldn't really be called a bottle. It was a three-inch high brown plastic cylinder with a white cap. Red letters across the cap said: PACKAGE NOT CHILD RESISTANT! The typed label was not only torn across top and bottom, it was wavy and peeling. A red sticker had been affixed upside-down on the back of the container. THIS PRESCRIPTION CANNOT BE REFILLED. Spraggue displayed it in the folds of tissue paper he'd wrapped it in, kept the label turned away from Hurley. *Phial* seemed too medieval a word. Maybe *vial*.

"So?" Hurley gave in and admitted curiosity with a grunt.

"Remember those prints I asked you to run, as a favor?"

"The ones your aunt lifted? You have to stop doing that. The department's drying up for lack of funds. We can't trace stuff for every . . ." Hurley ran out of steam and a faint grimace crossed his face. "You knew I was going to give you this lecture, right?"

"Right. So I brought something to trade."

"That—what is it?"

"Were those prints on file?"

"Yeah." Hurley didn't have to look the information up on any of the thousand odd sheets of paper on his desk. He knew. "But there isn't a whole lot I can tell you."

"You can give me a name."

"Martin Emery."

Martin Emery . . . Murray Eichenhorn. Same initials. But to go from such a neutral moniker to such an ethnic one. Why?

"And why were Emery's prints adorning your files?"

"Gun license."

"Then, as far as you know, he's a perfectly law-abiding citizen."

"Can't say anything else about him."

"Why not?"

"Jesus, Spraggue, you want blood? For all I know you're thinking of blackmailing the guy."

Spraggue rattled the bottle. "I have something to trade," he said. "Remember?"

"Something you obtained by breaking and entering?"

"Pete's sister gave me the key," Spraggue said truthfully, not mentioning that the presentation had taken place well after he'd picked the lock.

"Spiffy-looking lady, Pete's sister. Divorced, I hear."

"You want what I found?"

"If it's evidence in a police investigation—"

"Martin Emery," Spraggue said.

"Okay, but first you show me that bottle. If it has nothing to do with Collatos, if you just picked up some piece of plastic out of some dumpster to tempt me with . . ."

Spraggue held out the pill bottle. "Handle with care. Might have prints."

"You mean your aunt hasn't dusted it yet?" Hurley turned it slowly, studied the label.

"This mean anything?" he asked.

"I called my local pharmacist," Spraggue said. "It's a medication sometimes given to depressed people."

"I could use some of that," Hurley said.

"Martin Emery," Spraggue repeated softly.

"Look, suppose I were to say that I couldn't tell you anything about Emery because of certain judicial rulings, what would you assume?"

"Gag order?"

"No. Think about it. When can a person have a record, but not really have a record because nobody can touch it?"

"Ah," Spraggue said. "A juvie."

Hurley opened his mouth, shut it.

"A juvenile record for what?"

"That's what I can't tell you. Sealed is sealed. Even for a cop."

"Then tell me this. Did you happen to notice a cop at Collatos' funeral—"

"There were three hundred cops at—"

"Old retired cop, very short, just made the height limit, red face, broken veins in a knob of a nose, fat, sloppy—"

"Sounds like Sergeant Billy," Hurley said with a groan.

"Full name?"

"Hell, what was it? William O'Donnell. A legend in his own time."

"Bravery?"

"Stupidity. Drunkenness. Corruption."

"Know where I could find him?"

"The retirement fund would."

"Think Sergeant Billy would be as discreet as you are?"

"Discretion is a word Billy never heard of."

"Fine."

Hurley tapped the pill container with the end of a pencil.

"Was this hidden in Collatos' apartment? Where exactly did you find it?"

"How about in the medicine cabinet? In plain sight?"

"Shit. Not even Menlo could have been dumb enough to leave this behind. I'm not going to flush him down the toilet on this one."

"Don't you find it interesting that somebody planted his stash of pills in Collatos' bathroom?"

"I suppose. I can see stealing stuff out of there. I mean, anybody who followed the business in the papers would know that Collatos lived alone, know that the apartment was ripe for the picking. But why break in to put something there?"

"Maybe to let us know how Collatos died," Spraggue said.

Hurley gave him a long look, flipped a page in the file he'd been reading, ran his finger down the right-hand edge. "I think we've already got a handle on that," he said.

"That the JoJo Stearns file? The guy who turned up dead in the fire?"

"Stearns and a hell of a lot of other aliases, including a couple with a definite Greek sound to them."

"I doubt Collatos knew the creep just because they were both Greek."

Hurley fastened his eyes on the grimy window. Spraggue stared at the open file folder, upside down on the desk.

"The way Menlo figures it," Hurley said, "this Stearns has run up against Collatos in the past. Maybe Collatos makes things tougher for him than he has to because he's Greek. You know how sometimes cops are harder on their own? Maybe this guy's got a king-size resentment against Collatos. Collatos has been in the news lately, right? You see him in pictures with Senator Donagher, on the TV with

153

Senator Donagher. So our JoJo sees Collatos doing okay, knows he's going to run the marathon, decides to do him in.''

''Yeah, sure. And he knew all about the death threats on Donagher and decided to use them as a blind.''

''Why not?''

''You think he was that smart?''

''It's possible.''

''He decides to kill both of them? Why does he give the water to Donagher?''

''Ah.'' Spraggue could tell Hurley had been waiting for that one. ''Because Collatos might recognize him, even in his Little Mary Sunshine rig.''

''And he just feels in his bones that Donagher will share the stuff with Collatos?''

''It's a good guess. Collatos is the bodyguard. He probably tastes things. If you're running with someone . . . Maybe old JoJo even says to Donagher, share it with your buddy.''

''Maybe he even knew Collatos was allergic to speed.''

''It's possible.''

''Let me get this, Hurley. Are you guys planning to close this case? Just leave it at that? This JoJo Stearns, or whoever he really is, hates Collatos for reasons unknown, sets up a crackpot plan to kill him. Donagher almost gets taken out just for the hell of it? The end?''

Hurley stared out the window.

''What about the fact that old JoJo gets killed the next day? What about the arson blaze?''

''He could have been setting it himself, gotten trapped—''

''In his goddam dress and high heels? Come on, Hurley. If Stearns killed Collatos, he wasn't working alone.''

''Stearns is connected.''

''Huh?''

154

"What I said. Mafia. L.C.N. This may have been some move that came right down from La Cosa Nostra."

"Are you saying it's political?"

It was Hurley's turn to look blank.

"Frankie Bartolo," Spraggue prompted. "The man with the most to gain if Donagher doesn't make it back to the Senate. Rumor has it that Bartolo and the mob are not exactly strangers."

"I don't know anything about that. What I do know is that if it's mob business, we'll take one fast peek, report it to the Feds, and forget about it."

"I can't believe this."

"We get more unbelievable stuff in here seven days a week."

"As far as you're concerned, the investigation is over?"

"Hell, no, Spraggue. It's just that we're not facing the kind of heat we were—"

"Because you can put a paragraph in the papers that some guy who's suspected of giving Pete something that may or may not have killed him, is dead."

"Nobody expects you to third-degree a dead man."

"Quiets things down, a corpse. No pretrial motions by the defense."

"Look," Hurley said, "I'll go this far. I'll have these damn pills analyzed. I'll ask the M.E. whether they could have had anything to do with Collatos' death. I'll even send somebody over to talk to the super of Collatos' apartment, see if anybody broke in—"

"Thanks a heap."

"Jesus, Spraggue, there are a hell of a lot of other crimes going on around here. There are three million people in this—"

"Save the speech for the mayor," Spraggue said.

He walked out the door, slamming it the way Hurley would expect him to, ducked into the men's room. There, he pulled a notebook from his hip pocket, recorded the name

155

he'd read off the dead man's rap sheet, the one neatly listed under known associates.

He could read quite well upside down. He'd just had to get Hurley angry enough to forget to cover the page.

TWENTY-FOUR

Sipping lukewarm coffeed water at a luncheonette with cracked green walls even grimier than Hurley's, he devised plans to locate one Arnold Gravier, known associate of one JoJo Stearns, aka Joseph Stavropoulos, aka Joey Stavros, deceased. A trip to City Hall, the inevitable wait to check the Registrar's voting list . . . maybe the additional joy of a visit to the Assessor's Office or the Office of the Registrar of Motor Vehicles. . . . He plunked his fifty cents down on the speckled Formica countertop. A smudged black dial phone was nestled into the crook between the cash register and the March of Dimes canister.

"Do you have a phone book?" The doughy face of the waitress was frozen under sparse gray hair that no longer had any need of its restraining hairnet.

She rang up a sale, stared at him blankly, and said, "It's not a public phone."

"I wouldn't dream of using it. Just wondered if you had a phone book I could see. To check out an address."

"It's not a public phone," she repeated flatly, and walked away on feet so tired you could almost hear them groan.
156

The door creaked when he swung it open. She probably had to listen to it creak three hundred times a day.

The first phone booth he came to had no phone book, just a dangling metal snake with a bit of the ripped black cardboard cover still attached. He'd walked half a mile down Boylston by the time he found a sufficiently unmutilated book. He fought the wind and wrestled with the mechanism that held the volume in a position too awkward to peruse and thought nostalgically of the old-style phone booths, the ones that offered shelter, a beam of light, privacy.

There was no listing for an Arnold Gravier, but two A. Graviers headed the column. Probably Alice and Ann; women had long since learned the regrettable lesson that publication of a female first name in the directory was an invitation to the obscene phonecaller. He stuck a dime in the slot, dialed A. Gravier Number One, and let the phone ring twelve times. A. Gravier Number Two picked up the receiver on a spry two rings. A gentle flustered voice proclaimed herself 'just the housekeeper.' Mrs. Gravier was spending her afternoon at the Athenaeum, but would be delighted to return the call if the gentleman would kindly leave his name.

A man in a tan Burberry hovered half a block up the street, hands deep in his pockets, head down, kicking a scuffed shoe against the uneven sidewalk. Spraggue wondered if the man wanted to use the phone, but waited at a distance so as not to appear impatient. Between the sweet creature on the phone and the raincoated man, he'd probably located the two politest individuals the city had to offer.

He inquired after dear Mrs. Gravier's son, Arnold, and was firmly put in his place. He must wish to speak to some *other,* the voice said clearly, some *inferior,* Mrs. Gravier, and his name would no longer be required.

He tried the first number again, hastily, in case the Burberry man was still waiting. Not home. Or not answering.

The rain had thickened into a gluey mist. Spraggue dodged over to Newbury Street, entered an art gallery, and stared vacantly at some sinister deep-hued surrealist paintings he didn't like until the gallery owner, assuming fascination, interrupted his thoughts to quote prices. He started when she spoke, nodded briefly, and left her shaking her head at the oddballs who ventured through her door.

The man in the Burberry huddled under an awning across the street, a too small tweed rainhat perched on top of his wet gray-flecked hair.

Spraggue's first thought was that Hurley must have dispatched some aging flatfoot to tail him. Why? Had the captain set things up so that Spraggue would see Gravier's name in JoJo's file? Had he been selected for the role of guinea pig by the Boston Police? Or was the man in the raincoat some fatuous tourist out for a circuitous jaunt in a strange town?

That theory, at least, he could test. He made his way back to Boylston Street, crossing against the lights at the corner of Dartmouth. Going up the steps of the Boston Public Library—the old building, now the research library—he shot a quick look to his right. Tan raincoat was on the scent, negotiating the traffic-jammed street. Instead of the following the most traveled path, up the marble staircase to the second floor, Spraggue took a sharp right past the periodical room, then a left. He pushed open the door that led to the courtyard, crossed it, and entered the air-conditioned stillness of the new library building, the modern granite cube of a circulation library, added some ten years back.

He halted behind a shelf full of ponderous gray-spined

history books, read their titles for five minutes. A teenaged boy, wearing a black watchcap and bopping along to the rhythm of his silent Sony Walkman, entered through the courtyard door. No one else.

Spraggue exited the library through the revolving doors on Boylston Street. He crossed Exeter and entered the lobby of the Lenox Hotel, took a flight of stairs down to the telephone.

No answer at Gravier's. He looked up Senator Donagher's Boston number, dialed, and got a recording: "This is Donagher Campaign Headquarters. All our lines are busy now. Please hang on and the next available worker will answer your call." They started to play Muzak in his ear so he hung up. He fumbled through his pockets for his black Harvard Coop book, found the number Senator Donagher had given him the way you'd give someone a gift: My own private number; whether I'm in Washington or Boston, this'll get you through.

This time, Spraggue was almost sure the man who slurred an offhand hello in the receiver was the man who called himself Murray Eichenhorn.

"Michael Spraggue to speak to Senator Donagher."

"Senator Donagher is not available." If it was Eichenhorn, he wasn't breezing into any easy informalities.

"Then I'll speak to Mrs. Donagher," Spraggue said.

He could almost hear Eichenhorn swallow over the phone.

"Uh . . . hang on a minute, please."

There was a hurried, whispered, inaudible conference and then the unavailable Brian Donagher came on the line.

"What can I do for you?"

"When you were given that squeeze bottle, what did the woman say to you?"

Donagher hesitated, then spoke as if he'd made up his mind about something. "I've been through this so many times that I'm not sure I really remember. Maybe I'm not re-membering what happened anymore; maybe I'm just re-calling what I told the cops. It was so fuzzy when they first asked me. I was still in the hospital and . . ."

"Try. Word for word."

"Well, I remember the woman called to me, said my name. Hey Brian, or something like that."

"Did she seem at all familiar?"

"A lot of people call me Brian right off. They've seen my picture in the paper, seen me on TV. I'm one of the family. So, she said, Brian, have some water, or something like that. I was thirsty as hell—"

"And your wife wasn't where she was supposed to be."

"My wife . . . Look, Spraggue, Lila is not getting in-volved in this mess. I absolutely deny—" What started out a bombastic speech turned into a plea. "There's no reason to harass my wife. I'm telling you the truth, just the way it hap-pened. I was thirsty and I took the water and Pete looked at me, like to say, maybe the water's bad. I held it out to him, kind of like a joke."

"The woman say anything?"

"She said, go ahead and share it, or give your buddy some, or something like that."

"Is that all?"

"All I can remember. Then she promised to vote for me." Donagher sighed. "Are you making head or tail out of this? I'd sure as hell like to get rid of the cops at my door. My wife's afraid to send the kids to school. It's like living in prison, a state of siege—"

"The cops can do without another killing."

"It looks so bad. Especially with the election heating up—"

"I'd think it would give you a big publicity boost."

"Yeah," Donagher's voice was so bitter Spraggue regretted the gibe. "It's great. Senator hides behind cops.

160

Won't meet people. You think I want that kind of coverage? You think I care about publicity when my wife can't go out and buy a loaf of bread, my kids can't pedal their bikes around the block? You think I enjoy finding out what Teddy Kennedy must live with every day of his life?''

"Sorry."

"You're working on it, aren't you, Spraggue?"

"A little."

"Let me hire you. Then you can be on it full time."

"No, thanks," Spraggue said, craning his neck around and looking for the man in the tan raincoat. "By the way, you haven't hired anybody else, have you?"

"No."

"Good-bye."

"Wait, hang on a minute, Spraggue. Do you think I should?"

The receiver was still squawking sound when Spraggue pressed it down into the cradle. Hire someone? Nope. Fire someone? A definite maybe.

TWENTY-FIVE

He tried Gravier's phone number often enough to memorize it, plunking his dimes into the pay phone at the theater during intermission, calling from his apartment after the show, dialing between yawns into the early hours of the morning. Hostile-voiced Information confirmed that the number belonged to A. Gravier. At 9 A.M., Bell Telephone's business office declared the line in working order and suggested, with surpassing brilliance, that perhaps Mr. Gravier was out of town. Spraggue finessed the full name on the March bill out of the sweet young thing who handled the call. Arnold Gravier. Bingo.

He frittered away some time making breakfast, clearing the dishes. He had a script to study, a possibility for the next off-Broadway season, something his agent had described as "serio-comic Brechtian with a hint of Neil Simon." He read the first two pages, flipped it shut, and tossed it on the floor.

He stifled the impulse to call Sharon Collatos; he couldn't justify the intrusion with no news to impart. And the woman he wanted to talk to was the one in the photo on Pete's desk, the smiling, colorful, windswept girl, not the black Medea of the funeral or the desperate waif of the previous day.

He kicked the script across the room and decided to visit Arnold Gravier. Even if the man wasn't home, he'd have neighbors, neighbors who wouldn't mind spending a few minutes chatting with an old friend of Arnie's. Gossips who might talk too much or too little.

He felt foolish checking the shrubbery out front as he passed the high fence that sealed off his property from the street, but he had been followed from the police station yesterday. And if Hurley wanted to pick up the trail again, he certainly knew where to do it. No secret where to find one Michael Spraggue most evenings between eight and eleven o'clock.

He left the Porsche in the garage. Gravier's address was in the North End, on Hanover Street. The North End was one of the oldest sections of Boston, cut off from the rest of the city by a combination of the Central Artery and Italian clannishness. The streets were cobblestone, one-way, narrow enough to give the driver of the slimmest compact car pause. Parking was an adventure to be avoided; even if he were to beat the fifty-to-one odds and find a remotely legal parking

162

place, Porsches were apt to disappear in the North End. And then Mary would go out and buy him another flashy car, another engraved invitation to car thieves and reckless drivers. What he really needed was a battered, rusting-out jalopy, with a mammoth dent in the side, the kind of car that sent a message to aggressive drivers on the Southeast Expressway.

He was shoved out of the crowded subway at Park Street, walked down Tremont past the Granary Burying Ground, past the columns of King's Chapel, half hidden behind repairmen's scaffolding. He hurried across the cheerless bricks of barren City Hall Plaza, skirted Quincy Market to avoid the crush.

The smell of pancetta slowly frying in olive oil, of pungent Romano cheese, and fresh-baked bread made him regret having already eaten breakfast. Miniature multicolored lights twinkled from streetlamps overhead, left from the feast of St. Anthony, or any one of the myriad feasts, honoring the saints with parades and festivals, that periodically brightened the twisting streets of the neighborhood.

Arnold Gravier's building was three stories high, painted the same fading brown as its neighbors, a little further along in its state of disrepair. No yard to speak of, front or back. A clothesline waved three checked shirts out the second floor window like forlorn banners.

He kept walking, found a phone, and dialed the number with the usual result. He strolled back and mounted the warped wooden steps. The cramped vestibule disclosed the pertinent facts. The house was divided into three rented flats. First floor: two unrelated individuals, both designated by sexless first initials. Mrs. Eugenia Romero, the second floor tenant with the checkered shirts, wasn't afraid to list her entire name. 'Gravier' said the third floor entry, even less forthcoming than the phone book.

He backed out and circled the block. There were lights burning in the third floor windows. A blare from a radio on the second or third floor, hard to tell. Maybe Arnold Gravier took care to make his place look lived in when he was out. Maybe he wasn't out. Maybe he hated telephones. Maybe he was deaf.

Spraggue bought coffee and a copy of the *Globe* at a corner variety store, settled himself in the schoolyard across from the Gravier place, and played the innocent, catching the rays of the friendly sun.

The Editorial and Op-Ed pages had three columns dedicated to the upcoming election. The *Globe* editorial was pro-Donagher as expected, the *Globe* being the more liberal rag in a two-newspaper town. The *Herald* would assuredly be pro-Bartolo. The second column was a rehash of campaign promises by both candidates, a compare-and-contrast job pointing out that both candidates had said the politically expedient at the appropriate time. The third, under the byline H. Marsh, discussed the media coverage of the campaign. Spraggue sighed and folded the paper in half, scrunching over to shield the page from the glare of the sun. Damn, but he was getting tired of the media turning its own people into minor league celebrities, interviewing each other instead of the newsmakers. He had started to turn the page when the name "Heineman" caught his eye. H. Marsh excoriated Channel 4's new "glamour boy" for tearing apart Senator Donagher in stories that were supposed to be news, not commentary. How much more would Marsh have written had he known of Lila Donagher's friendship with Edward Heineman?

The street noises grew louder, the sun warmer. Spraggue was glad of the length of the Wednesday *Globe*. It gave him plenty of reason to prolong his stay on the bench, enough anyway to avoid arousing suspicion—

The sudden quiet made him wary, that was what he diagnosed later. The radio inside A. Gravier's apartment

164

had been turned off. Spraggue waited, staring at the same paragraph for five minutes without really seeing it.

Jaunty steps descended the front stoop of the brown house on Hanover Street. Spraggue peeked over the top of the newspaper just in time to see the man in the tan raincoat head down the street.

The same man who'd followed him from police headquarters yesterday.

TWENTY-SIX

The man in the tan raincoat couldn't have negotiated his disappearance more neatly if he'd known he was being followed. He pushed through the double doors leading to the central market building, the most crowded of Quincy Market's jammed lunchtime locales. Spraggue abandoned caution, ran up the steps in an effort to keep the raincoat in sight. The long, narrow hall was wall-to-wall people, lined with fast-food stands. The clamor of cohorts greeting colleagues from nearby Government Center over pizza or knockwurst or seafood salad crushed his ears. He shouldered his way through the tide, muttering haphazard "excuse me's" to outraged patrons, made it as far as the central rotunda.

Tan raincoats. Three were in sight, none of them on the back of the man with the gray-flecked hair who might be A. Gravier. Already Spraggue had passed six possible exits, cut-offs to the right or left galleries of the building. From the rotunda, the tan raincoat could have exited any one of a dozen ways, including the stairs to the vaulted dome. Spraggue hesitated on the first landing, revolving like a slow-spinning top, climbed further, seeking the better view.

From the second floor, the marketplace spread out beneath him like an intricate moving tapestry. People turned into blobs of color: a dark head surrounded by purple, a blond head in blue. Too much tan. Too much gray. Directly below, the wooden benches and tables melded into the wooden floor, the cacaphony of laughter and words deafened. A constant hunt for the rare empty table took place. As soon as one was vacated, figures sprang upon the seats like famished vultures.

Outside, with the pale sunshine for a backdrop, the scene turned into a Breughel frolic. Constant movement, vivid color—almost a dance. Spraggue circled the rotunda. Gave up the chase. Sat on the corner of a precarious bench.

Was Tan Raincoat Arnold Gravier? Or was Tan Raincoat a cop? Had he been sent to spy on both Spraggue and Gravier? Had Spraggue just witnessed the ransacking of Gravier's apartment?

The man had played the radio, turned on the lights. He'd bounced merrily down the front steps, ignoring a perfectly good back alleyway that would have served far better as an unobserved escape route . . . He'd acted like the apartment's rightful tenant, which made him Arnold Gravier. But he didn't answer his phone.

Why not? And why did he spend his time darting through the streets of the Back Bay? What did Tan Raincoat know about the arson that had claimed the life of JoJo Stearns? What did he know about the murder, if indeed it was murder, of Pete Collatos?

Spraggue wondered what Pete's killers would be charged with, just in case he should happen to stumble across them. What was the charge for spiking drinking water? Not first-

166

degree murder. It would be harder than hell to get the district attorney to call it first-degree murder. Even though premeditation was evident, intent was not. What if the target were actually Donagher? What if—

Shit. Spraggue consoled himself with the fact that he'd discovered something about his shadow, that he'd probably be able to pick him up again. He headed over to the Government Center MBTA stop. Maybe they'd meet while waiting for the train. If it arrived with its customary dispatch, most of the world would have time to parade by.

He had to wait in line to buy a subway token. He passed a telephone and, on impulse, called Sharon Collatos. The operator told him to dial one first and try again. Deposit fifty-five cents for the first three minutes.

Sharon sounded eager. She'd been trying to reach him. He was almost disappointed to learn that it was about her brother.

"I got something in the mail today, from Pete."

Spraggue computed dates. "From Boston to Chelmsford in seven days? Did it come by water buffalo express?"

"Well, it could have been delivered anytime within the past three days. I haven't been reading my mail."

"I'm glad you answered your phone."

"I thought it might be you. . . . I mean, I have been trying to get in touch and . . ."

"What did Pete send you?"

"I'm not sure. It looks like some ordinary envelope. I don't know if he meant to send it or not. Maybe he put the wrong thing in the mail. It makes no sense."

"Did he ever send you things?"

"On my birthday. Christmas. Not envelopes."

"I'd like to see it."

"I want to show it to you."

"Hang on." Spraggue ran his tongue around his lips, thought quickly. "I'm booked this afternoon. I've got a show at eight and I won't be out till eleven . . . You couldn't meet me for dinner, could you? Somewhere in Cambridge, near Harvard Square?''

"I suppose I . . ."

"There's one of those Cambridgey salad-and-quiche places on Huron Avenue. Or a good Spanish place right on Boylston.''

"The Iruña? Behind the wrought-iron gates, across from the Galeria? I'd like that. What time?''

"Would six be too early?''

"I'll be there,'' she said.

The wait for the train wasn't bad. No tan-raincoated watcher lurked.

He switched to the Red Line at Park Street Station, waited again, got off at Central Square and walked down Pearl Street to Magazine Street, into the heart of the Cambridge Riverside community, where gentrification warred with the old neighborhood. Every other house was spruced up with fresh paint and elegant hanging greenery in just washed windows. The bright touches made the other houses look even worse by contrast—peeling paint, sagging porches, dusty, smudgey windows, some broken and replaced with slabs of plywood. The renaissance seemed to have halted fifty-fifty. He saw no signs of present renovation, no moving vans. The trend had died midstream, leaving an uneasy truce between the old and the new, the revitalized and the dying.

Sergeant Billy lived in a dying house, untouched by paintbrush or repairman. A lived-in-all-your-life house, so that you no longer noticed the crumbling eaves, the shabby curtains, the worn steps leading up to the blistered front door with the dull brass knocker.

Spraggue checked the street for tan raincoats before beating a tattoo on the door. He heard slow shuffling steps after a five-minute wait.

He had trouble reconciling the memory of the spit-and-polish uniformed, if red-faced, codger of the funeral with the down-and-outer who blocked the doorway, old eyes blinking in the sunshine. It was as if the uniform had held him together. In a tattered robe, a miasma of whiskey surrounding him, the man seemed to have blurred, expanded, softened. Spragguer wondered if his conversation would be intelligible.

"You sellin' somethin'?" the man began belligerently. "I ain't puttin' this house up for sale even if you was to offer me the mayor's own Parkman House."

"No," Sprague said.

The man's bloodshot eyes narrowed suspiciously. "No, what?"

"I'm not selling, Sergeant Billy."

The name had a transforming effect. The old man tried to pull his belly in. "Sergeant? Do I know you?" He tilted his chin and scratched the three-day stubble on his face.

"I know you. About you."

"You from one of these goddam socialist agencies? Gonna ask me personal questions? Make me beg for a goddam handout?" Billy's fingers tightened on the door-handle.

"Nope."

"Well?"

"Aren't you going to guess anymore?"

"No. I'm gonna slam the door in your face is what I'm gonna do."

"I used to be a private investigator," Sprague said. "You used to be a cop. Maybe that gives us something to talk about."

Billy trumpeted a laugh. Sprague was glad the man's mouth wasn't any closer to his nose. "I retired," he said. "What's your excuse?"

"Somebody over at District One said you might be able to help me on a case."

169

Spraggue could have sworn the man grew two inches before his eyes. He wiped a hand across his face, tugged the front of his robe closed, retied the belt under his bulging stomach, made a curious burping noise and moved out of the doorway.

"Come on in," he said. "You want . . . um . . . coffee or some other liquid refreshment?"

"No," Spraggue said quickly. "Just a little of your time. The use of your memory."

"Memory," Billy muttered. "One thing I've sure got is memories." He motioned the way into a dark curtained sitting room that smelled as musty as it looked. The furniture was uniformly dark and heavy, built to last. The curtains were dust-coated green plush. Spraggue wondered if they'd ever been opened. He sat in the armchair Billy offered and tried not to cough when a puff of dust exploded around him. He wondered when Billy had last used this room, this dead formal parlor. He probably lived in the kitchen or on a back porch, wherever the TV and the radio were kept. This room was for company.

"Memory," Billy repeated. "I guess guys on the force today just shove numbers into computers. Every once in a while I suppose they could use somebody with a memory about people instead of fingerprints and numbers and times and dates. That's where some of us old guys could help. But no way. Pension you off and be glad to see the back of you. And I guess I should be glad for it. The streets nowadays ain't safe, even for a cop."

"I saw you at Pete Collatos' funeral."

"Collatos . . . Collatos. Yeah, that's the one last week on the Sunday. I didn't know him, mind. I go to all the funerals of the boys in blue. The cops and the ex-cops. Least I can do and a chance to see the old guys. Gets pretty dismal, huh, when the only place you see your friends is at funerals."

"You knew a lot of people there?"

"A few. A few. Are you headin' someplace particular?"

"I saw you talking to someone I know. Martin Emery."

"Ah, Marty! Marty. Talk about a surprise. Maybe twenty years and I knew him right off the top even if he was dressed up in a three-piece suit the like of which I never thought to see on a boy like that. I heard his voice, good and clear, and it made me stop and stare, I can tell you. I've got a better memory for voices than I do for faces."

"You recognized Marty's voice and you went over to say hello."

"Sure. We did a lot of talking, me and him, in the old days, I can tell you. He's the one you want to know about, is he?"

"Yes."

"Hope he's not in trouble. Looked like he'd gone straight as a ruler, that three-piece suit and all."

"I take it you knew him professionally."

"You could say that. I got him in off the streets a couple of times. He was running with a bad crowd. I took him in to Juvenile Court maybe three, maybe four times. Never saw him after he was seventeen or so. Figured he'd wised up or moved out of the neighborhood, Southie that was. Guess he knew he'd get different treatment as an adult. They don't mess around with you once you're over eighteen. Off to Walpole."

Walpole was the maximum security state prison, not someplace you got sent for drunk and disorderly, not someplace to house a runaway. "What kind of stuff was Marty up for as a juvenile?"

Hurley was right. The man had lost his discretion in a bottle years ago.

"Breaking and entering, mostly. A little street robbery. He tried that afterward, when we'd convinced him he'd never make it as a burglar. Left his signature all over the place. Never could pick a lock worth shit. I could take a look at the doorhandle, go straight from the site of the burglary, and pick the kid up before he even had a chance to pawn the loot. I got to thinking maybe he just pulled a job when he got lonely, so I'd go over and have a word with him. I liked the kid. No father and his mother not what she should be. I'm glad Marty's made something grand out of himself.''

"How did he pick locks?''

"Well, he never had any money, you know. And he wasn't as good with his hands as the other kids. They could make a set of picklocks just like pros. But Marty used his mother's long hairpins. Too thick. He'd mess the door up terrible.''

He stayed as long as politeness demanded. Billy hated to see him go. It was as if Spraggue had completed some ancient circle. Sergeant Billy had comforted Marty—now Murray—long ago. And now Spraggue comforted Billy.

No tan raincoat waited outside the house.

He fumbled in his pockets as he approached a phone booth near the bus stop on Mass Ave. He'd have to start carrying more change. If Ma Bell switched over to the twenty-cent call from pay phones in the Boston area, he'd be in trouble.

He asked for Hurley in Homicide.

"Parnate,'' he said when the right voice grunted hello. "I checked it,'' Hurley said. "It's the trade name for tranylcypromine, which is a monoamine oxidase inhibitor.''

"No shit.''

"Anything else I can do for you?''

"On you, Hurley, smugness sounds good.''

"I get to try it out so infrequently.''

"Just what is a monoamine what's-its-face?'' Spraggue asked.

"They call it an MAO inhibitor for short.''

"I like it. Cute and snappy. Could it have anything to do with Pete's death?"

"Sure could."

"Did it?"

"There is absolutely no way on earth to tell."

"You're kidding."

"I wish I was. This I can tell you. If Pete was taking that medication, then that hit of speed, that minor hit, would have killed him as sure as a tank running over a field mouse."

"How?"

"His blood pressure would have shot up to about 300 over 200. Incredibly high—as if the dose of speed had been a hundred times what he actually got. He would have ruptured an artery in his head. It just would have blown up."

"Like it did."

"But it can't be proved that he ever took this drug."

"You've found his doctor?"

"Think you're dealing with an amateur? Prescott on Beacon Street. Never gave him anything stronger than tetracycline. Never recommended a shrink. We're asking around, but—"

"But you can't put in time on a crime that's been solved, right?"

"Right."

"But I can," Spraggue muttered as he hung up.

TWENTY-SEVEN

He had to check twice to make sure the dark woman in the silky coral dress was really Sharon Collatos. Then he quickly reevaluated his impulsive invitation to dinner. Pity had been part of the motive; he'd extended the invitation like a lifeline to a sinking exhausted swimmer. This Sharon Collatos, chin high, color in her cheeks, clad in a garment that lost detail in its overall impact, turned heads. This Sharon Collatos was a washout as an object of pity; no sinking swimmer, but the proud pennant on the topmost mast of the Coast Guard rescue cutter.

The mustached Latin waiter looked as if he enjoyed guiding her across the room.

"Hi." She turned suddenly shy when she saw him, not knowing whether to expect a businesslike dinner or the date she had dressed for.

"You look terrific," he said immediately. It wasn't the most tactful opening in the world, but he knew he'd have to say it sooner or later. She blushed. The compliment apparently made her think, as he had feared, not of how well she looked tonight, but of how she'd looked two days earlier. And acted, clinging to him in Pete's study.

"I'm getting myself together," she said flatly. The waiter held her chair.

"Obviously."

"Went back to work today. I teach. High school. It

helped. Made me realize I'm not the only one in the world who has to deal with death and disaster and pimples.''

They opened tasseled, red leather menus, scanned choices printed on fake parchment. ''The Spanish dishes are good. So's the steak.''

''Paella,'' she said. ''And the stuffed avocado if you're going to have an appetizer. I've been here before, years ago . . .'' She turned her head and glanced back toward the door, at the clutch of small tables with pristine white cloths, dotted with tented scarlet napkins, the hallway leading to the other narrow room. ''Hasn't changed.''

''You want wine? A drink?''

''No. I might get maudlin again.''

''We'll skip it then. I can't drink before a performance.''

''Have you been acting long?''

''Long enough.''

He hadn't meant it as a brush-off, but she was sensitive to every nuance. Her hand jumped to her leather bag. ''I brought Pete's letter,'' she said, all business.

''Relax,'' he said. ''I'm sorry. We'll get to the letter. We have to start by exchanging life stories, don't we?''

''Not if you don't want to.''

''Let's do it slowly,'' Spraggue said. ''A little at a time.''

''That bad?'' she said, smiling.

''How did you wind up out in Chelmsford when you used to eat dinner at the Iruña in the Square?''

''That alone would take us through to dessert.''

''Fine. Begin.''

He'd expected a protracted tale of indecision, love, rapture, disgust, divorce. Instead he got a cool, lucid, unsentimental account of a marriage that hadn't made it and a career that had.

''Would you like to see a play tonight?'' he asked.

"I don't have a ticket."

"House seats could be made available. I won't be able to sit with you."

"What show?"

"*Caucasian Chalk Circle*. I think."

She laughed. "I'd love to see it."

"Good."

The paella and steak appeared and disappeared. None of their talk had the nervous patter of strangers trying desperately to impress. When they tired of old tales, they talked current events; when they tired of that, they talked about Pete. That led back to the letter.

She held it out over the starched white tablecloth. Their hands brushed during the transfer. She did have wonderfully long dark eyelashes.

Pete's communication wasn't much to look at. The envelope was standard business size—plain, white, cheap—a Woolworth's special. The postmark was blurred, but the word *Boston* was evident and a date could barely be made out.

"How the hell could it take so long to deliver mail from Boston to Chelmsford?" Spraggue muttered.

Sharon shrugged.

The envelope contained only one item, another smaller envelope. Spraggue held it up to the light, carefully, by the edges, even though the paper seemed too smooth for fingerprints. He stared at it for a full thirty seconds before its significance sank in.

"What is it?" Sharon asked anxiously.

"Your brother showed me five envelopes three days before he died. The envelopes Senator Donagher got his hate mail in. Pete expected there to be six envelopes, but there were only five. . . . He assumed that the police had kept one. That's what he said."

"Why mail an envelope to me?"

"Presumably, because it was important."

"Yes?"

"I'm just thinking out loud. Don't expect major revelations here. Okay. He sent it to you because he knew it wouldn't be safe in his apartment, because someone else wanted it. . . ."

"Maybe."

"I think the postmark is April twentieth."

"That's what it looked like to me," Sharon said.

"The day after he died."

"That means somebody else mailed it. Who? Why?"

"Suppose," Spragg said slowly, "Pete stuck it in the mail Sunday, Sunday night. The post office doesn't pick up mail Sunday night."

Sharon took a pocket calendar out of her purse. "Monday, then, the nineteenth."

"Patriot's Day," Spragg said. "No mail."

"So Pete could have mailed it before he . . ."

Spragg stared at the smaller envelope, the three lines of typed text: *Senator Brian Donagher; 55 Sparhawk Street; Brighton, MA.* "He did mail it . . . he must have mailed it right after he called me. . . ." Spragg pushed his dinner plate away, smoothed his scarlet napkin over the tablecloth. He placed the two envelopes on it, side by side, then placed the smaller one above the larger one.

"What is it? What do you see?"

"Look." He tilted the envelopes in her direction. "Look at the typing. The envelope with Donagher's name on it. Then the one Pete typed with your name on it. They were typed on the same machine. See that blocked *o*, that off-center *t*?"

"What does it mean?"

"Your brother knew who sent the warning letters to Donagher."

Sharon held her water glass to her lips, sipped, set it down

177

with unsteady fingers. "You think that's why he was killed?"

He blew out a sigh of exasperation. "No. I don't think so. Dammit, I don't know. I've been working on the theory that he was killed because of something he learned while he was a cop, when he was working with the Arson Squad. Now this."

"Confuses everything?" she said and Spraggue wanted to lean over and kiss her for the sympathy in her voice.

"Yeah. Not only do we get our choice of how your brother died, we get our choice of why somebody killed him."

TWENTY-EIGHT

She was holding her ground at one of the small round tables in the lobby where they'd agreed to meet after the show. Her caramel-colored sandals, hooked over the metal rung of a folding chair, impeded the progress of a surly teenager who pushed a broom impatiently across the polished floor. The sweeper couldn't have been more pointed in his invitation to depart. Sharon ignored him and smiled up at Spraggue with such warmth that he didn't bother with his planned apology about how long it took to part spirit gum from skin.

"Terrific," she said. "I laughed out loud and I applauded my hands red. I'd almost forgotten what a real play with real actors was like. And you! I didn't even recognize you as the doctor—what's his name? Niko Mikadze, or Mika Loladze? How many roles did you play?"

"Four. Right in the program, ma'am."

"I'm glad you did the prologue. It's so rarely done like that, with the actors assuming the roles for the story right onstage."

"Ah. You know the play."

"I wish I could bring my kids to see it."

"Your kids?"

"Oh." She laughed. "Not my kids, the ones I teach. No biological kids."

"Maybe you can."

"Nope."

"Why so definite?"

She ticked the reasons off on stubby, unmanicured fingernails: "Bad language; money; logistics; location. The parents of the kids I teach are Boston's suburban escapees. They're convinced that entering the city limits is tempting fate. They gobble up every newspaper account of crime in the evil city. If you are not raped, you will be mugged. If you are not mugged, your car will be stolen, vandalized, and burned."

"Where did you park, by the way?"

The teenager had fetched a mop and a bucket of water. He glared at the lobby's intruders, prepared to spill water on their feet if that were necessary to evict them.

"Behind the Harvard School of Education. They never used to require the relevant sticker." Awkwardly, she stuck out her right hand for a handshake. "Thank you for the play. I did enjoy it."

"Hey, I didn't mean you should run away this instant and check on your car."

"Well . . ."

"Come have a drink with me."

She consulted the slim gold band on her wrist. "It's late. Even the places around here should be closed by now."

"My house is five minutes' walk."

Her eyes narrowed. "You're still high from the applause."

"Otherwise I wouldn't have asked."

"If I did come, it would be just for a drink, just to talk."

"Just for a drink. Just to talk," he echoed.

"I shouldn't leave my car at the school," she said, weakening.

"We'll get it now. You can park in my driveway."

The floor washer was so pleased by their departure he started whistling.

They strolled down Appian Way in the cool night breeze, staggering over the uneven brick sidewalk. Spraggue used it as an excuse to take her arm.

"Did Pete ever talk about me?" she asked.

"Enough so I knew he had a sister who didn't like him being a cop."

She drove her battered Dart like a veteran of Boston traffic. He gave her directions: a right on Brattle, another on Fayerweather.

"This house," he said. "The top two floors are mine."

"I like old houses."

"Are there old houses in Chelmsford?"

"My husband's choice. He didn't like anything older than twenty. I found out later that held for women as well as houses." She had a warm, low laugh without a trace of self-pity.

"Don't slam the car door. I try not to let my downstairs neighbor know when I come in; it keeps her guessing."

"Does she guess about who you come in with, too?"

"She's no nosier than the usual tenant."

"It's your house?"

"Yep." Spraggue touched the lightswitch and led the way up the stairs. "My house, my hobby. I started by fixing up the first floor apartment. My enthusiasm waned by the time I moved upstairs."

"It's a lovely place," she said. Then she got flustered and asked abruptly about progress on Pete's case. Spraggue wondered if she'd been out with a man since her divorce, whether her jitters were the result of a rotten marriage, bad experiences since then, or just a reaction to the past week.

"First, the drink," he said firmly. "Tell me where else you've seen Brecht."

She sat on a jade green cushion that set off her coral dress, insisted she'd be more comfortable there than in the huge brown chair, shrugged off his apologies about the lack of furniture. She'd gone to college in Oakland, bought a subscription to San Francisco's American Conservatory Theater with money earned as a part-time typist. They'd done *Mother Courage* and *The Good Woman of Setzuan*. Years later, she'd seen a memorable student production of *Caucasian Chalk Circle* at the Boston University School of Fine and Applied Arts.

She took a firm grasp on her wineglass, reddened as if she'd only just realized she'd been talking for some time, and asked how long he'd been acting. Then she realized she'd tried the question before, at the restaurant, and blushed redder still.

"That's a tough one," Spraggue said from a recumbent position, head on blue cushion, across the room. He'd settled some distance away from the nervous woman, convinced that any attempt to get closer would have terminated the evening. When he'd approached to hand her a wineglass, she'd backed off. "Would you accept 'all my life' as an answer?"

"Not a very good one."

"A long time, then."

"Why did you go into acting?"

"I guess the usual reasons. I didn't know who I was—and I had the unsettling feeling that if I did, I wouldn't like myself very much. So I started being other people. And I was good at it. And by the time I decided I liked myself well enough to possibly do something else, all I was trained for was acting."

"Well," she said, "I thought you were very good tonight."

"Thank you. Good is exactly what I am."

She started to say something, stopped, and took refuge in the wineglass. "You don't sound pleased about it," she said finally.

"Pleased, displeased, what difference would it make? I'm a good actor, not a great one. On a wonderful night, I am very good. I hold my own with the Harvard Rep, but I don't shine, I don't blaze out the way Underwood does—"

"He played Azdak?"

"You didn't have to check the program for that one."

"He had a much more forceful, more interesting part than you did." Her words spilled out so quickly that she coughed.

"He had the kind of part I'll never play. He has that something extra that all the technique in the world can't give you. Me, I'm more a chameleon than a star."

"A chameleon is a useful thing to be."

"Part of it's my training. I learned to act in England. I was taught to fit the proper form to the passion, not to seek the passion and worry about the form later. And part of it is just something lacking in me."

"Passion?"

He wished it were earlier in the evening. Or later in a

relationship that hadn't had such a rocky beginning, so he could ask her to stay the night.

"Forget it," he said. "I shouldn't talk after performances. Or drink."

"I'm enjoying the conversation. Or I was."

"Sorry."

"The applause gave you a lift. You're hitting the corresponding low."

"You're kind."

She looked away, motioned towards the two cardboard boxes near the kitchen door, used them as an excuse to turn the conversation away from her virtues. "Why did you bring that stuff over from Pete's apartment?"

Sprague sighed. Collatos might as well have been in the room with them, between them when they walked side-by-side down the street. "Because I don't understand it. He had no business having police files in his closet. Hiding them. And they're old files. From before Pete ever thought about being a cop . . ."

"Don't be too sure about that," she said. "It's all I can ever remember: Pete playing cop."

"I thought I'd go through them, see if I could make any sense out of them. If you don't mind."

She coughed again, straightened up on her cushion, and looked around the room, puzzled.

"Do you smoke?" she asked.

"No."

"I didn't think so. No ashtrays. But—" She closed her eyes and inhaled, said, "Don't you smell it?"

"No."

She forced a grin. "I'm overly sensitive to smoke—allergic, I guess. But I could swear . . ." She sat as still as a portrait on her jade green cushion. Her brow wrinkled and she breathed in deeply, nostrils flared. "Definitely. Not cigarettes, but something burning—"

It happened fast. Not only could Spraggue smell it, he could see the faint mist rise through the room, hear the crackle of the flames. He eased the front door, the door to the stairway, open a scant two inches, saw only a wall of flickering yellow tongues. He slammed it shut, grabbed Sharon by the hand, pulled her along to the kitchen, soaked towels in the sink.

"Put this over your nose and mouth."

She chewed the color off her lower lip, said faintly, "Will we have to jump?"

"Not if we can get down the back stairs. God, I hope Mrs. Wales isn't sleeping." He pounded on the floor, yelled "Fire!" twice in a voice that would have thundered off the rail of the third balcony. He helped Sharon drape the dripping towel across her face. "Listen, it may be smoky in the hallway. You might not be able to see. Hold on to me. I know the way."

"Okay," she said, firmly gripping his right hand.

He pressed his other hand against the back door. The wood was so hot it scorched his palm. Fire at the front door, fire at the back. Was the first floor of the house completely involved in flame or had the fire sprung from two sources? Why hadn't the smoke alarms sounded their shrill warning? Why in hell had he invited Sharon home? When he knew he'd been followed earlier, when his shadow might be connected to an arson ring?

"Can you climb trees?" he asked.

"Yes—when I was a kid—What are you doing? Why can't we use the stairs?"

"We'll have to go out a window." He led her back into the dining room. The big, center window was still sealed with plastic tape against last winter's icy draughts. He removed half the paint on the window frame ripping it off, then heaved up on the sash. His shoulders protested, but it didn't budge. Stuck tight.

"Back off," he said, grabbing a chair. "I'm going to break the glass."

It resisted, finally shivered into a thousand glittering shards. He ran the legs of the chair around the edges of the frame to dislodge the jagged remnants.

Then he remembered Pete's files, trapped in cardboard boxes on the floor.

"No," she said, sensing his intent, "don't go back for anything. Let's just get out of here. Nothing's worth it—"

"Careful of the glass," he said. "Get your head out the window and scream for help. I'd rather climb down a fireman's ladder than an oak tree."

The boxes were near the kitchen doorway. The smoke, the towel over his mouth made breathing difficult. He reached around and tucked the ends of the towel more firmly under his shirt collar. A stream of sweat inched down his back.

He'd brought the boxes in from the cab one at a time. Now, he hefted one on top of the other, knelt beside them, and jerked them both off the ground. He staggered back toward the window. The top box blocked his vision.

"Out of the way!" he said to Sharon. His words came from between clenched teeth. He bent his knees and consciously straightened his back. His arms felt like they were about to pull out of their sockets. He positioned himself in front of the window. "Give the top box a shove. Now. Good."

They both pushed the second box off the sill, heard it thud in the darkness, a long way down.

The room was getting murky, hazy with stinking smoke. They crouched on the floor, towels pressed to faces, hanging out the window, yelling.

He could hear Sharon screaming with part of his mind,

see the smoke rising with another, was dimly aware that the towel had slipped down over his shoulder. Fireman's ladder or no, it was time to get out.

"Okay," he said to Sharon. "Let's go."

"Where?" She stared out the window. "I can't see."

"Just below the sill—here, reach out and feel it—the ivy is as thick as your wrist. About four feet down, it intersects with a tree branch. It's a good, solid, sturdy climbing tree. I use it when I lock myself out."

"You first, then," she said. "You've got experience."

"Get your shoes off. I'll go down as far as the tree and then I'll wait for you. Okay?"

She nodded. He tried to gauge the depth of fear in her eyes, but they were opaque. Reason said he should be the first to climb down, so that he could coach her along the way. But what if she panicked, froze?

The door to the kitchen burst into flame.

Sprague tossed his shoes into the night, crawled out the window. His shoulders ached. Bark scraped his fingers raw; awkward twigs poked at his eyes and mouth. He remembered the upward climb as a frolic; executed always in daylight, with only inconvenience at risk, it had nothing to do with this nightmare descent.

He grabbed the tree trunk, hollered: "Now!"

Framed in ghostly firelight, she balanced on the sill. He could hear her feet scrabbling for holds in the wall's ivy spiderweb, count each of her rasping breaths. He called her name, caught her ankle as it snaked down into his reach, and set her foot on a strong, adjacent branch.

They talked each other down to the blessed ground.

TWENTY-NINE

Every light in the Chestnut Hill mansion was aglow, from the round stone turret to the flood lamps on the lawn to the old-fashioned gas lampposts that lined the driveway like runway beacons for a weary pilot. Aunt Mary had answered his 3 A.M. phone call, delighted at the prospect of a late-night chat. Her tone had altered with his message. She must have woken the house.

He screeched the car to a halt at the peak of the curve near the front steps, flicked off the headlights, put a hand on Sharon's shoulder. She had drowsed through most of the journey from Cambridge. He didn't know if her sleep was feigned or real, a normal or abnormal reaction to shock. For someone who'd had to deal first with her brother's death, then with narrow escape from a burning building, he thought she was doing fine. Let her sleep. Let her unconscious try to sort out the muddle.

Sleep, exhausted as he was, held no lure for him—not with the memory of the inferno racing like a just seen movie behind his eyes, not with the acrid smell clinging to his hair, his clothes, not with the aching rasp of smoke caught in his throat.

The scenes replayed themselves, loops of film trapped in his memory: the gust of flame that had burst through the second floor window not two minutes after their escape; the frenzied search for Mrs. Wales, finally found, safe and cry-ing, huddled like a bag of old clothes on the front lawn; the sucking, crackling hiss of tearing flames; the eerie light. The scream of approaching fire trucks. The utter, total helplessness. The relief. The rage.

Oh, but the fire had spread quickly, so fast he never doubted for a moment it had been set. Every face in the nightclad crowd of neighbors, he'd scrutinized, searching for the familiar face of the raincoated man. Only neighbors, arms crossed defensively across their chests, murmuring in fear and wonder. When a section of the roof collapsed in a shower of sparks, they'd breathed a long drawn-out "ah!", like spectators at a fireworks exhibition.

The windless night, the streaming hoses, the battering, breaking axes wielded by the black-slickered firemen, had kept the blaze from spreading to surrounding homes.

He tried not to run through the final loop of film: the dismal corpselike remains of the house, streaming water and smoke. Shattered windows. Muddy grass. It ticked on through the projector and he felt a cold, hating rage, a bitter anger he'd hoped never to feel again.

Sharon stirred and mumbled. His hand was too heavy on her shoulder.

"We're here," he said. God, but he was tense. He had to practically pry his left hand from the steering wheel. All the way over, he'd glared at the speedometer, holding back, denying the need to drive fast, flat out, reckless, to let some of that rage escape, burn off. He shook her arm. "Do you want me to carry you?"

She lifted her head, peered at the whirl of lights, and blinked.

He came around to her side, opened the door and helped her out, gave her a hug to steady her, and started for the front steps. Mary had the door open before he reached it.

"Dear Lord, Michael," she said, in a welcoming rush, "what have you gotten yourself into now?" She kissed him on the cheek, perched on the toes of tiny red fluff house slippers, enfolded Sharon in a warming embrace, urged them into the library, rang for coffee, all the while keeping up a steady flow of comforting, meaningless chat.

"You woke Pierce up at this hour?" Spragbue said as he guided Sharon to the green velvet sofa. "I don't think you pay the man enough."

"Don't worry about him," Mary said. "He owes me too many gambling debts to even consider quitting." She took her cue from Spragbue; if he didn't want to talk about the fire, she would ramble on about other things. "My dear," she said to Sharon, "forgive me for saying it, but you ought to be put straight to bed. You look even more exhausted than my nephew, who is, I trust, sorry for dragging you into this mess."

Sharon tried to smile. "I think I dragged him in."

"No one ever has to drag him a quarter of an inch. He volunteers. He plunges off the deep end with scarcely a glance at the rocks below. Even as a child—I won't go into the horrid details now with you ready to drop. I've had the south guest room prepared, Michael, for Miss Collatos—"

"I'll take her upstairs, Aunt Mary." He smiled reassuringly at Sharon. "You need a guide in this place. Souvenir maps at the door."

"Don't badmouth the old relic," Mary said with a maddening smile. "I've had the tower room prepared for you. You may have to come home for a while."

Spragbue sighed.

"Follow me, please, ma'am," he said to Sharon, taking her unresisting arm. He led her up the curving formal staircase that rose from the marble-tiled foyer. She was starting to take notice of her surroundings.

"Michael," she said with a puzzled frown. "What is this place?"

"My aunt lives here."

"Your Aunt Rockefeller?"

"My Aunt Hillman. Mary Spraggue Hillman."

"Spraggue with two *g*s Spraggue."

"Right."

"Unbelievable," she said as they traveled down a wide corridor papered in ivory and gold. "I could get lost in here." Their footsteps were muffled in thick golden carpeting. Tiny crystal sconces lit their way.

"I did, when I was a kid."

"Did my brother know about . . . about this?"

"About what?"

"I'm sorry. I didn't mean—"

They turned into a narrower hallway, trod along a deep rose Oriental runner that warmed the cream-colored walls. The carved mahogany molding at ceiling and floor glistened.

"Your room is the fourth doorway in the Oriental corridor. Here it is. There's a bath attached, and if I know my aunt, there is a new toothbrush in the medicine cabinet and a selection of nightgowns in the closet. Press that button in the morning and you'll get breakfast. Oh, and your dress cleaned. I don't think Dora's up to see to it tonight, but she may waltz in. This place runs on odd hours."

"Who else lives here? Besides your aunt?"

"Pierce. He's the butler and chief card player. Dora cooks. There's a chauffeur who's so old my aunt has to drive him around, and a gardener, but I think he has a room in the gatehouse."

"What your aunt said—about coming home. Is this yours?"

"I think of it as belonging to my children."

"Are you . . . Do you—?"

"No. I don't have any kids."

She took her cue from his tone and didn't ask any more questions for a while. Her eyes made a search of the room from left to right, lingered on the silk-embroidered Chinese

190

tapestries, the huge canopied bed. She giggled, but the noise came out strained. "Are the sheets satin?"

"They might be." Spraggue put his hand on her chin, tilted her face up, and brushed her lips with his mouth. "I wish we could check them out. But you're giggling and I've never heard you do that before, and you're totally exhausted, and possibly in what people call a state of shock. And my aunt would probably interrupt us by sending Pierce in with a glass of warm milk at a crucial moment."

He had to lean far over to kiss her; she was so small.

"Good night," he said.

"Where will you be? What are you going to do?"

"I don't know."

She turned away. He could hear her deliberate deep breathing, see her back straighten. When she faced him again, her mouth had stiffened into a line of resolve. "Look," she said, and her voice had iron in it, "it may have been your house, but it was my brother and I'm not planning to go nicely off to bed, thank you, while you plot revenge alone."

"Go to sleep. Nothing major is going to happen tonight, believe me. I'm too damn tired."

He left her there, gazing into the gilt-framed mirror, retraced his steps downstairs.

Back in the library, Aunt Mary stared at him and he could read a hundred questions in her eyes, some dealing with the length of his stay upstairs. Pierce poured him a cup of steaming coffee. He shook his head, and the butler, with an upward flick of an eyebrow, brought the cup to Mary instead.

"The radio is calling it arson," Mary said. "I've been monitoring the police band since you called."

He sank onto the green velvet sofa, noticing that Dora or

191

Pierce or someone had smoothed out the indentation of Sharon's head on the pillow.

"Are you all right, Michael?"

He leaned forward, elbows pushing into his thighs, chin and mouth pressed into his triangled hands. "Great."

She nodded at Pierce, who took his silent leave, closing the oak doors behind him. Sprague shut his eyes and listened to the clock tick, to the swishing of Mary's slippers across the parquet floor, the splashing of liquid in a glass. She put the brandy glass in his hand, startling him by her silent approach. She waited until he'd downed half the glass.

"Michael—" she began.

"Please. No questions tonight, Mary Paper?"

"The *Globe*?"

"Writing paper, please."

"In the desk."

She followed him to the huge mahogany block that sat in the exact center of the vast Oriental rug, opened the top right-hand drawer and set a sheet of blank stationery on the maroon leather blotter.

He didn't bother sitting in his great-grandfather's leather armchair. He leaned over, lifted a pen out of a marble block and wrote, handed the piece of paper to Mary. Two lines of scraggly print danced across it.

"Tomorrow at nine o'clock," he said. "I want these two men here. Can you get them for me?"

She studied the list. "Will they want to come?"

"Hand them a line. Either of them should be willing to dance to any tune you want to whistle."

"Nine o'clock."

"Get me up by eight. I'll wake Sharon. She's got to be in on it. And I'd like you and Pierce to be available too."

"No explanation?"

He tried to stretch his mouth into a taut smile.

"Tomorrow," he said.

THIRTY

Spraggue shifted his weight forward in the huge leather chair. The change of clothes he always kept in the tower room felt stiff, unworn and overstarched. They didn't stink of smoke, though, and he was grateful for that. He'd spent almost an hour last night—this morning—standing under a pounding, steaming shower, trying to get the burning stench out of his hair, his nostrils, out of his mind. He nodded up at Pierce who stood ten paces inside the library's double doors.

"On schedule?" he asked.

"To the minute."

"How are they doing?"

"They're staring at their wristwatches. Mr. Heineman arrived first, showing a great deal more politeness than one is used to from a member of the press. I sat him in the west parlor as you instructed. Mr. Eichenhorn followed ten minutes later. More of a nervous type, wanted me to know he had no time to waste. I ushered him into the west parlor also."

"Reactions?"

"Definite recognition on both sides. Cordial hellos of great wariness exchanged. I should say Mr. Eichenhorn seems more apprehensive about Mr. Heineman's presence than vice versa, but that may merely be a sign of the times. Who could possibly make the news media uneasy?''

''Another reporter.''

''Very true.''

''Show Eichenhorn in. Then make polite noises at Heineman and reassure him that Mary will be with him soon.''

''Done.''

Pierce closed the heavy doors on the way out. Spraggue moved away from the desk, crossed the Oriental rug, the parquet border, and mounted the wrought-iron stairs to the open balcony that ran around the second story of the massive room. He would be able to see Eichenhorn. Eichenhorn wouldn't see him. Not at first.

''Mrs. Hillman will be with you in a moment,'' Pierce rumbled, holding the door, ushering Eichenhorn inside. ''Please take a seat by the desk.''

''I'm really running late—'' Donagher's campaign manager began. Pierce must have frowned at him. Pierce's frown left people unable to finish sentences.

''I'm sure you won't have long to wait,'' the butler intoned. The doors banged shut.

Eichenhorn took his time meandering over to the desk. His suit looked rumpled and hung across his narrow hunched shoulders no better than it would have hung on a bent wire hanger. He whistled under his breath as his eyes scanned the shelves of leather-bound volumes. He admired the Cézanne over the mantle, strolled across the room to the bay window, whistled softly again before sinking into the smaller of two leather armchairs in front of the desk. Spraggue took the steps noiselessly, cleared his throat when he was some six feet behind Eichenhorn.

The campaign manager jumped, half turned in his chair, stared. His lips compressed into a tight line and he shook his head.

"I told the senator I shouldn't come. Not today, not so early in the campaign."

"And he said?" Spraggue settled himself in the chair behind the desk.

"He said we couldn't afford to ignore Mary Spraggue Hillman, that with a flick of her checkbook, she could win us the race."

"Donagher's a smart man."

"What do you want? Do I get to see your aunt or was that just a come on?"

"It was a kindness. I thought the questions I have to ask you might be less embarrassing here, in private, than they would be in Donagher's company. Or at the police station."

"What questions? Why the hell should I answer any more of your questions?" Eichenhorn stood up. "I'm going to tell the senator about this. He'll be—"

"You recognize the man you were sitting next to out there?"

Eichenhorn had turned away and taken two steps towards the double doors. He pivoted on one heel, his face a wary mask. "Some TV news guy. Channel 4. I think the name is Heineman."

"Very good. If you walk out the door, I'm going to invite him to take your place here. And I'm going to tell him what I would have liked to ask you, if you hadn't been in such a hurry."

Eichenhorn retraced his footsteps. "Such as?"

"Sit down. Would you like some coffee?"

"No. You're pressuring me and I don't like it."

"You're going to like it even less. Sit down."

Reluctantly, indignation puffing up inside him like air in an inflating balloon, the man sat.

"I want to know where you got the bottle of Parnate," Spraggue said.

Eichenhorn stared. "The bottle of what?"

"Parnate, Mr. Emery."

Eichenhorn's fingers clutched the arms of the chair, then balled themselves into fists. He said, "I don't know what you're talking about."

"Let me tell you then. It won't take long and you may find it entertaining—and conclusive, the way I did. Act One: at a funeral an old cop calls a guy I know as Murray, Marty. The old cop could have been drunk or mistaken."

"Yeah."

"Act Two: a bottle of pills appears in a dead man's bathroom, *after* the police have already searched it. I notice some marks on the front door lock of this dead man's apartment, the marks of a not very talented housebreaker. Are you following this?"

Eichenhorn nodded.

"Act Three: the fingerprints of the man called Murray turn out to be the same as those of a boy named Marty, a boy who used to pick locks so badly the cops could always nail him—"

"Those records are sealed. You can't use them in court."

"I didn't say anything about court. I said something about TV news. Something about a slip of the tongue while I'm talking to a reporter. I'll be very sorry. I'll say I was misquoted. Senator Donagher's going to be very pleased to learn he has an ex-burglar as a campaign manager. So are the voters."

"What do you want?"

"I want to know whose medicine you planted in Collatos' bathroom. And why."

"Jesus—"

"And it better sound good."

Eichenhorn shoved his wire-rimmed glasses back on his narrow nose, wiped his hand across his forehead. "Are you taping this?"

"Not now. This is your chance to come clean, off the record. When Heineman joins us, if he joins us, then we'll do some recording.''

Eichenhorn closed his eyes and bowed his head; his Adam's apple bobbed up and down in his scrawny neck. He glanced behind him before he spoke, started off whispering, as if that would defeat any undetected listening device, frustrate any unseen eavesdropper. "The way I figured it,'' he began shakily, "it would get the heat off the senator. The sooner Collatos' death is cleared up, the sooner the whole fracas dies down, the sooner the papers go back to printing political stories instead of crime stories. See? So I wanted it out of the way. It was the wrong kind of publicity. Donagher doesn't need stuff like that.''

"And you just happened to have a bottle of pills handy that would make the whole story, the whole accidental death garbage, come out right. Whose were they?''

Eichenhorn shrugged.

"This isn't hard to figure,'' Spraggue said. "You live at Donagher's place. You didn't want those pills over there, so they have to belong to you or Donagher or Donagher's wife or one of the kids. If I had the time, I'd just check the medical records of every member of the Donagher machine—''

"They're confidential. Medical records are confidential.''

"There is very little information that can't be bought in this world. Understand that. But I don't have a lot of time to play around with. So I am asking you to make a choice. Either tell me where you got the bottle of Parnate, or meet the press as a reformed burglar. Maybe Donagher will weather the storm. Maybe he'll even keep you on, bluff it out, say he knew about your record all along and he's all for rehabilitation. But my bet is that it would be a big mistake to admit openly that your right-hand man, a man who is, I'm sure, lusting for appointed office in the government, is a crook. People might assume that all politicians are crooks, but they hate to see it spelled out in the papers in black and white.''

''They're my pills.''

''Who's your doctor?''

Silence.

''Who suggested that you plant them in Collatos' medicine chest?''

''I was working on my own,'' Eichenhorn said faintly. ''I thought it would be easy. I mean, why the hell shouldn't Collatos have been depressed? I thought the cops would find the bottle and close the case, say he'd been taking those antidepressant pills and then the hit of speed on top of it killed him. And that would be the end of the story. We could get on with the campaign. I planted them too late, I guess.''

''It was a stupid thing to do.''

''I can see that now. I've done a lot of stupid things in my life and the one thing I've learned from my mistakes is not to compound them by screwing people who've been good to you. I'm not going to talk to you about anyone else on Donagher's staff. I'll resign. Then your goddam TV reporter won't be able to hurt him.''

Spragge stared into the opaque blue eyes behind the gold-rimmed glasses, and found unexpected steel. Murray's long fingers gripped the armrests. His knuckles were white as chalk. He sat as straight as Spragge had ever seen him sit, with his shoulders flung back, as squared as nature would ever let them be. Eichenhorn had drawn the line; he'd rat on himself, not on others.

Spragge found himself admiring the defiant man in the chair more than he'd thought possible five minutes earlier. He said, ''There are a couple of other items I would like.''

''What makes you think I'd give you anything?''

''They're too trivial to fight over. I can call Donagher and get them on the phone. Or get him to order you to give them to me.''

"What?"

"Number one: a list of people on Donagher's staff."

"And number two?"

"A list of all the places Donagher and Collatos went the day before the marathon."

"That's all?"

"That's all."

Eichenhorn sighed. "I don't suppose I could bargain with little items like that," he said.

"Try."

"If I give them to you, now—I have Donagher's appointment book with me—would you wait until after the election to tell the press about me, about Martin Emery?"

"You're a rotten burglar," Spraggue said.

"I know. But I'm a good campaign manager." Eichenhorn tried a sickly smile. "I'm not even a bad person. I haven't done anything illegal since—"

"But you insist those pills are yours?"

Eichenhorn swallowed. "Yes."

Spraggue rang the buzzer on the desk. "Pierce will show you out as soon as you've written down the timetable for Sunday and the names of Donagher's staff workers."

"What's it worth to you?"

"I won't say anything to the press for now. Not today. The election is still a long way off."

It took ten minutes for Eichenhorn to write out the lists, five more to relay instructions to Aunt Mary, shake hands with a puzzled Heineman, kiss Sharon on the cheek in a manner far more brotherly than he felt. At ten fifteen, Spraggue left the house.

THIRTY-ONE

The Porsche was where he'd left it, but Mary's chauffeur had polished it until it gleamed. Might as well have smacked a steal-me-first sign across the front bumper. The windshield sparkled so brightly he was afraid he wouldn't be able to see out of it. The gas tank, close to empty when he'd careened up the driveway in cold anger, had been filled. He wondered if the parking tickets in the dash compartment had been laundered.

Half a mile from the house, where the twisty driveway looped in front of the stone gatehouse, he pulled the car over and stopped.

He couldn't have stayed ten minutes longer at the mansion. Already childhood memories were closing in: the sensation of unseen wheels turning, of unheard oiled machinery grinding relentlessly away. His shoes had been polished, his rumpled, sooty clothes removed while he slept. Life under great-grandfather Davison Spraggue's slate roof was lived in the old man's shadow. It had a rhythm foreign to this generation's renegade Spraggue, a seductive and hateful rhythm.

The windows of the gatehouse were dark and bare. Mary had probably done her worst and fired the gardener. Spraggue slid across the seat and out the passenger door, walked up the flagged pathway, peeked in the half-glassed door. Empty. He could move his things temporarily to the gatehouse, whatever things he had left. Aunt Mary wouldn't like it. Well, she didn't have to face the ghosts in the tower room.

He walked back to the car, got in.

What would he have left to put in the gatehouse? His fingers tightened on the steering wheel. Furniture he didn't give a damn about; he hadn't had any furniture to speak of on Fayerweather Street. He'd had a drawerful of yellowing theatrical programs, some photographs, a few trifling oddball gifts . . . Kate's letters. Visible, tangible backups for wayward memory, physical evidence of the fine-drawn threads that webbed him to others. The two paintings his mother had loved . . .

Why fire? He flexed his shoulders, loosened his hands on the wheel and let them drop forward into his lap, forced himself to consider the fire dispassionately, from a distance. To warn him off? Off of what? To destroy? Destroy what? The files he'd brought in from Pete's house that very day, possibly under the nose of secret watcher? He hadn't noticed, had hardly shot so much as a glance out the cab's rear window. The reckless between-lanes driving of the cabbie, the memory of Sharon Collatos' shower-damp face, had occupied his thoughts much too completely. Was the object to be destroyed the envelope Sharon had brought, the one that he'd pocketed at the time of the fire, the one that he'd transferred to this new stiff jacket?

Had the arsonist meant to kill? Had he waited, shivering in the bushes, for homecoming footfalls on the concrete path, for lights to blossom in the upstairs windows?

Mary, he knew, would understand his need to escape, realize that he wouldn't feel up to any social banter with the rage still in him, compounded by the distaste he felt at his role of inquisitor. Hadn't taken much to get poor Eichenhorn quivering. Maybe he should audition for nastier parts: Reverend Parris in *The Crucible,* Iago, Richard III.

Mary would begin to unravel one end of the ball of yarn. Mary understood what had to be done.

God, that it were as simple as picking at a ball of yarn until the one lost end came free. It was more like probing a tangled skein of writhing serpents knotted on the floor, trying, barehanded, to isolate three, possibly four, poisonous heads, before one rose to strike.

He jammed a clenched fist into his palm. He needed activity to ease the rage, needed some physical release. He thought about jumping out of the car, racing madly three times around the gatehouse, and the absurdity of the image almost made him smile. He had to keep everything clear, everything under control, especially now, with the goal so near, with the serpents' heads in view.

Aunt Mary, Pierce, Sharon, Heineman had two assignments between the four of them. Mary had already begun; by the time he'd consumed breakfast, she'd had the contents of both cardboard boxes—all the files that had escaped the police search of Pete's apartment, the fire, the fall to the ground, the rocky ride in the trunk of the Porsche—spread out across acres of vast dining room table. She would have an eager aide in Sharon, a reliable one in Pierce. Heineman had invaluable sources of information. And Heineman had agreed to help, knowing the results might affect Lila Donagher. Spraggue wondered how the newsman would react if the facts tended to show Lila in a less than favorable light.

If Pete had been killed by a double dose of poison, one or more hits of nonlethal Parnate coupled with one hit of nonlethal speed, the origin of the more exotic drug was vital. That was the second item Mary and company would have to discover. After the mammoth task of reading, sorting, making some semblance of sense of the police files, they'd have to sift through medical histories, lie to doctors and pharmacists, check newspaper files. Another monumental chore that might come to nothing, might wind up smashed against a rock of medical ethics.

He pulled the list of Donagher's Sunday appointments out of his pocket and smoothed it on one knee. The third serpent head belonged to him.

10:00 A.M.	Mass at St. Columbkille's with wife and kids
11:30	Handshaking at Dunkin' Donuts, Market and North Beacon Street
12:00	Lunch at home; meeting with staffers
1:30 P.M.	Running (Location?)
4:00	Televised interview with Edward Heineman, Channel 4
5:30	Eliot Lounge
7:30	Pre-Marathon dinner party at home

Assuming that Pete had tagged along like the faithful bodyguard he was, assuming that he'd stayed with Senator Donagher like a shadow, one of those locales was the key. At one of those places, Pete had turned up the missing envelope, along with a typewriter that matched. And at one of those locales, had Pete's assassin found him, slipped him a drug in a drink?

Spraggue closed his eyes. They felt like they'd been rolled in grit. How long before the race would the drug have had to be administered? He'd have to check that out, have Mary check that out. . . .

He heard the click of the car door opening on the passenger side and jumped.

Sharon Collatos turned her back to him to sit down, drew her legs in, and swiveled on the seat to face front. "You can go now," she said.

"Wait a minute—"

"Your aunt said I'd probably find you here, pulled over by the gatehouse, thinking or asleep."

"She was supposed to—"

"Keep me nice and safe and close to home while you went out and had the fun. Well, they've got plenty of researchers back there, believe me. That Heineman guy has got sources you wouldn't believe. He's plugged into everything. And what he isn't plugged into, your aunt's got covered. So they don't need me to hunt and fetch."

"Neither do I."

"Oh yes you do. A man asking questions alone is conspicuous. A man with a woman is casual. A woman can ask questions and get answers a man can't. You'll see."

"Did my aunt rehearse you?"

"I'm going with you."

"Last night was bad enough. I'm not setting you up for target practice."

"How do you know it wasn't the other way around? That I didn't put you in danger? That whoever set the fire wasn't following me, not you? Are you always this self-centered?"

"Which question do you want me to answer first?"

"Where are we going?"

He pointed at the top of the list. "Church."

She smiled and said, "But I didn't bring a hat."

THIRTY-TWO

The priest at St. Columbkille's Church was averse to discussing the affairs of his most illustrious parishioner with individuals he strongly suspected of being undercover reporters for the heathen press. The rectory next door had two typewriters—one ancient manual, one electric—neither of which proved to be the one Pete Collatos had used to type his sister's address.

Dunkin' Donuts had a smiling, cooperative waitress, and strong, hot coffee, but no typewriters. The lady behind the counter remembered Donagher's Sunday visit, thought he was just about as handsome as a movie star, and was definitely going to vote for him.

By the time they'd blitzed down Eichenhorn's list as far as the Eliot Lounge, both of them needed a drink. Spraggue pulled one of the backless imitation red leather stools away from the pale oak bar and Sharon slid onto it with a sigh. As he sat on the next stool over, Spraggue heard a thunk and looked down. Sharon's shoes lay on the red tile floor. Her stockinged feet rested on the brass rail at the base of the bar.

"Tired?" he asked, raising one eyebrow.

"Your aunt said her secretary had the same size feet I did, but she didn't warn me about the woman's devotion to style. These things are torture traps. The heels must be four inches high."

"What'll you have?" the bartender asked.

It was only three thirty, but the lounge had a healthy sprinkling of customers. Three men fed quarters into the video games on the lower level. A middle-aged couple held hands across one of the small round tables against the far wall, underneath a collage of framed photographs of famous runners: Bill Rodgers, arms raised in victory, laurel wreath encircling his brow; Alberto Salazar, collapsing into the arms of another runner. Two men sat at the bar, one young, one old, one stool between them, marking their separateness. They had the remote look of businessmen a long way from home.

"Wine," said Spraggue. "Red. Not chilled."

"White," said Sharon. "Cold."

To the right of the bar, a sign read: Only 353 days until the Marathon. At the Eliot, the watering hole for Boston's elite runners, the site of the annual postrace bash, they took their marathon seriously.

To the left of the bar, a TV set droned. The two businessmen glanced at it every once in awhile.

"You're not a drinking man," said Sharon.

"Not hard liquor. A confirmed wino."

"I never know what to order in a bar. I'm not fond of beer and most hard stuff tastes like the medicine I hated when I was a kid. And if you order one of those sweet drinks—you know, Brandy Alexanders, and stuff like that—the bartender gives you that look, that isn't-that-just-like-a-woman look." Her smile twisted ruefully. "On the whole, I stay out of bars."

"I'd make a rotten bar fly, too."

"You make a good investigator," she said, shrugging her shoulders in her too large suit jacket. "You're relentless." Spraggue wondered whether the gray suit had come from the same secretary. It was certainly more appropriate for the work they'd been doing than last night's coral dress. Ah, that coral dress.

"Spraggue?"

"Huh?"

"Where were you?"

"Someday I'll tell you. I'm sorry. What were you saying?"

She took a careful sip from her too full wineglass. "The bartender doesn't look too friendly."

"That's because we ordered wine. Scotch is a good bar drink. Bourbon. A shot of rye. A beer. Look, I'll talk to the bartender and you call my aunt, all right? See if she's turned up anything and tell her our next location will be Channel 4, over on Soldiers Field Road. She can reach us there if disaster strikes. Or inspiration."

"Okay."

The bartender, whose name was Johnny, didn't like answering questions; he went as far as asking to see Spraggue's investigator's license. He didn't get into reading the fine print, like the expiration date. He didn't have access to a typewriter. He said, with a wry twist of his mustached mouth, that his patrons rarely required one. Didn't keep a notary in his back pocket either. He did recall seeing Senator Donagher and Pete Collatos the Sunday before the big race. He remembered them complaining about the crowds out running earlier that afternoon.

"Where was that?" Spraggue asked.

"Got me. My guess is they were running a track. Wouldn't complain about crowds on some random street. Complain about traffic on the streets, let me tell you. Some of those cars, man, they aim right at you, try to give you a thrill. I'd rather run a track. Level, too."

One of the men from downstairs requested change for a dollar, fodder for the insatiable video game. As he passed a crumpled bill over Spraggue's shoulder, he joined in the conversation.

"You want to know where the senator ran the day before the race?"

"Hey, Joey," the bartender said, beaming a welcoming grin at the stringy pale-faced Pac-Man addict. "How are ya? Yeah, man, Joey was here. All the guys were here."

"Give Joey a drink," Spraggue said.

"Just a beer," Joey said. "Thanks, man."

Sharon returned, slipped unobtrusively back onto her barstool. She hadn't put her shoes on to go to the phone. Her bare feet combined with her too large suit made her look like she'd been caught dressing up in her mother's clothes.

"Sure," Joey said, bragging a bit, caught up in the importance the others gave his words, "I know where the senator ran. Cause I kidded him about running the day before, you know, the day you're supposed to rest up, and he said, hell, a couple of times around 1.8 wasn't gonna kill him."

"1.8?" Spraggue said.

"Yeah, man. 1.8 miles. The Chestnut Hill Reservoir."

THIRTY-THREE

The Porsche sported a glowing red-orange parking violation ticket stuck under the windshield wiper. Spraggue stuffed it in the glove compartment. Sharon gaped at the number of relatives it joined.

"Dear God," she said. "Is that your hobby?"

Spraggue shrugged.

"Don't you fear the Denver Boot?"

"It's a game I play with the city of Boston. See, sooner or later, this car is going to disappear; every other decent car I've owned has been stolen while legally parked in Boston. Whoever rips off this one is going to get a bonus: a lifetime supply of parking violations. Can't you just see some joyriding son-of-a-bitch coming out of the package store half-drunk to find his newly stolen chariot wearing the boot? I look on it as an experiment; I want to see who gets the car first: the crooks or the cops. I'm betting on the thieves."

He could have taken Commonwealth Avenue all the way to the reservoir, but a line of sullen drivers crawled along, honking at left-turners and parking place scouts, so he turned right and got onto Storrow Drive, traced that all the way to Parsons Street, then zigzagged through Brighton back to Commonwealth. He parked in a tow zone and Sharon shook her head reproachfully.

The afternoon had turned gray and chilly. A low-hanging layer of clouds blotted out the sun and a sharp breeze belied the season. The reservoir trail was almost deserted. Spragque hoped the absence of runners was due to the promised rain, not the fear of a random sniper. He stopped a few panting college students to ask if they'd been out the day before the marathon. Faint hope. No takers. He and Sharon circled the reservoir once. She shivered.

"Want to wait in the car?"

Her temper flared. "I don't know why you're doing this, but if you're doing it, I'll go along."

"Did my aunt hire you to be my bodyguard?"

"Nobody hired me to do anything. Nobody hired you either, so I'm told."

"I'm working for myself."

"I could pay you—"

"Forget it."

"I can't forget it. Michael, look at me. Are you doing this because of what I said at the funeral? Are you doing it for me?"

"Why?"

"Because I'm not a reward."

"What do you mean?"

"I've kissed you; you've kissed me. Once I think it was desperation and once relief. I like you. I do. But I don't want to have that hanging over me. The idea that you would do something like this, something dangerous, so that I would— Well, just don't play knight in shining armor on my account."

"Wouldn't dream of it. Too uncomfortable."

"I'm serious."

"Me, too. I learned a long time ago never to confuse women with trophies."

"Well, I'm no prize, believe me. I'm an over-the-hill, dumpy, divorced schoolteacher—"

"Go sit in the car. It's not locked. You're a beautiful woman in a foul mood. Either that or your feet are killing you—"

"And I haven't noticed any typewriters in the goddam bushes," she said, ignoring his protest, making no move to leave.

"Neither have I."

"Then what are we doing here? Your poor aunt thinks we're at Channel 4. She said she might pack everything up and go over there. Heineman's got some files he's anxious to look at, and they'd be able to check out all the typewriters while they keep on with their research."

"She'll wait for us."

"That doesn't answer my question."

"Your brother went here; we go here."

"And what do we do?"

210

"What investigators generally do. Wait. Listen. Absorb. Waste time. Hope for divine guidance."

"How long do they generally wait? On a cold day?"

"Want my jacket?"

"No." The response was automatic, a reflex of independent stubbornness that made Spraggue smile. He stopped and stripped off his windbreaker.

"All right," she said, reluctantly. "Yes. I do."

He helped her drape the jacket over her shoulders. The contact, the isolation, the windy chill made him draw her into the circle of his arms. She stepped back, turned away.

"It wasn't just desperation and just relief, you know," he said. "I think there might be some basic chemistry involved, a little bit of attraction . . ."

She kept her head down, stared at the brown, dead grass, slipped the arms of his windbreaker over those of her own borrowed jacket.

"You're freezing," he said, when she failed to respond. "Goose bumps and all. Want to race me over to the Rodgers Running Center? Warm you up."

"Run in these shoes? I can barely walk. Mine—"

He remembered. Abandoned on the second floor of the Cambridge house. Burned or drowned. Ruined. Delicate leather straps charred to black dust. Along with— He blocked the thoughts, but the rage must have translated itself into speed. Sharon tugged at his arm.

"Could we go a little slower?"

"Sorry."

They succeeded in crossing the complex intersection at Beacon Street and Chestnut Hill Avenue only by ignoring the traffic lights completely. Bill Rodgers Running Center boasted a blue and gold sign. They descended a few steps to the basement level doorway.

One lanky, bearded man slouched behind the cash register to the left of the door. Another, this one with a blond beard in contrast to the cash register man's dark beard, knelt on the wooden floor, busily lacing a shoe on a woman customer's foot. Everyone in the place was uniformly thin. The WeightWatchers next door would go out of business if they had to depend on the clientele of the Running Center.

"Can I help you?" the dark-bearded man asked. He had a voice as soft as his silky beard.

Spraggue made sure his words were loud enough for all the runners in the store to hear. "I'm looking for anyone who was racing around here the Sunday before the marathon."

After thirty seconds of dead air, a blond teenager standing by a magazine rack muttered, "Jeez, there must have been millions of people out running."

"It's important," Spraggue said. "Did anyone here run around the reservoir the day before the marathon?"

With a clatter of feet, a few other customers, intrigued by the loud voices, came down three steps from the small ground-level room that held, besides merchandise, many of Rodgers' own trophies, as well as a glass case containing the running shoes he'd worn to win his first Boston championship in '75.

A woman with thick blonde hair stopped pushing hangers around a circular rack of colorful racing tops and said, "I did."

Spraggue asked the follow-up question quietly, so certain was he of the negative response.

"Did you happen to see Senator Donagher? Running with a dark, curly haired man."

The blond-bearded sales clerk who'd been fitting shoes stood up. "Pete Collatos?" he asked.

Spraggue nodded.

"If you're a reporter, nobody here wants to say anything

212

for the papers. They've made a big enough hash of it as it is. You read them?'' he said indignantly to the woman who'd agreed to buy a pair of blue Adidas. ''You'd think running was a hazard to your health. Probably written by some guy with so much belly flab he can't even see his feet.''

''I'm not a reporter,'' Spraggue said. ''A friend of Pete's. I was wondering if he came in here that day. That Sunday. Were you open?''

''Not actually open. Not to the general public. But we weren't actually closed either, if you know what I mean.''

''Did Pete come to the party?''

''He might have. I know he was in that week. Senator Donagher, no, I don't think so.''

Spraggue sighed. If Donagher hadn't come in, then Pete hadn't either. Me and my shadow travel together.

''Do you have a typewriter here? In the office?''

''Michael!'' It was Sharon's voice, quiet but electric. It sliced through the room like a surgeon's scalpel and everyone turned to look at her.

She was standing by the bulletin board to the right of the door, her left hand uplifted, pointing at a fragment of paper pinned to the upper right-hand corner of the crowded board.

''Pete wrote that,'' she said in a faraway voice. ''I think.''

In the midst of much folded newspaper articles, ads for running clinics, chiropractors, and practitioners of sports medicine, folders extolling races, some upcoming, some held months ago, was a scrap of paper, folded over and tacked shut. *B.D.* it said on the outside fold. Brian Donagher.

Spraggue removed a blue pushpin, took the note down, unfolded it. The room was so still he could hear Sharon breathing.

Sorry, was all it said. *Back soon. If you need me, call 555-8945.*

Spraggue read the number twice.

It was one he knew well.

THIRTY-FOUR

In the next six hours, Spraggue learned many things. He learned that the dun-colored metal chairs in the barren Channel 4 conference room were not designed to be sat in for six hours at a stretch. He discovered that the hitherto viceless Ed Heineman chain-smoked cigarettes that smelled like old worn socks, and kept a bottle of cheap bourbon in the locked desk drawer of his second floor office. He couldn't be sure that Sharon always liked to work with her shoes off; the shoes given her by Aunt Mary were so uncomfortable she couldn't stand them. He didn't have much left to learn about Mary's working habits. He knew that she had a habit of humming soft tuneless mumbles under her breath. Nothing could cure her of it as she was totally unconscious of doing it. After a while her humming blurred into the background, like the spurting radiator and the clicking, heeltapping, typing office sounds outside the conference room's closed door.

He learned that none of the thirty-eight typewriters at Channel 4 had been the one Pete Collatos sat down at that Sunday to type his sister's address on an envelope.

Heineman sat at one end of the long rectangular table, Mary at the other, separated by their likes and dislikes of cigarettes and humming. Spraggue and Sharon shared one of the long sides of the rectangle, leaving the window view of the Charles River unobscured except for Pierce's balding egg-shaped head.

At 7:30 P.M., Spraggue glanced at his watch and experienced a jolt of true panic before remembering that the opera was being performed that night. No play tonight. No applause.

The objects of study had started in a pile at the center of the table, been distributed by a grab-bag method and, by general agreement, were passed, once studied, clockwise around the table. Every hour, on the hour, the assembled company took a five-minute break during which complaint was the main order of business.

For the first hour, Spraggue pored over the files he'd discovered at Collatos' apartment, old files, dating back twelve, fourteen years, that Pete had had access to as liaison to the Arson Squad. He read them the way he'd told the others to read, as if studying for a major exam. You weren't sure what questions were going to be asked. Memorize all relevant facts, names, dates. Take notes.

The second hour he read the medical examiner's report on Collatos' body, followed by the same doctor's commentary on the remains of JoJo Stearns.

The third hour, he studied the list of Donagher's staff workers provided by Eichenhorn, read the biographies Pierce, Mary, and Heineman had researched during the day: Martin Emery né Murray Eichenhorn; JoJo Stearns; Arnold Gravier, the tan raincoat man; Lila Donagher née Lila Bennett; Senator Brian Donagher. Heineman had, on request, provided his own résumé to round out the pile.

The fourth hour, he spent deciphering Mary's spidery scrawl concerning the drug Parnate.

He learned that Parnate (tranylcypromine) is the most commonly used nonhydrazine monoamine oxidase (MAO) inhibitor and is not toxic to the liver. He read a lot of other multisyllabic mumbo jumbo. He scowled in Mary's direction but she was busily reading and humming and not visibly affected by his glare. He suspected that she had cribbed her entire report on the drug straight from some medical textbook, or worse, that she had not, and understood clearly the entire complex mechanism of the drug. You could never be sure with Aunt Mary.

He learned that Parnate is structurally related to amphetamine. That MAO inhibitors are not specific for MAO but inhibit many normal enzymatic functions and therefore patients taking Parnate should not be given other drugs affecting the central nervous system. That such patients should be warned against the use of alcohol.

He remembered that he had entertained uncharitable thoughts about Pete Collatos after that last late-night phone call. That one of those thoughts had been that Collatos was drunk.

He learned that MAO inhibitors are readily absorbed by the intestinal tract. He knew that already. No needles. No needle marks. Pete had swallowed the substance that had killed him. But when? How? Why?

He put his elbows on the table and cradled his forehead in his hands.

"In 1964," he read, "Parnate was withdrawn from the market because of its marked interaction with many drugs or foods. It subsequently was replaced on the market with the restriction that it be used only in hospitalized depressed patients.

"Cheese, natural or aged, has been implicated as a cause of hypertensive crises in patients treated with these drugs. An average serving of such cheese contains enough tyramine to cause a marked rise in blood pressure. Other foods high in tyramine that have produced this toxic syndrome are red wine, chicken liver, yeast, coffee, pickled herring, bean pods, and canned figs. Deaths have been reported in patients who have ingested moderate amounts of these foods. Symptoms include increased body temperature, marked rise in blood pressure, severe headache, and in those cases in which death resulted, intracranial bleeding. In addition to tyramine, other sympathomimetic amines, such as amphetamine, should not be taken by patients receiving MAO inhibitors.''

He reread the list of foods. "Pickled herring, bean pods, canned figs . . ." He suspected Mary of adding those three items in a vain effort to interject some humor into her dry text.

"God." Sharon gave out a sigh that startled the rest of the group. "I'm not even seeing this stuff anymore. It's all starting to blur together. Meaningless figures, names I never heard of . . ."

"I haven't got a clue yet," Mary admitted sadly. "Or, if I do, I haven't yet recognized it as such."

"I wish we could just dump all this stuff in some computer," Heineman said, "and pull out the right answers."

"Wouldn't work." Spraggue yawned and stretched his arms out over his head. Something in his neck gave an audible popping sound. "To use a computer, you have to program it. To program it, you have to know the questions. You have to know the questions to find the answers."

"So what are the questions? What are we looking for?"

"Oddities. Coincidences. Repetitions. Anything that strikes you as unusual."

After a pause, Mary said hesitantly, "Well, I think the only oddity is Lila Donagher. She seems to disappear from time to time, just take off for New York. Her children don't go with her, and that's the only time she seems to be separated from them. The gossip is that she's being treated for alcholism—"

"Lila's no alcoholic," Heineman interrupted.

"She doesn't drink like one," Spraggue agreed, thinking back to their lunch at the Harvest.

"Exactly my point," Mary said. "She may have been receiving treatments for depression. Possibly alcoholism is more forgivable in a politician's wife than depression. Remember the fuss over poor Senator Eagleton? I vote for Lila as the person most likely to have access to Parnate."

Spraggue said. "It's not enough though."

"Damn right, it's not enough," Heineman said defensively. "She's a damned fine woman. She liked Pete Collatos—"

"Better than she likes her husband? She was supposed to hand Donagher his water bottle. She never showed up. If she had access to Parnate—"

"Who kills a spouse like that?" Sharon interrupted. "Today? With divorce so simple? No-fault divorce?"

"Husbands kill wives; wives kill husbands," Mary said. "Read the newspapers."

"Yes," Sharon countered. "But in crimes of passion. Not coldbloodedly. With the gun in the nightstand drawer. With a kitchen knife. Not with fancy drugs and devious schemes."

Heineman gave a vigorous nod as if he'd personally scored the point and Spraggue said, "I think we'd better get back to work."

"How much longer—" Sharon began.

"Until everybody's seen everything."

Pierce bent unblinkingly back to his task. He hadn't uttered a word in several hours.

"Or until we go blind," Mary said cheerfully.

They toiled on. The radiator droned regularly now. Mary had found a tune and was humming variations. Heineman

218

went out twice for cigarettes. Sharon slid her feet in and out of her shoes, wincing. Pierce took to rocking backwards on the legs of his chair until Mary reprimanded him for making her nervous. Her remarks almost opened the way for a free-for-all. Tempers were wearing thin.

"Oh," Heineman said. It burst out of him like a muffled explosion. He stared at his reading, ignoring the fact that it had happened.

"What?" Spraggue said.

The reporter started, looked quickly at his wristwatch. "I didn't realize it was so late," he said. "I've got a story I have to finish up for tomorrow night. My secretary should have reminded me. I told her where to reach me—"

His unsteady hands tried to shuffle the piece of paper he was reading under one of its fellows.

"Excuse me," he said. "This shouldn't take more than ten minutes. Just checking a source."

Spraggue's eyes met Mary's across the table. His eyebrows went up and, quietly, he pushed back his chair.

He opened the door cautiously. The hallway was clear. Spraggue closed his eyes and heard faint footsteps. To the left or right? He chose the left, guided by memory. Heineman's office had been to the left. He remembered the name plaque on the door.

He walked quickly now, silently, staying close to the side of the corridor, his right shoulder an inch from the cinderblock wall. He took a right at an intersection, pausing and peering around the corner before committing his body to the turn. He saw a door swing shut: Heineman's office door.

He stood outside the door in the darkened hallway, pressed his ear against the smooth-grained wood and listened. First, a whoosh, as if another door had opened and closed, then nothing. He twisted the doorknob and walked into Heineman's secretary's domain. Empty.

Applying his ear to the inner door, he heard the unmistakable sound of someone dialing a telephone. The noise was faint and far away. Heineman's voice was a distant, undecipherable rumble.

He glanced quickly at the secretary's desk. A red light shone on a beige, touch-tone telephone. Line 1 was engaged. He slid along the beige carpeting, holding his breath, carefully lifted the receiver.

"Listen," Heineman was saying, his normally mellow voice as tense as Spraggue had ever heard it, "Put Mrs. Donagher on immediately. This is urgent, understand?"

Spraggue thought it was Eichenhorn's voice on the other end, wasn't sure. Whoever it was didn't want to bother Mrs. Donagher at this ungodly hour.

Heineman said, "Goddammit, just get Mrs. Donagher. You'll be sorry if you don't."

Spraggue's eyebrow shot up. He heard reluctant acquiescence from the unidentified voice, followed by a click on the line. It took almost five minutes for Lila to come to the phone. Spraggue, crouched over the desk in the dark, hoped Heineman wouldn't give up. If he heard the receiver slam, he'd have to bolt out the door. Or confront the reporter.

"Lila," Heineman said eagerly.

"Ed, honey, is that you?" The voice was Lila's, but different. It had a wildness about it. Spraggue wondered if she'd been drinking.

"I have to know something fast. Answer me, tell me the truth, and we can find a way out. I'll protect you—"

Her laugh rippled across miles of telephone company wire. "Do I need protecting?" she asked incredulously. "Is this really you, Eddie? Say the password."

"Lila—"

"Come on, I was fooled once by that damned snoop and I'm not going to be fooled again."

220

Heineman cleared his throat and mumbled, "And now here's Channel 4's own Ed Heineman."

"Okay." She giggled and the giggle almost got out of control. "Now what are you so upset about?"

"Your name . . . It's listed on everything as Lila Bennett."

"My maiden name. Yes." She seemed puzzled, maybe wary.

"Didn't you tell me once that wasn't the name you grew up with?"

"I may have."

"Then it isn't?"

"What is this all about?"

"Di Bennedetto." Heineman said. "Not Bennett."

"I'm surprised you remembered," she said. There was an icy stillness in her voice, as if she'd snapped abruptly out of an alcoholic haze. "Ed, I can't stay on the phone chatting over old times in the middle of the night. I'll call you later, okay?" She waited for a nonexistent reponse. Two clicks followed.

Spraggue got ready to sprint for the door but before he put the receiver down he heard quite clearly, over the phone, not through the doorway, Heineman's moan. "Oh, Lila," he murmured. And again, "Oh, Lila."

Spraggue left him in his office, raced back to the conference room. Mary was shuffling through the file Heineman had abandoned in his hurried exit.

"I think this is the sheet he shoved under the rest when he left," she said in answer to her nephew's inquisitive stare. "It's from Collatos' police files." The piece of paper had been folded in thirds, creased, smoothed out. The top right-hand corner was missing, the result of a jagged tear. The paper was brittle, crackled as he touched it. It bore a smudged date: 3/14/68.

"Di Bennedetto," Spraggue said. "Does the name mean anything to you?"

Aunt Mary repeated it twice, under her breath, hummed a few notes of her tune, snapped her fingers. "Of course it does. But not in conjunction with all this." She waved her hands at the cluttered tabletop. "Someone named Di Bennedetto is one of the untraceable straw owners of that building I want to buy on Commonwealth Avenue, the one I've been after you to tell the police about."

Spraggue ran his finger down the worn page. L. DiBennedetto was listed as a property owner in the North End, a property owner whose buildings seemed to have had a marked attraction for spontaneous combustion.

"I haven't gotten to the financial reports yet, Mary," Spraggue said. "How did Donagher come up with the money to afford his original campaign?"

"The same old tune," Mary said. "A wealthy wife."

"Oh, Lord," Spraggue said under his breath, and then loudly, "Get Heineman out of his office and keep him here. And then call the police. Tell Hurley, no one but Hurley, to meet me at Donagher's. Fast."

THIRTY-FIVE

When Spraggue jerked the car door open, Sharon scuttled past him, barefoot, and scrambled into the passenger seat.

"I'm going with you," she said. "I won't be any trouble. There's no point in telling me to stay put."

"I wouldn't dream of it," he said. "You're terrific."

"You're wasting time."

The house on Sparhawk Street was dark except for a rectangle of light in a third floor dormer and a glow from a side window on the first floor. The street seemed deserted. Spragrue parked right in front of the house, in a tow zone, wondered as he did so whether Donagher still had police protection, whether the so-called protection was slumbering as soundly as the rest of the silent neighbors. The wind groaned like a bow drawn across a cello's lowest string; it made him shiver.

Sharon followed on her noiseless bare feet while he hurried up to the front door, and rapped sharply with a bronze, bull's-head knocker, waited for a count of ten, rapped again. This time they heard reluctant footsteps pad across a wooden floor, heard a deep yawn as the door creaked open.

Eichenhorn blinked at them, started to say something, thought better of it, and began to close the door. Spragrue pushed against the wood and Eichenhorn, surprised, drew back. "Hey," he said in an injured tone, "what the hell do you think you're doing? I could call the police. Shoving your way in here in the middle of the night—"

"Where's Mrs. Donagher?"

"Where's—?" Eichenhorn shook his head in disbelief. "It's—it's past twelve o'clock. I suppose she's sleeping. She gets up early with the kids. What do you care?"

"Half an hour ago she was talking on the phone. Is she upstairs? Is Donagher home?"

"Brian's—he's in his study. Wait—!"

Spragrue burst in through the doorway. The room was as calm as a still-life drawing. The senator glanced up from the armchair in the corner, dog-eared the page he was reading in a bound document, stuffed a pair of reading glasses into his pocket. He said nothing, but his look was one of gentle inquiry, first directed toward Spraggue, then at his outraged campaign manager, finally at Sharon.

"I have to see your wife," Spraggue said.

"Oh, come now," Donagher said. "No melodrama, please. No bursting into the house after midnight with threats. I'm tired. My wife is tired. She went to bed hours ago."

"Did she?" Spraggue said, suddenly wary. "Wake her up."

"Murray," Donagher said. "I think you'd better call Captain Menlo."

"The police should be on their way."

The senator stood. "What is this all about? Who is this woman? What are you doing here at this time of—"

"It's about your wife. I'd rather not accuse her when she's not here to defend herself."

"She doesn't need any defense, as you put it. She's not on trial."

"All right," Spraggue said. "Let's talk about your wife. She's had a secret all these years, maybe more than one secret. But at least one absolutely vital secret that she had to keep quiet. And you invited a man into your house who could have blown her whole life sky-high."

"My wife—" Donagher began with indignant spluttering, regained control and continued with intense sarcasm. "Are you crazy? Lila? What secrets—"

"When you married her, you thought her name was Lila Bennett."

Donagher nodded. His mouth moved but no words came out.

"It may be. She may have had it legally changed. But it was as L. Di Bennedetto that she inherited real estate all over Boston. And as L. Di Bennedetto she became part of a scam to raise real estate values and then burn that real estate down for the insurance."

The senator took his reading glasses out of his pocket, started to put them on with shaky hands, changed his mind, and placed them absently on the end table near the chair.

"No one connected L. Di Bennedetto with Lila Bennett who was Lila Donagher," Spraggue continued. "It happened years ago, when you were first married. There may not even be enough evidence for a criminal prosecution. But she was terrified that the facts would come out and be exposed in the press. Terrified that they might influence a judge when she filed for divorce, that they might make her, in the eyes of the law, an unfit mother, that she might lose the children—"

"She hasn't filed for divorce, not yet—not until after the election. She promised—"

Spraggue's eyes narrowed. "Senator, we have to talk to her, before the police arrive—"

"Have you told them any of this?"

"No."

"Do you have to?"

"She killed Pete Collatos. Because he was putting the pieces together—"

"I don't believe you."

"Ask her."

"Murray." Donagher took four or five deep breaths before making the decision. He sat down, folded like a sail bereft of breeze. His head sank slowly to his hands and his call to his campaign manager was faint and muffled. "Ask Lila to come down here."

Eichenhorn, puzzled, nodded. He took the stairs two at a time.

"Oh, God." Donagher's soft words exploded in a room so quiet the ticking clock sounded like a giant metronome. "I know I shouldn't be thinking things like this, not now, but it will ruin me . . . I've worked so hard . . . I've done so much and there's so much left to do. I've got a deskful of legislative proposals: tax reform, gun control . . . Things I've worked for my whole life. So much I could do—And now this. It will take everything away. I might as well withdraw from the Senate now, before the election. How can I justify going on? Lila will need me. The kids . . ."

Donagher let his head drop back into his hands. They waited long enough for the silence to get uncomfortable. Sharon sat on the sofa and folded her legs up under her. In profile, Spraggue realized how much she resembled her dead brother—not just in the dark coloring, the round forehead, the prominent chin. He'd seen that resolute defiance in other brown eyes than hers, in this very room, when Pete Collatos had told his old friend of his intention to catch the anonymous letter writer.

They heard Murray's steps echo downstairs, twice as slowly as they'd gone up.

"She's not in her room." Eichenhorn said. "Or she's not answering. The door's locked."

"Hurry up," Spraggue was already in the hallway, pushing past Eichenhorn on his way to the stairs. "Do you have a key?"

"Lila!" Donagher hollered on his way up the stairs. He used the bannister to help himself negotiate a sharp turn at the landing and stopped outside a heavy oak door. "Lila!" No answer. "Murray," he said urgently to the man who was trailing behind, "Go upstairs and make sure the kids don't come down. Tell them it's okay, but under no circumstances to come down. Then get back here."

Spraggue said. "We'd better call an ambulance."

"No. Please. She may just be asleep. She sleeps heavily . . . She may have forgotten to unlock the door. It might be stuck. She may—"

"You're clutching at straws."

"Please. Help me break the door down. If there's any way to keep it quiet—I'm begging you."

226

The two men put their shoulders against the door, backed up, thudded against the door.

"Let me kick it in," Spragger said grimly.

"Can you?"

"I can try."

Donagher stood back. The door quivered with the first kick, gave off a shower of splintering wood. The second kick knocked it wide.

"Oh my God," Donagher mumbled.

Lila was dressed for a sleep much less permanent than the one she seemed to have achieved. Her nightgown was white, dotted with small pink roses. Her hair, brushed into a smooth, yellow silk curtain, partially hid her face. The smell in the air was alcohol and vomit. The pill bottle anchoring the sheet of paper to the bedside table was empty.

Donagher moved first. He snatched the note off the table, flinging the pill bottle on the floor. He kept repeating those three words—oh my God, oh my God—over and over.

"Call an ambulance," Spragger said.

Sharon was a foot from the bed, her hand on Lila Donagher's motionless shoulder. "I'll start CPR—" she began.

"No!" Donagher pushed her away with a force that made her stumble. "Don't touch her. Leave her alone."

"Is she dead?" Eichenhorn breathed, just outside the door.

"She will be if you don't call an ambulance," Spragger said. "She will be if your boss doesn't let us help her."

"Murray," Donagher said. "Don't call. She'll be okay. Get these people away from here. They're trying to pull something political. If Lila gets carried out of here on a stretcher, it's political suicide. We can bring her around ourselves. Black coffee. We'll make her throw up, make her walk off whatever she took.''

Spraggue absorbed the tableau: the motionless, rag-doll form tossed across the king-sized bed; the senator, tousle-haired, wild-eyed, shielding her; Sharon, kneeling on the braided rug, searching for a way through Donagher's defenses.

"Get away from her.'' Donagher's face was twisted, his voice an ugly snarl.

One minute everything made sense one way and the next minute everything had tilted and rearranged itself into a new pattern.

"Murray,'' Spraggue said, his dead monotone more threatening than Donagher's snarl. "What was the diet Donagher and Collatos went on two weeks before the marathon?''

Donagher froze.

"What the hell?'' Eichenhorn said.

"Tell me if I have it right. And if I do, get an ambulance fast because Donagher killed Collatos and he's trying to kill his wife. No cheese, right? No alcohol? Nothing rich in tyramine because tyramine reacts with Parnate. If Pete had eaten anything wrong the week before the marathon he might have died too soon and it wouldn't have looked like Donagher was the target; it wouldn't have thrown us off the scent, it wouldn't have given Donagher a sympathy vote and all that publicity . . .''

"Brian,'' Eichenhorn said and his voice was a plea, a plea for a denial that didn't come.

"He's trying to stall,'' Spraggue said, "hoping that help will come too late—because if Lila dies, he can still blame it all on her. Go and call an ambulance!''

Eichenhorn, when he moved, walked as stiffly as an old man, stumbled down the corridor.

"No!'' Donagher called after him. "Don't call!'' He

lunged toward the doorway, but had to stop to keep Sharon away from the bed.

The doorbell rang.

THIRTY-SIX

The chiming bell echoed through the first floor, up the stairs, into the room where Lila Donagher lay motionless as a wax statue across the king-sized bed. It froze everyone in place: Eichenhorn in the corridor, shoving his gold-rimmed glasses up the bridge of his nose, disbelief in the round 'o' of his mouth; Donagher, twisted, undecided whether to stop Murray or bar Sharon from the bed; Spraggue blocking the bedroom door.

"Answer it, Murray," Spraggue said, moving a few steps inside the bedroom.

"No." Donagher shouted. "It's a trick. I wouldn't do anything to hurt Lila."

"Get the door. They'll break it down," Spraggue warned.

The campaign manager came unstuck and moved haltingly toward the landing. The senator must have seen him as a greater threat than Sharon because he ran forward to stop him, into the space Spraggue had ceded. Closing in from behind, Spraggue grabbed Donagher's gesturing right arm with both hands, at wrist and elbow, twisted it cruelly—up, behind the writhing politician's back.

Donagher sagged as if he'd given up, kicked backward

suddenly, landing a stinging blow on Spraggue's shin, wrenched his arm free.

"She's got a pulse!" Sharon shouted, bending over the still form on the bed.

Donagher struck first. The punch hit the fleshy part of Spraggue's neck, cracked against his jaw. It made Spraggue stop thinking of Donagher as a respected senator gone mad, made him remember instead Pete Collatos cold on a stretcher, a house full of blackened memories.

The senator may have seen the change in Spraggue's eyes. He dodged back toward the bed, tried to push Sharon away from his wife.

Spraggue seized the man by the shoulders, sent him crashing into the wall. Donagher slumped, clung to the wall. But he was stronger than he looked—quick, wiry, and crafty. When he turned, he came out punching.

Afterwards, Spraggue couldn't remember what had happened. Rage blinded, deafened him, cut him off. The pulsebeat humming in his hears exploded into a roaring ocean of sound. In the rush of blows, some of Donagher's must have connected, but he shook them off. Then Donagher was on the ground, his upturned face shocked and bloodied. Spraggue picked him up as if he were a stick of wood, buried his fist in the politician's stomach.

"Stop it!"

Spraggue heard the words before he understood their significance. It sounded as if someone were shouting at him from down a long tunnel.

"Stop it!" Sharon was screaming in his ear, pounding on his shoulder. "You'll kill him."

Spraggue's arms fell to his sides. Donagher sank to the floor, cradling his head, moaning.

Sharon stared at Spraggue for a long moment, ran back to Mrs. Donagher. "I'll breathe for her until the ambulance comes."

Spraggue bent down, seized the senator, spun him around, grabbed his arm in the hold that had set off the fracas, hauled the man to his feet.

"You're breaking my arm—" Donagher struggled, his skin patchy, his breath coming in gasps.

"I'd like to break your neck," Spraggue said in a voice so quiet it silenced him like a shot. "Pete worshipped you. He thought you were the best goddam thing that ever happened to him. And you told him to keep on running while you lay down and played possum, knowing he'd die."

Eichenhorn raced down the steps. Spraggue's progress, pushing the senator ahead of him, was a crawl by comparison. He didn't want Donagher to trip, by accident or design. By the time they got downstairs, the front door was already ajar, the porch light blazing. Captain Hank Menlo loomed on the doorstep, a smaller uniformed cop behind him.

"Shut the door!" Spraggue said quickly, too late. The huge man and his shadow stepped over the sill. The uniformed attendant slammed the door and twisted home the locking bolt.

Donagher stopped struggling.

"Let him go," Menlo ordered. Spraggue loosened his grip. "Do you want to prefer charges, Senator?"

"Officer," Eichenhorn's tenor practically squeaked. "Upstairs. Mrs. Donagher . . . she needs an ambulance . . ."

"About time, Menlo." Donagher straightened his shirt, rubbed his arm. He had his voice back. His breathing was almost normal. He sounded as confident as he did on his promotional campaign radio spots, but the blood still oozed from a corner of his mouth. "There is a woman upstairs who joined this man in breaking into my house. Have your man bring her down here—and tell him to ignore anything else he might see. Only to bring that woman downstairs."

Menlo nodded and the short, dark cop headed for the stairs. When Spraggue stepped out to challenge him, the cop patted his holster and looked questioningly at his boss. Menlo cracked a smile that had no humor in it. "Not yet," he said.

The cop bypassed Spraggue and bounded up the steps.

"Murray," Donagher said calmly, "go into the kitchen and wait for me."

"I can't. . . . I . . . Mrs. Donagher . . ."

"You'll do what I tell you," Donagher said. "Now."

Upstairs, a woman's scream was cut short.

"Get an ambulance," Spraggue said. "If Lila dies, she's going to take the rap for all this."

A flicker of understanding lit Menlo's eyes. Spraggue could almost see the machinery turning—weighing, evaluating, stacking and restacking the chips. Then the captain motioned Donagher to his side, drew his revolver, and herded the other two men into the front room. "No phone in here? Good. Nobody leaves until I say so." The rest of Menlo's words were addressed to Donagher in a whisper too faint for Spraggue to catch.

Eichenhorn collapsed on the couch, removed his glasses, rubbed his eyes. Spraggue stood by the mantel, searched the room—first for an escape, then for some sort of weapon—regretted that he no longer carried a gun. The dark cop half carried, half dragged Sharon Collatos into the room, dumped her on the rug. She had angry tears in her eyes, the crimson mark of an open hand splayed across her face. The cop had bloody scratches down one cheek. He backed out of the room, quickly, warily, guarded the doorway with his hand poised above his holster.

Sharon shook off Spraggue's hand when he tried to help her up.

After a long five minutes, Menlo reappeared, coughed. "The senator says that his wife wrote a letter before she took her life and that perhaps I'd better read it before I involve the authorities any further.''

"It's too late for that—" Spraggue said.

"Exactly," Donagher interrupted smoothly. "It's too late for Lila; but it may not be too late to salvage something from this tragedy. That's what I was explaining to Captain Menlo."

"She's not dead yet—" Sharon began.

"Menlo's been in it all along, hasn't he?" Spraggue said. Eichenhorn, on the couch, turned to stone.

"It all fits. Menlo is in charge of arson liaison. Menlo is a rotten cop. Menlo flourishes on the force, keeps getting promoted while other, better cops, get fired. He must have found out about your little arson fortune a long time ago, Senator. He must have been bleeding you for years. Menlo must have told you about a young eager-beaver cop who was getting too damn close to your secrets."

Spraggue looked at Donagher for confirmation, got nothing but a blank stare.

"Then Collatos got laid off and Menlo breathed a sigh of relief. But you didn't, did you, Senator? You had to know how much this Collatos character had guessed or discovered. Once Menlo told you Pete had pulled those old files, he was as good as dead. Menlo knew Pete well enough by then to know he'd keep on looking and, eventually, he might have found out the source of your early wealth. Pete was like a dog on a scent once he got started. A good cop. Not like some who'll follow any stink that leads to money, who've forgotten the aroma of justice if they ever smelled it."

"Want me to shut him up?" the short cop asked.

"So you set it up with Menlo to hire Collatos as your personal bodyguard. I've always hated your guts," Spraggue said to Menlo, "But I'm not sure you knew Donagher intended to kill him."

"I didn't," Donagher said harshly. "Not then."

"Or did you plan Pete's execution together? No, I doubt the senator would trust his brainwork to a cop. The senator had the medicine, thanks to his wife's previous illness . . . He had the mob connections from his earlier arson scam. I wonder what the senator's record is on organized crime legislation?

"Didn't your wife suspect anything when all the property she owned under her old name, her father's name, burned so advantageously? Or did she trust you to handle all her business affairs?"

Eichenhorn picked that moment to stand and announce, "I'm going to call an ambulance."

"Sit down," Donagher said. "That one won't be any trouble. I know enough about him to guarantee silence."

"But Spraggue," Menlo said, "is another story altogether. And the woman."

"Any other cop would have been too smart to type one of those envelopes on his own typewriter," Spraggue said. The words brought purple into Menlo's face, made his foot tap the wooden floorboards. "Did Pete know for sure when he visited you that Sunday, or did he just come to ask you why you'd lifted the envelope? Was he surprised when he typed a line on your typewriter and found it matched the type on the threatening envelope?"

Menlo took his gun out of his holster. Not the police standard six-shot S&W—a .357 magnum.

"No," Donagher said hastily. "We have to think this out. We have to set the stage. I heard a burglar; I called the police. After all the threats, after Pete's death, naturally I'd be uneasy. I call you and you see them running from the house. You call out, he turns. You see a gun. You shoot. The girl's in the line of fire. How's that? We can plant the guns later."

Eichenhorn shook his head. "I can't—" he said.

"You damn well can. Or there'll be three deaths."

Spraggue said, "There'll be three deaths anyway. Isn't it going to strain the public credulity to imagine that you had burglars in the house the same night your wife committed suicide?"

"It would sure as hell strain my goddam credulity," Hurley said. He had his gun drawn as he came out of the shadows of the hallway. The walkie-talkie at his waist crackled. Sirens wailed and blue flashing lights split the night.

Donagher broke for the front door, was outside in a flash. Hurley yelled into the walkie-talkie.

"There's nowhere far enough for him to run," Spraggue said.

Sharon dashed for the stairs.

THIRTY-SEVEN

The ambulance came and went—khaki-clad paramedics eased Sharon to one side, took over Lila Donagher's arrhythmic breathing, shifted her onto a stretcher, vanished with their burden so rapidly they seemed like creatures from a disjointed dream. Police cars came and went. Heavy black shoes beat a path up the walk of number 55 Sparhawk Street.

Whispered conferences were held in corners. The governor, red-faced and irritable, abruptly wakened and hauled over to Donagher's in the official limo, was closeted with aides in the kitchen. Someone tipped the press and what had seemed like madness moments before seemed now like a model of organized sanity as the newshounds joined the fray.

When he wasn't wanted for questioning, Spraggue sat in the senator's armchair, elbows on knees, head bent forward. He laced his fingers together at the back of his neck and closed his eyes, imagined himself elsewhere, on a different stage.

He saw Senator Donagher, running out into blackness, endlessly falling, opened his eyes and focused on the rug.

Hurley prodded his shoulder.

"Tell it once more," he said. "For the superintendent."

"Shit," Spraggue said. "Can't you get a tape recorder?"

Hurley waved a microphone in front of his eyes. "Straight from headquarters. This time for posterity."

Spraggue closed his eyes, composed his thoughts. He spoke with no inflection. "Some of this is guesswork. Some of it is fact. You'll have to sort it out."

"Go ahead."

Spraggue was aware of a shifting of furniture, of additional faceless people entering the room. He waited for silence, began.

"When Donagher decided to go into politics, he didn't have the money to get into it in a big way. I think he ran for state auditor or something and lost. It must have cost him a lot to lose. In cash, in self-respect. His wife had some money, but more than that, she had property. Buildings in Roxbury, the North End, in Back Bay, Jamaica Plain, God knows where else. Maybe Donagher tried to sell them. Maybe that was when the mob approached him. Maybe he went to them because he couldn't get a good price. But, no matter who initiated it, he became part of a scam to increase the value of his wife's holdings, increase their value on paper, and then burn the buildings and collect the insurance. His name never appeared in any transactions. Buildings passed between straw owners connected with the mob and

236

L. Di Bennedetto. Every time a building was sold, its property value increased. No money changed hands."

"Do you know the exact location of any of these buildings?" Sprague didn't recognize the questioning voice, didn't look up.

"One of them is 312 Commonwealth Avenue. The scam is still going on."

"How did Collatos get involved in all this?" Hurley asked.

"Doing his job. He was working for Captain Menlo, assigned to liaison work with the Arson Squad. Maybe he couldn't figure why so little progress was being made. He was a maverick sort of guy. A little slow on the uptake, but once he got ahold of an idea, he kept at it. He probably saw Menlo's little cache of secret files, either stole them or copied them, took them home to work on. Maybe he put them aside to deal with later. He didn't know he had hold of one end of a live stick of dynamite."

"But Menlo did," Hurley added.

"Yes. And he told the senator. And the senator ordered him to get the files back, to find out what Collatos was after. But then Collatos got laid off."

"And Donagher couldn't leave it alone."

"He may have been obsessed with the upcoming election, with the idea that someone was going to tell his opponent, that Collatos was actually working for Bartolo. Donagher was uneasy. He wanted to get next to Collatos."

"Go on," Hurley urged softly.

"Donagher dreamed up the anonymous letter campaign. Menlo helped him out. Donagher probably did the letters himself. Those letters always bothered me. They were so damned meticulous, so obsessive. . . . Of course, Donagher would be careful, snip out words from the paper rather than print them. He couldn't afford to be linked to those letters. And he'd naturally spend more time on the makeup of

237

the letters than the contents. He didn't care what they said, as long as they could be used as a reason to hire Collatos. He had Menlo do the mailing. And then Donagher called the police department for protection, and Menlo made sure that Collatos was touted for the job."

"Once he met Collatos, Donagher must have realized he'd made a mistake."

"I'll say. Pete made friends with Donagher's wife, started asking her innocent questions about her upbringing that must have made Donagher shiver. Donagher was having a hell of a time. Election coming up. His wife thinking of leaving—"

"Stay with what happened next."

"What I think happened. Donagher decided he'd-have to get rid of Collatos. He wanted to do it in a way that would not only leave him unsuspected, but would actually help his reelection. The marathon was obvious. Donagher wasn't going to make any great time, wasn't going to be the contender he'd been when he was young. But if somebody made an attempt on his life at the marathon, that would be news. And he fixed it so that, if the political assassination attempt idea wasn't accepted, Lila would come under suspicion. She was the one who was supposed to give him water at the top of Heartbreak Hill. Even if someone did figure out that the act wasn't political, but personal—an attack on Donagher the man, not Donagher the senator—our boy must have felt he could keep the wraps on under the guise of protecting his beloved wife. Maybe he even threatened to say she arranged the whole thing, tried to murder him. Maybe that was supposed to keep her in line until after the election. We were never supposed to get Pete as the target."

"And you think Pete already had that Parnate stuff in him?"

"I don't know if we'll ever be able to *prove* that Pete was given Parnate. If Donagher's campaign manager hadn't
238

made a misguided attempt to shield the Donagher family, I'd never have even heard of it. Question Eichenhorn. He must have had a powerful reason for getting it out of Donagher's house. Maybe it suddenly appeared in Mrs. Donagher's medicine cabinet. Maybe he saw Donagher trying to stash it someplace. Maybe the senator clammed up when Eichenhorn asked him about it. But it's the only way Pete's death makes sense.''

"How does it work?" Hurley prompted softly.

Spraggue shut out everything but the memory of typed words on paper. The tape recorder hummed insistently. It was the only sound in the room. ''Let me see what I can remember. The drug doesn't take effect immediately. Donagher probably started feeding Collatos doses of it a week, maybe two weeks before the race. Collatos, when I met him running around the reservoir, back when it all started, told me that Donagher had both of them on some kind of crazy diet to prep for the race. That diet would have been crucial to Donagher's plan, because Parnate reacts with so many things. Donagher had to keep Pete under his nose all the time, regulate his behavior. That was easy; Pete hardly left his side. Pete probably got Parnate ground up in his spaghetti sauce the night before the race. He probably got a hit in his coffee just before the marathon began.''

"Then you're saying that the sniping at the reservoir was staged?" Hurley said.

"What better way to make the public believe in a later attempt on Donagher's life?"

"But how could Donagher count on his wife not showing up, not being there at Heartbreak Hill to give him water?" The question floated over from across the room.

"I hope you'll be able to find that out for yourself, by asking her. The story she gave me was that she and her husband had a fight before the race. Donagher waited until the morn-

239

ing of the race to tell her he wanted her at Heartbreak. He issued an order instead of asking her. He pushed all the right buttons, knowing that he'd provoke a certain reaction. You don't live with a person for all those years without learning how to manipulate that person. And Donagher was a master manipulator."

"Then Donagher got in touch with JoJo?"

"I doubt Donagher had to get involved in the nitty-gritty. He called on the people who'd helped him before, when he needed money to get into politics. They provided a sniper for the reservoir scene, a flunky to hand over the tainted water—" Sprague lifted a hand to his forehead, pushed forefingers and thumb against his temples. "God, yes, pick up a guy named Arnold Gravier; he's in this thing up to his neck. He burned my house down trying to get rid of Pete's files—and me."

"We've been looking for him—"

"The mob picked JoJo for his acting ability, and his expendability. He may have been on a hit list already. Once JoJo was dead, all direct connections to the senator were severed—"

"Of course, a lot of the deal required us not to identify JoJo as the killer—"

"Right. Because JoJo was arson connected, mob connected. He made us wonder if the target might have been Pete all along. But then Menlo stepped into the investigation and shut the door. Even you," Sprague paused and focused his eyes on Hurley. "You had a dead man; you had a killer. You weren't planning to scratch around for the story behind the facts."

"I got here," Hurley said flatly. "I've been tailing Menlo since you called. That's what I call cooperation. Tailing another cop sucks. How did you get onto Menlo?"

Sprague said, "The minute I got involved with Pete, Menlo was all over me. He even gave me his card so that I could call him if I heard anything else from Donagher's direction. Earlier today, I saw the same phone number Menlo had so kindly shoved in my face on a note Pete Collatos had left for his boss, pinned to the bulletin board at Bill Rodgers Running Center. Either Donagher never got it, or he never took it down. It said that Pete had left Brian on his own that Sunday for a brief spell while he went to call on Menlo. And I knew that Pete had discovered something that day—he called me and told me so. He sounded drunk—or sick.'' Spraggue raised his hand abruptly to his forehead, realized as he did so that the gesture was pure Pete Collatos. His hand shook. ''Dammit.'' he said. ''Find somebody who was at that party! Find out if Pete went off his diet, had a glass or two of red wine with his spaghetti. If he'd been dosed with Parnate, that would explain his sounding so wrecked on the phone. . . . Maybe one of Donagher's guests could testify to Pete's reactions to the food and drink. Then a doctor could verify that those reactions were consistent with Parnate—''

''That's not much to give a jury—''

''It may be all you have if Donagher doesn't break down and confess.''

Hurley said, ''Why didn't Pete tell you what he'd found?''

''Someone came into the room. Donagher, probably. And Pete didn't realize the significance of what he'd stumbled across. Maybe he thought he'd grabbed onto some stupid police-department con: cops write anonymous letters to politicians so that the terrified politicians will hire laid off cops for bodyguards. Revenge for all the tax cuts that hurt the department. Lord knows what Collatos must have thought when he realized one of the anonymous notes was typed on Menlo's machine. But he wouldn't have wanted to tell Donagher about it. Not yet. Collatos would have wanted more evidence before he accused a cop—even a bum like

241

Menlo." Spraggue's recitation ground to a halt. His throat hurt.

"Any more questions?"

In the ensuing silence, Hurley pushed a lot of buttons, detached the microphone from the tape recorder.

"I have one," Spraggue said.

"Yeah?"

"Have you found Donagher?"

"MDC unit called in half an hour ago. Saw a guy standing by the Charles River, near Soldiers Field Road. Just staring at the water. Thought they had a drunk or a potential floater, so they took him in. Collapsed in the prowl car. It's Donagher. Took some kind of drug. They've got him over at Mass General. No word, yet. But to my mind it's as good a confession as we'll ever get."

"Don't bank on it," someone said. "If he recovers, his lawyer'll tell us he was distraught over his wife's attempted suicide."

"She still among the living?"

"They think she'll make it."

"Another question," Spraggue said. "Two. Can I leave now? And where's Sharon Collatos?"

Hurley put a clumsy hand on Spraggue's shoulder, scanned the room looking for objections, found none. "She's waiting in the hall. Go home. I'll be in touch."

Sure, Spraggue thought, go home.

Sharon was asleep on a spindly bench in Lila Donagher's colonial foyer.

"Morning," he whispered close enough to her ear to smell the scent of her perfume.

"Mmmmmphf," she said.

"Time to go home."

She sat bolt upright, blinked.

"Thanks for waiting," he said.

"I called your aunt. Ed Heineman went to St. Elizabeth's to check on Mrs. Donagher. Your aunt says—"

"I know. Come home."

"Right."

Spraggue leaned down and kissed her, hard, on the lips. "Thank you," he said.

"What for?"

"For saving a life, two lives, three—"

"Whoa. I would be honored to accept partial credit for Lila Donagher, but—"

"If you hadn't stopped me upstairs, I could have killed Donagher—and if I had—"

"You'd have stopped on your own."

"Maybe." He smiled crookedly. "I'm glad you came along."

"So am I."

Spraggue sat on the bench next to her, took her hand. "How are you holding up?"

"I don't know. . . . I feel so empty. Like none of this ever happened. Like the past two weeks have been one horrible endless day." She shrugged her shoulders. "I don't know how I'm supposed to feel. Revenge is supposed to be sweet, but—Donagher—I liked him; Pete liked him. He was just a guy who messed up. . . . And Pete's dead."

"Want to get out of here?"

She nodded silently.

The street was almost back to normal. The police cars had ceased flashing their lights; the neighbors had retreated to their beds. The first streaky clouds were changing from black to gray.

There was a huge red sign blocking the front window of the Porsche. It said: Do Not Move This Vehicle. The dreaded Denver Boot was affixed to the right front wheel.

One elderly gray-haired woman who hadn't been able to get back to sleep peeped out from behind her lace curtains and pursed her lips at the shameless couple laughing and hugging right there on the street in front of the house where all that commotion had been.

ABOUT THE AUTHOR

Linda Barnes was born in Detroit and has a theatrical background. She now lives in the vicinity of Boston with her husband, where she is on the Board of Directors of the Mystery Writers' Guild. Ms. Barnes has won "Mystery Scene" magazine's award for "Best P. I. Novel of the Year" and the Anthony Award. She was nominated twice for the Shamus Award and was a nominee for the Edgar Award. Her latest novel is THE SNAKE TATTOO.